THE
INCREDIBLE
BANKER

By the same author

Devil in Pinstripes
If God was a Banker
I Bought the Monk's Ferrari
The Bankster

THE
INCREDIBLE
BANKER

Ravi Subramanian

RUPA

Published by
Rupa Publications India Pvt. Ltd 2011
7/16, Ansari Road, Daryaganj
New Delhi 110002

Sales centres:
Allahabad Bengaluru Chennai
Hyderabad Jaipur Kathmandu
Kolkata Mumbai

ISBN: 978-81-291-1877-6

Ninth-impression 2014

10 9

The moral right of the author has been asserted.

Printed at Yash Printographics, Noida

Dedicated to my wife
Dharini and my little doll Anusha

10 January 2004

Malkangiri, Orissa

THE rickety state transport bus was the last to leave the small run-down bus stand in Malkangiri. On board, apart from the driver and the conductor, were sixteen people, all making their way to Bhubaneswar via Koraput – a neighbouring town. Till the early nineties Malkangiri was a part of Koraput but it was carved out as a separate district in 1992. The vast dense jungle of Malkangiri was home to several tribes. Dotted with steep ghats, plateaus, valleys and wooded hills the area was beautiful, though secluded and lonely.

In one of the blocks in Malkangiri, Ganjali, the local coordinator of an NGO was resting in the dark and isolated balcony of the dak bungalow. The bungalow was about twenty-five metres away from the main road connecting the highway passing through the town to the bus depot. The only people in the bungalow were Ganjali and the caretaker. A lone bulb glowed dimly in the hall of the bungalow threatening to go off anytime, casting surreal shadows on the walls. Some would have found the scene intimidating but not Ganjali. Even though Bhubaneswar was where he carried out most of his lobbying he was not new to Malkangiri. The caretaker in the dak bungalow didn't know that, since Ganjali was staying there for the first time.

'Why is the dak bungalow empty? Does no one come here?' he asked the caretaker.

'People do come, sahib. But they mostly leave before night falls. They stay back for the night only if they miss the bus or if something urgent comes up.'

'Why?'

'Because this place is not safe, sahib. You are an outsider, so you do not know what happens here. Please do not venture out in the night. Just put off the lights and go to sleep. These are bad times.'

'I am anyway waiting for the bus to come. I will be leaving in an hour's time.'

'Oh yes, yes. I completely forgot, sahib!' the caretaker said as he went his way. 'Good for you. Very good.' Ganjali saw his back disappear behind the weak wooden door of the balcony as he lifted his legs up, bringing them to rest on the railing. The bus would be here any time, he thought. He patted his bag and felt the consignment. It seemed to be in order. There was another bag in the bedroom. He decided to gather it on his way out.

After a wait of around thirty minutes Ganjali heard the rumble of the bus in the distance. He got up immediately, went into his room and picked up his bag. On his way out, he tipped the caretaker a few hundred rupees which lit up the caretaker's eyes. The sound of the bus was getting closer. He ran out of the main door towards the gate and then on to the road, to the bus stand.

He was the only person at the bus stop. Not a soul in sight. Even the stars had forgotten to light up the sky. Had his wait at the balcony not gotten his eyes used to the darkness, the blackness of the night would have blinded him.

A couple of honks told him the bus was not too far. Within a few minutes he could see the headlights of the bus coming his way. It was an antiquated bus, looking like parts loosely held together by nuts and bolts and kept in place by layers of mud and dirt. It screeched to a halt at the bus stand. Ganjali got in through the door at the far end of the bus. There were enough seats for him to choose from. He quietly picked the one towards the front. Sitting on top of the rear wheels made him nauseous. In any case most people were sitting in the front and he just followed suit. A few stared at him wondering why he got in through the back door if he had to walk all the way to the front for a seat.

The bus moved. It was a journey which would take him another five hours to reach his destination. By daybreak he would be in Bhubaneswar, from where he had to take a flight to Mumbai where his family lived.

Reminiscing, he went over the events of the past few days: the hostile meeting with the tribals, the work his organisation had started there, the apathetic local administration and allegations of working against the government. His wife had warned him it would not be easy but he was extremely passionate about the cause of the tribals and he had, against all odds, taken it up. Both his grandparents belonged to this region and he had not seen any progress in the tribal areas since the time his parents decided to leave Malkangiri and moved to Mumbai in search of a better life for themselves and their children. He rested his head on the window grill as thoughts of his wife and kid haunted him. It had been a month since he had seen the innocent smiling face of his child which he knew he would never see again. A tear squeezed itself out of the corner of his eyes. He wiped it off hurriedly, reminding himself that he couldn't afford to be emotional or weak. This was the time to demonstrate his strength, the strength of his team, his group and the entire movement of which he was an integral part. The work he had begun had to be completed. He looked at his watch. It was twenty-five minutes since he had left the dak bungalow. It was time for the action to begin, for him to do what he had set out to. Everyone around him was sleeping. He counted. There were eleven Special Police Officers (SPOs) and constables in the bus. The others were tribals making their way to the city to buy essentials. He stretched to his left and pulled out his bag from below the seat. It was heavy even to drag. Bending down, he opened it and pulled out a tiffin box. A couple of wires were sticking out. He tugged a bit at the green wire, removed the tape covering it and joined it with the red wire sticking out from the other end. He closed his eyes and said his prayers.

≈

It was six in the morning when the shrill ring of the phone broke Ganjali's wife's dream sequence. She first thought it was the alarm on her cellphone going off. But when she got hold of her cellphone, she realised it was not the alarm. She got out of the bed and picked up the call.

'Hello.'

'Ji mein Malkangiri se bol raha hoon (I am calling from Malkangiri).' The person spoke in Hindi with a heavy Oriya accent.

'Yes, who is this?'

'Madam...,' the person on the other end rattled on.

Ganjali's wife was too shocked to react. It had happened. How much she wished what the guy was saying was not true! She stumbled back to the bed, clutching the side of the bed for support. Something inside her told her every bit of what she heard was true. Picking the remote, she switched on the TV and nervously surfed a few channels till NDTV 24x7 came on. All she could see were advertisements. She waited for the ad break to get over. Her heart was beating faster than ever. Finally news started flashing on the screen. And there it was! Something which she had feared, so wished would not transpire.

'Breaking News' screamed the ticker at the bottom of the screen. 'Naxal attack in Malkangiri kills seventeen. All passengers including eleven SPOs killed in a dastardly late night attack.'

Tears rolled down her cheeks as she looked at the picture placed on top of the TV. It was Ganjali's favourite picture. Clicked during their wedding reception, he always held her eyes looked mesmerising in that picture. The same eyes were now glistening with tears. She would never see Ganjali again. He was on that ill-fated bus targeted by the Naxalites in Malkangiri. That was what even the caller, a representative of the Orissa government, told her when he gave her the news. She closed her eyes. Something which she always did when she was stressed and jaded. Her clenched fists were the only indication she was trying to gather strength to deal with the situation. Ganjali would never come back!

Fort, Mumbai

'YOU throw a stone and you are likely to hit a banker' was a common saying in the old business district of Bombay, lined with greying stone buildings. And two out of three times it was sure to find a foreign banker. Banks, brokers, fund houses, investment bankers – all could be found in intimidating numbers in the one-kilometre radius of the Bombay Stock Exchange. The Reserve Bank of India (RBI) too had its offices in the neighbourhood so that the seemingly subdued and subservient higher ups of the foreign banks could be summoned by the top brass of the RBI as and when required.

The perception in the banking circles was that the RBI looked at the foreign banks with a jaundiced eye – as organisations that would try to push the limits of regulation until someone in the corridors of power would wake up and realise their transgressions. At such times the foreign bankers would merely feign ignorance and apologise. The global financial meltdown worsened the situation for the foreign banks as it became a dirty phrase in the wood-panelled alleys of RBI.

Ronald McCain had just got out of bed on a Thursday morning. He usually got up early on Thursdays as he had a team meeting with his entire set of direct reports. Referred to as 'morning prayers', he had started this routine a few months back. Over time he had noticed many of his direct reports had started delegating this weekly meeting to their team members. This peeved him and he made it mandatory for his direct reports to inform him and take his concurrance in case they were not attending. Quite a headmasterly approach to running a bank, but that was Ronald McCain for the uninitiated! His team hated these Thursday morning meetings when Ronald would go on a rampage. What made it worse was these meetings began at 8 a.m. Such an early start in Mumbai meant that people had to leave home at 7.15. This resulted in a great deal of discomfort for his team members and under-the-breath abuses for Ronald.

However Ronald had a point. 'We must be through with our morning prayers and be back in our seats by the time our first branch throws open its doors for the public.' And when the CEO of Greater Boston Global Bank (GB2) says something, the employees don't have much choice but to listen.

Ronald McCain and his wife Sarah had relocated to India from New York a year ago. Ronald was taking over the reigns of the Indian business of GB2 from Girija Vaswani, who had run the bank admirably for over three years. Ronald was sent to India with a clear objective. 'Bring the bank at par with the GB2 culture across the globe.' A resoundingly clear but difficult-to-execute objective. Difficult because of a problem typical to most of the foreign banks in India: Indians were smart, high on intellect but loved to argue and debate. These were exactly the kind of qualities the management of these banks in the more developed western countries frowned upon. Traditionally, most of the Asia-Pacific regional offices of foreign banks had found India to be the most difficult country to work in. They encountered the maximum push back and most perplexing questions and debates in India. 'Indians argue a lot,' they would say – a statement bordering on racism. GB2 was no different.

Those were the days when a number of banks across the globe were collapsing. The 'invincible' tag associated with some banking groups was fast being relegated to archived pages of banking journals. Losses in the US led to a knee-jerk reaction the world over. Aggression was replaced by caution. The global banking mantra of 'Grow at any cost' was replaced by a desire for 'profitable growth'.

Banking in India, particularly retail banking, seemed to be the most affected. Traditionally banks in India looked at retail banking as an area for investment, to build a bank for the future. The thinking of the management was simple – 'Acquire customers now. Once we get them in, we will figure out a way to make them profitable'. This challenge, which the banks had conveniently left for a later date, remained what it started off as – a challenge. Thus most of the foreign banks, even the ones with a strong retail banking proposition globally, had a very confused strategy in India. Almost every bank in India was incurring significant losses, in its retail banking business.

The Singapore office of GB2 realised the gravity of the situation and wanted to bring in certain changes in the management structure and style to ensure maximum alignment to overall organisational goals and strategies. But it was not going to be possible with the old Indian management in place. The traditional Indian way of running these banks was not good enough in a difficult time, or so thought the management team based in Singapore. Hence, Girija had to make way for McCain to take over the reigns of GB2 in India in late 2008.

That Thursday morning, McCain was not in his element. He had just heard from the Singapore office that they had declined his overall growth plan and strategy paper. Twelve months back, when he shifted base to India, his global office had unequivocally endorsed the broad direction he had outlined for the bank. They had supported him. But this time they had communicated to him, in no uncertain terms, that they were not happy with the strategic plan – a three-year strategy docket the India team had put in place. His strategic vision had been suddenly found weak and wanting – without any conceivable reason being offered.

Were the events of the last four days responsible for this sudden shift in the stance? He couldn't pin it down. The Asia-Pacific regional office's perception about India was not close to complimentary by a stretch of even the most charitable imagination. They often said that India made 'huge commitments' but never delivered. There was a credibility problem that the Indian team faced in its interactions with the global management.

'India is a country of glorious powerpoint presentations' was the regular party gossip and often a water-cooler conversation in the Singapore office. He had to change it and he only had two options – either try to change the work culture and make the Indian team execute well, or change the people who created obstacles in execution of strategic plans.

In any case there was no time to sort out this debate in his mind. There was a bigger battle lurking in the shadows. How was he going to handle that? He thought of talking briefly about the strategic plan in the morning prayers but he knew it was going to be dominated by the issues that had started to rock GB2 in India, especially over the last four days. This was clearly one of the biggest and gravest challenges GB2 had faced in the recent times.

Ronald was quite disciplined. He had a fixed morning routine – a routine he rigidly followed every single day. His morning cup of coffee was followed by twenty minutes of rummaging through the newspapers – he read five of them every morning. A quick shower was preceded by ten minutes of jumping around with Oodie, his dog who had dutifully followed him from New York to Mumbai. And then he would set off on his morning jog from his Malabar Hill residence down the Marine Drive, past the Police Gymkhana, crossing the Wankhede and Brabourne stadia on his left, till the Oberoi at the far end of the Marine Drive. He would then head to Oberoi Belvedere where he would shower quickly, change into his formal suit which his driver carried for him and head to office after a light breakfast. This regimen helped him keep fit, physically and mentally, to run a large bank in India, especially in a demanding environment.

Despite this hectic morning schedule, Ronald was the first in office that Thursday. He normally was the first one in on any given day. A stickler for punctuality, he made no bones about the fact that he hated latecomers. 'Do not steal bank's time,' he would tell people in meetings. 'The bank pays you for coming at 9.00 a.m., so please be in by 9.00. If you stay back and work till late to compensate your inefficiencies, it is your problem. The bank does not expect people to stay late,' he would thunder in the town hall meetings. And to be fair to Ronald, he made it a point to leave every single day at 6.30 p.m., whatever the compulsion.

He spent a few minutes at his desk clearing his mails. Quite a peculiar style he had – Ronald would never read anything marked as 'cc' to him. His secretary would read and give him only the priority mails. 'If a 'cc' has been marked for me, it's only for covering one's ass... which I refuse to cover. If people make decisions, they should learn to live with them. If I start reading all such mails, I will only be reading mails the whole day,' he had once told Sherlyn, his secretary.

At 8.00, he headed to the boardroom for 'morning prayers'. One by one, every business head made a presentation before Ronald and the team. But that day Ronald had a specific agenda in mind. He had two issues to cover. But he left it for the end, after all the business heads had spoken. He didn't want his agenda to even remotely influence their updates.

The corporate bank head spoke about three new large deals in the pipeline. Ronald was quick to point out that he had been hearing the same three names for the last three weeks. 'Closure... we need closure on these deals,' he said forcefully; in fact he said it as forcefully as could be considered civilised in a formal forum of mature adults. The treasury spoke about rising cost for funds and the need to ramp up low cost deposits by the branches.

The retail head, Ramneek Chahal, spoke about the initiatives he had taken to bring the entire team together and how he was building 'camaraderie' among his team members. His update revolved around bragging about how he was getting the team to work with each other, cutting across individual businesses and thinking of the bank as a whole. The entire management team sniggered as he said this.

Considering the fact that the losses in the retail banking sector continued to mount, much to Ronald's displeasure, the entire team was a bit put off that the retail banking team was not focusing on loss reduction but on the less important issues such as boosting employee morale and engagement. Tough times called for tough measures, but the retail banking team in India didn't quite see it that way. Ronald had already made up his mind to ease out the head of retail banking, so he did not bother much about giving feedback to Ramneek or on wasting the entire top management's time on what Ramneek had blabbered. Being conscious of time, he wanted the meeting to get over by 9.00 and hence kept pushing everyone.

The marketing team was the next in line. The head of marketing was carrying a number of props to support her claim for the work done that week. She had just begun her discourse when the door opened. Sherlyn walked into the boardroom and straight to Ronald. She bent down and whispered something into his ears. The colour on Ronald's face changed. Fair-skinned as he was, the blood gushing through the veins to his cheeks made them turn red.

'Can this wait?' he asked. 'I will be back in fifteen minutes.'

'Vardarajan claims it is urgent. If you want I can tell him you will call back the moment you are out of this meeting.'

Ronald turned towards Saurabh Bhambani, the Head of Compliance, and then looked back at Sherlyn. 'I am coming. Give me a minute.' The blank look on Saurabh's face made Ronald decide against making Varadarajan wait.

Sherlyn nodded and left the room.

'Gentlemen, I will be back in a couple of minutes. There is an urgent call I need to attend to,' and Ronald, too, followed Sherlyn. The moment he left, pandemonium broke out into the room. Everyone looked at Saurabh with eager eyes, wondering what had happened. Vardarajan would not normally call and Ronald would not leave a 'morning prayer' for anything less than 'very important'. Saurabh Bhambani just shrugged his shoulders, disappointing all the quizzical eyes focussed at him. He obviously had no clue. They had never in the past called the CEO directly.

Back in his room, a worried Ronald walked up to his desk and picked up the extension. 'Line 1,' Sherlyn had whispered to him as he walked past her desk.

'Good Morning, Mr Varadarajan. How are you?'

'Am good, Mr McCain! Hope you are doing well too.'

'Of course, I am. Thank you. How come you called so early in the morning?'

'Mr McCain, the governor wants to meet you today. Will it be possible for you to see him in his office at your convenience?'

'Today seems a bit tight, Mr Varadarajan. Will it be ok if I speak with him, or else I will ask Sherlyn to fix up a mutually convenient time?'

'If you could just hold on, Mr McCain. The governor says it's very urgent. Let me check with him again. Please bear with me, sir.' Varadarajan was too courteous for his comfort.

'Sure.'

After a moment's pause, Varadarajan was back on the line. 'Mr McCain. Thanks for holding the line.' He was overtly polite. 'The governor has requested that you see him today. He says it is very urgent and cannot wait. It cannot be discussed over the phone. May I request you to accommodate this request?'

'Ok, what time would suit the governor?' This was not something which would happen on any normal day. If the governor of the RBI sought a meeting with the CEO of a bank, in this manner, it spelled trouble. And if there was indeed even a hint of trouble, there was no point aggravating it by being hard-nosed. McCain knew it better than anyone else.

'He asked me to tell you that any time that fits in your schedule today would be fine by him.'

'I will be there in an hour's time. Will that be all right? Second half of the day is packed with external meetings, which will be difficult to reschedule. The morning is full of internal meetings but I can move them around and come.'

'I will tell the governor that you will be here in an hour. Thanks for accommodating, Mr McCain. Really nice of you.'

The moment he kept the phone down he had a queasy feeling in his stomach. His instinct told him something was terribly wrong. It was weird, the way the conversation had gone. Vardarajan was extremely secretive. He most probably knew the reason for this meeting but didn't drop any hint. He spoke as if he was requesting McCain for a meeting but it was not a request. It was an order. Had RBI taken serious offence to the issues that had cropped up in the last few days? Ronald wondered.

He dialed a number on his phone and picked up the headset. 'Sherlyn, please call Saurabh. Ask him to come to my room immediately. And also tell the rest in the boardroom that the "morning prayers" are over. They can go back to their respective offices.' Ronald was quick and curt.

Within two minutes Saurabh Bhambani was in Ronald's room.

'You wanted to see me, Ronald? What did Varadarajan call for? Anything important?'

'Yes, Saurabh. I have been summoned to see the governor of RBI in the next one hour. Are you aware of anything that I must know before the meeting? In fact he hasn't even told me the agenda for the meeting. He just wants to meet me in person and that, too, urgently.'

Saurabh's face looked as perplexed as Ronald's. 'Do you think it's connected with the investigation, Ronald?'

'Don't know,' said Ronald, as he picked up his jacket from the sofa and walked out of the room. 'Will tell you when I get back,' he added as he walked out into the lift lobby and pressed the lift button.

Early 2007 (A Few Years Ago)

Deputy CEO's Office, GB2
Fort, Mumbai

SANJIT Banerjee, the then Deputy CEO of GB2, was sitting in his office in a very pensive mood. In front of him was the latest RBI audit report on the retail lending business of GB2.

As part of a regular inspection process, the RBI had directed their auditors to spend over three weeks at the bank premises and audit the processes, controls and service delivery. And it was not looking good. GB2 had got over forty-six comments from the RBI, which were basically observations on matters that did not adhere to the guidelines issued by the RBI. An audit comment from the RBI was viewed as negative by every bank management.

In the entire history of GB2 in India the number of observations raised by the RBI had never hit double digits. But this time it was forty-six. Something had gone terribly wrong. A few voices in the bank management opined that the RBI was being vindictive and this was reflective of their approach to foreign banks. Sanjit had stepped in and nipped such talk in the bud. 'The RBI had no reason to be vindictive. GB2 was a clean bank,' he had said.

Was it the aggressive growth phase that they had got into? Was it lack of control or inferior process knowledge? Should they induct fresh talent? Would they get to where they wanted by just forcing a reshuffle and putting in seemingly smarter and more capable people in key roles? He did not have any answers. What made it worse for GB2 was that almost all the comments that the RBI had made last year still remained unsolved. No one in GB2 had bothered to act on the issues raised.

The starting point for preparation for any audit was the previous year's audit report and every organisation began by picking up the last audit report and evaluating its processes. A repeat of audit comments in subsequent reports was seen as an absolute lack of control, or at times even lack of intent on the part of the management to fix issues.

These problems were compounded by the fact that two months back an internal group audit had also identified the same set of issues. Yet again these issues remained ignored.

'It can't be systemic. Globally our processes and controls are the best in the industry. It is completely a failure on the part of our people. A clear lack of delivery! They have been terribly lax in the implementation of the issues raised by the audit team,' Sanjit kept rationalising to himself.

In a bank like GB2 even one audit comment was blasphemy, but here there were forty-six of them. It was enough to set alarm bells ringing. And unless he was seen to have taken stringent steps to fix it, his own job would be in jeopardy. As a Deputy CEO, he was directly responsible for all operational issues of the bank.

No wonder there was doom and gloom spread all over his room when his secretary, Sherlyn, walked in. 'Sanjit, Deepak Sarup is here to see you. He has an appointment with you at 11.30. You still have ten minutes. You haven't had any visitors since morning so I thought I'd let you know.' And she smiled. Her smile failed to cheer Sanjit up.

'Send him in. This is important...'

In the next couple of minutes Deepak walked into Sanjit's room, smartly dressed in a dark grey, pinstriped Louis Philippe suit. The smell of naphthalene and camphor from the 'just out of the trunk' suit mildly filled the room. Sanjit felt under-dressed in comparison. Deepak was certainly dressed to impress. It was not often that employees at his level were called by the Deputy CEO for a meeting and he made sure to look the part.

'Good morning, sir,' said Deepak stiffly as he walked into the room.

'Hey Deepak! Good morning. It's always good to see you.' It was clear that Sanjit was trying to put on a very cool behaviour as he did not want Deepak to see through the tension that had gripped him recently. 'Come on in.' Sanjit's handshake was very firm.

Both of them settled on the leather sofa in the corner of Sanjit's room. Deepak had hardly interacted with Sanjit in the past; there was neither an opportunity nor any need! He was the cluster manager for the four branches of GB2 in Mumbai for over two years now. In his chain of command, he reported to the country head of Branch Banking who, in turn, reported to the head of Retail Banking, Ramneek Chahal. Ramneek, too, had just moved into this role a couple of months back, from his erstwhile role as the head of Branch Banking.

An 'A-rater' for the last three years, Deepak held a prominent place in the talent pool of the bank. The 'talent pool' in most companies consists of high-potential individuals who the organisation feels can be groomed for larger roles. Deepak's biggest strength was that he had worked in every unit of the bank and was well-versed with the nitty-gritties of retail banking.

'Deepak, I am not too sure if you are aware why I have called you here.' Deepak drew a blank. He got the summons from Sherlyn and here he was at the appointed hour.

'Ok, then let me start from the beginning. We have just gone through a group audit almost immediately followed by the RBI's annual audit. The group audit was disastrous and the RBI audit was even worse. On the lending side of our business, we have got the worst audit report ever in the history of the bank. I'm really concerned.'

'I can understand, sir,' Deepak replied.

'You know my worry, Deepak? I believe that all this is due to a change in attitude towards audit and controls. And for me...this behaviour is highly contagious. It's like an airborne virus people catch from each other. And when that happens, Deepak, people change. And then they change other people. That's how one man's approach becomes the cause for an entire organisation's downfall.'

'Yes, sir, I agree,' Deepak said, nodding. Deep inside he was wondering why Sanjit was telling him all this.

'Deepak, I called you because I have seen the good work you have done on the branch banking side. I want you to move to the Credit and Risk team as head of Internal Audit and Control for that unit and get down to fixing all the issues that affect their core controls. I want you to bring in a culture of self-restraint, discipline and audit and control. You have to reign in the cowboys there and bring in a semblance of sanity.'

'But Sanjit...,' Deepak didn't know what to say. 'I have never worked in the Credit team before.'

'Deepak, you understand lending. You have worked long enough in the bank and in product management for asset products to understand that side of the business. All your branches and clusters have always been rated satisfactory in their audits. That shows your focus and diligence in dealing with audit and related issues. Process control comes naturally to you.'

Deepak was quite thrilled to be praised by the Deputy CEO. 'Sanjit, I don't want to be a pain in the back but that post is graded at the same level as the current one, and I have already been in this department for over two years. I have been a consistent 'A-rater' and a talent pool member. Why would you move me to a position which places me at the same level as I am currently working in?'

Sanjit's response to Deepak's question was a masterpiece. 'Because, my friend, the situation we are in is nothing short of a crisis. And in a crisis you pick your best man for the job. The reasons you are stating for not taking up this job are exactly my reasons why you must take it up. We need the skills of an 'A-rater' and the genius of a talent pool member to see us through this crisis. If we do not get our credit shop in control, we will be in deep, deep trouble.'

Deepak was at a loss for words. Thoughts deserted him. Sanjit's forceful appeal rendered him speechless. Besides he couldn't have refused the Deputy CEO of the company.

'I understand your point of view. This is an unprecedented situation. Forty-six comments on an RBI audit do not augur well for us and something needs to be done about it quickly. Assuming that I move in, how long would you want me to perform that role? And what happens to me after that?'

'You know that you have a reputation here, Deepak. Everyone values you and thinks highly of you. Don't worry, you will be taken care of. I would expect you to be in this position for twelve months at least. See us through the next audit and I will move you to a good position in business or sales, depending on what is available at that point in time. This organisation does not forget favours and by taking on this assignment you would be doing GB2 a favour.'

Deepak bought into the plan. Relief surged through Sanjit's body as Deepak stepped out of his office. The same evening, after speaking to Ramneek Chahal, Sanjit announced the appointment of Deepak Sarup as head of Internal Audit and Credit Control for the lending unit at GB2.

Dear Members of the Governing Council,

It gives me great pleasure to announce the appointment of Deepak Sarup as the Head of Internal Audit and Credit Control with immediate effect. Deepak will be responsible for managing the entire audit process across the lending business of the bank and implementing the actionables arising out of the group audit and RBI audit comments on a priority.

Deepak brings with him a wealth of knowledge from the branch banking team and is expected to take on this challenging assignment for a minimum of eighteen months.

I request you all to extend all possible assistance to him as he steps into a very difficult and challenging role. I wish him success in his new enhanced role.

Regards,
Sanjit

When Deepak saw this message, he was miffed. The message spoke about a minimum tenure of eighteen months, but his commitment was only for twelve months. This 'googly' was unexpected. He decided to confront Sanjit.

'Deepak, if everyone thinks you are going to be there for twelve months, no one will take you seriously. Even you would not take yourself seriously. It will take you three months to settle down and in another three months people will start counting the number of days you will hold on to this position,' Sanjit coolly responded.

'I don't want others to know about the understanding we have reached. I am quite happy to confirm this to you separately by mail that will remain between you, me and the HR manager.' Deepak looked convinced and didn't ask any more questions. Sanjit, to him, seemed an honest guy.

Within the next fifteen days, Deepak gave up his cluster and took up the audit and control role in credit with a mandate to rein in the business and credit teams and oversee the implementation of all the audit comments. He had his hands full.

17 December 2009

Fort, Mumbai

Ronald McCain's mind was bubbling with various conflicting thoughts as he entered the lift. What could it be? Why did the governor of the RBI request to see him at such a short notice? 'Request....' He let out a scornful laugh. *He was summoned.* Ronald had no choice but to go and see him. He didn't want the RBI governor to get annoyed.

What disturbed him the most was that Saurabh Bhambani, whose Compliance team normally managed the equation with the Reserve Bank, had no clue about this meeting. In the past all such requests were always routed through the compliance team and that, too weeks in advance. This was the first time he was called directly and without any real notice. Something had to be drastically wrong.

'Why can't these guys manage relationships with the regulators? Why can't they keep them happy? Do all foreign bankers in India have inflated egos when it comes to dealing with regulators, or is it only the GB2 folks?' Ronald was deep in thought.

He had heard that Citibank dealt very well with the regulators and hence sometimes even got away with murder but GB2 seemed to always end up rubbing the regulators the wrong way. How many things would he have to change? Had he made a mistake by accepting this assignment?

The lift opened and he stepped out on the corridor that led him to his private parking lot. His BMW-7 was parked there and the driver was ready with the engine and the air-conditioner on, holding the door open for him to get in.

He slid into the comfortable bucket seats at the back and waited for the driver to get in.

'RBI chalo,' he told the driver. He had learnt a smattering of Hindi to get by. The driver was an old timer and didn't need any further directions.

Within minutes the car was on the main road, negotiating bumper-to-bumper traffic and heading towards the office of the epitome of all banks in India.

Ronald took over thirty-five minutes to traverse a distance of four kilometres. All along he had only one thought on his mind. Why? Why? Why? Was it in any way linked to the current investigation? Did RBI find anything suspicious? Had his bank screwed up on anything? Or maybe it was just a casual visit. At times, the governor sought inputs from foreign banks on certain policy issues which impacted them. Maybe it had something to do with that. It could be anything. 'I should keep my calm,' he said to himself, again and again, but...it was all futile.

Early/Mid 2007

GB2 Offices, Mumbai

D EEPAK spent the first few days reading the group audit and the RBI audit reports. They were quite scathing. It took him some time to get his act together as it had been a while since he had worked in lending business. But the basics don't change over time; it was not too difficult for him to come up the curve. Within a week's time he had identified the core issue. He knew where the problem was. Sanjit was right. It was clearly one of will, of the desire to change in a few people in leadership positions. While the people down the heirarchy were reasonably capable, in the absence of proper guidance and leadership they had drifted.

In the second week, he prepared a detailed action plan for everything that needed to be done. It took him three days to work out a comprehensive makeover strategy. Soon he shot off a mail to Sanjit.

Dear Sanjit,

Please find enclosed a checklist of activities which I have prepared after going through all the audit comments. If we are able to implement the proposed steps over the next sixty to ninety days, we should be able to come clean on any audit that is conducted by our internal auditors or statutory authorities.

To implement this checklist I will need some resources to work with me. To start with, I would like to request you to allow me to hire four people. I will be requiring these four people to assist me in executing the action plan and meeting the stringent deadlines.

As the current crop of people in credit team is aligned to a particular way of functioning, I would not like to move any of them to these roles. I seek your approval to hire these resources from the market, or from other units of the bank.

I look forward to your thoughts on the activity list and also your approval on the headcount.

Regards,
Deepak

Within five minutes he got Sanjit's reply.

Dear Deepak,

I am extremely happy with the progress you have shown. You have made a huge difference to our credit controls team. Well done! Please treat the headcount as approved.

Regards,
Sanjit

The mail was marked to the entire top management of GB2. Deepak's chest swelled by a few inches with pride.

Over the next sixty days Deepak's importance grew manifold within the credit department. Riding high on the sponsorship of the Deputy CEO, he began to be abrasive with people. Given the background to his entry into the credit team, no one took him head on. Even the incumbent head of credit, Bhisham Sen, did not dare to lock horns with him.

Deepak was a one-man army. He was there with an agenda. With a problem to fix. And his only trip in life, for the time being, was to get the bank a satisfactory audit next time around. However, the line between arrogance and firm determination is a blurred one. And when Deepak crossed that thin line, no one knew. He was becoming a pain to deal with. This became apparent in the last week of July 2007.

It was month-end time. Month-ends in any sales organisation are very hectic and action-packed. Apart from the occasional screaming and shouting by the supervisors at sales guys who hadn't met their monthly targets the atmosphere in the office was festive.

Every sales business in the country including the financial services business experiences a sudden spurt in sales towards the end of the month. All of a sudden deals start getting closed, obstacles to the closures are removed, people start working more efficiently, customers come out of nowhere and deals start getting juicier for the customers. And this sudden positivity defies all logic.

This was true even for the loan business, especially the home loan business. In almost all the banks about 35-40 per cent of the home loans for the month were booked in the last two-three days of the month. Surprisingly, there were no records to suggest that 35-40 per cent of property deals were closed in the last week of the month. Then why did home loan sales only shoot up towards the end of the month? Even the smartest of managers couldn't crack this mystery. Various ways to stagger the loan disbursal evenly over the month, including incentivising the sales staff, had failed miserably.

Though such a month-end upsurge was welcome at any time of the year, it didn't come without its bag of problems. Month-end sales ut tremendous pressure on the entire system, which at times could ad to a breakdown. People were required to work late into the ight, even on holidays, which frustrated them. The entire support ystem would be on its toes to handle the level of throughput and ometimes that created chaos and confusion.

Karan Punjabi, GB2's Regional Head of Mortgage in western ndia, was marshalling his team that month-end. It was already the wenty-sixth of July. Five days to go for the month to end and there as a weekend in between. Karan was far short of meeting his monthly arget of ninety-six crore – he was off target by about forty-two crore. hings needed a desperate push in the last few days so that he could uch the magical number of ninety-six crores. In fact he was aiming r hundred crore worth of loan disbursal from Mumbai. A very npressive figure to quote in front of the entire management team.

It was late evening and Karan was having a cup of coffee with s sales guys and a few credit guys. He was a great motivator and brilliant team player who was rated very highly by the senior anagement at GB2. Deepak passed by. He looked at Karan and opped to ask, 'What are you folks doing here?'

'Month-end na. So we are getting the mortgage loans booked d disbursed,' one of the sales managers working under Karan lunteered.

'Why don't you guys work during regular days in a month? You n't need to work so hard and so late on a month-end!' He couldn't lp being sarcastic even when he was in no way involved.

'You have seen it yourself when you were on the other side in anch banking, Deepak. What's new?' said Karan and added after pause, 'as if you don't know how a sales team works.'

'Oh, yes, yes, I know. But that does not necessarily mean that I bscribe to everything that goes on.' He was nasty and aggressive.

'Hmm...that's your opinion. And I guess an opinion is like a asshole. Everyone has one. You have the right to yours, my friend. Karan was not the one to keep quiet. Deepak's caustic commen were the last thing he could tolerate as he was already annoyed du to his team's average performance that month. 'Come on, guy Let's not waste our time here,' he said as he walked out, leading h bunch of sales guys.

As expected, Deepak, too, was not thrilled with the way the tabl were turned. He was only trying for a smart repartee which backfire. The way he was insulted in front of the sales guys left him fuming. Ho could Karan do this? His dislike for Karan was legendary anyway.

There was a history to the Karan-Deepak story. Both of the were branch managers at one point in time in GB2 in Mumba Extremely competitive, smart and well-regarded. It was difficult choose the better of the two.

Competition often breeds dislike and that's what happened to th two of them. Over time, they reached a stage where they just couldn stand each other. What made matters worse was that Karan scored ov Deepak in the next promotion as he was seen as more of a peopl man and his ability to lead teams was apparently more evolved tha Deepak's. This peeved Deepak and he saw it as a loss of face.

Since then Deepak had always remained one level below Kara in the organisational hierarchy, even though he thought of himse to be more capable and efficient than Karan. That evening's tiff w yet another chapter added to their hostile history. Karan's sma comeback had left him angry and insulted. He had to do somethi to get back at Karan.

That day Karan was able to disburse loans worth only four cro He had four more days that month to disburse loans worth thirt eight crore left to meet the monthly target of ninety-six crore. F sat with his sales team that night to take stock and was reasonably confident that with the number of deals they had in the pipeline, he would be able to meet the benchmark easily. So, he didn't need to lose sleep. He went back home confident he would be able to beat the monthly target.

When he reached office the next morning, he was surprised to see some activity on the credit floor, very unlikely so early in the morning. The place was swarming with people. 'What were so many people doing there?' he thought. On a normal day there would be six or at the most seven underwriters there. (Underwriters are people who look at a loan application and approve or decline the loan.) That day they were double strength than their usual number. And none of the sales guys were around. He had in fact received quite a few calls from his sales team in the morning, which he did not responded to because he was driving to work.

He walked in that direction to figure out what was going on. And then he saw *him*. As he walked towards the credit team a head rose from the cubicle.

'Good that you came in. In fact I was going to call you.'

'And why would that be?' Karan was already beginning to get irritated.

'Karan, I do not want any sales guys on this floor today. I don't want them to be talking to any of the credit underwriters. We are doing an audit and we want to make sure everything is in order and not influenced by sales.'

'That's fine, Deepak, but don't you think your timing is wrong? We have four more days for the month to close and we cannot afford a disruption like this. And what is the agenda? What is the purpose of this audit? This was not on the plan. Has this been signed off by anyone?'

'It's a surprise audit. We planned it last night. We were a trifle worried about the quality of work on a month-end. If the entire system is so stretched that it is on the verge of collapse, how do you expect things to be normal? How do you expect an underwriter who normally works ten hours a day, to work for sixteen hours on a month-end and deliver the goods with the same efficiency? How can they look at loan applications with the same level of diligence if they are so overworked? How do you expect a valuer who values five properties a day to go out and value twelve of them in a day and still give you the same output? So, we want to make sure that in your quest for numbers the bank's interests are not compromised. Every loan that you book these days is in the range of 60-75 lakh. One loan going bad can wipe out the benefits that all month-end loans give you cumulatively.'

Deepak had a point. But this was not the right time to play it across. Karan figured out that it was futile going after Deepak. He knew that he had to raise this issue somewhere else. He stormed into the room of the credit head, Bhisham Sen.

'Bhisham, this is not done.'

'What, my friend?'

'Deepak can't be auditing us on a month-end. I am quite happy facing the music if there are any mistakes but I don't want him jeopardising my business at this crucial time.'

'What are you talking about, Karan? What has Deepak done?'

It was clear then. Bhisham was clueless about what Deepak was up to. Karan explained to Bhisham in painful detail what transpired between Deepak and him the previous evening and what Deepak was doing that morning to even the score.

Bhisham heard Karan out and grasped the issue. He instructed Deepak to back off and told him that audit could be done after the month was over. Deepak was not happy, but Bhisham was his boss and he could not have questioned his orders.

He immediately withdrew his team from the audit and moved them out. However, the sixty minutes that he spent with the underwriters wasted their precious time and impacted them. They suddenly became extremely worried about the consequences of any mistake that they may make. They were worried that a witch-hunt would begin in case of a goof-up, which would make life miserable for them. They became overcautious.

All the underwriters started spending unduly long time on the loan applications. If they spent twenty minutes in the normal course on a loan application, they started taking forty, which impacted their output. Applications could not be cleared at the speed required to meet the month-end targets and started piling up at the tables of credit underwriters for a decision.

Karan was getting frustrated with this slowness but he could not push the underwriters beyond a point. They did not report to him directly. And if he did push them he could have been accused of manipulating credit for the sake of business, which was not viewed well in GB2.

Karan and his team could only disburse eighteen crore in the last four days and thus fell short of his monthly target by twenty crore. For the first time in his career at GB2, Karan had missed his target by that huge a margin. What also hurt him was that the morale of his sales team was affected. Nothing really motivates the sales team more than achieving targets. Money and incentives are secondary. The adrenalin which gushes when you see your targets being overrun has to be felt to be believed. The entire team felt let down. They had in the pipeline cases to get to the target, but because of the fear which had set into the minds of credit underwriters due to Deepak's action, they were not able to close the pipeline deals.

In lending, it is said that credit is all about mindset. And the credit team in GB2 was just not in the right state of mind to deal with pressure, and Deepak obviously deserved the *credit* for that. The damage had been done.

When Karan raised the issue with his boss, he did not get much support. He was bluntly told that he should manage stakeholders better and should push things which were in his control rather than make excuses post a poor month. He got the message. The entire episode was not seen as a deliberate screw-up by Deepak but as a poor excuse by Karan for not having met the desired numbers.

Sudden access to the seat of power had turned Deepak Sarup brash and evil. Radically different from what he was when he was in the branch-banking world! And subtle victories like this one over Karan only made him more determined and wicked.

1 August 2007

Bandra, Mumbai

THE shrill alarm bell woke up Savitha. It was six in the morning and she was already fifteen minutes late. Life had been hurtling at a hectic pace for her. Her day usually began at 5.45 a.m. After a hurried cup of coffee, which was the only time she had to herself, her day would take off, almost at breakneck speed.

Her daughter Aakansha had to be packed off to school at 7.30, by which time Savitha had to cook her lunch, get her ready and be at the gate by 7.25 – at least five minutes before the school bus arrived. After bundling her into the bus, she would get ready and leave for work by 8.30 a.m. to reach office just in time at 9.00. In the afternoons, the maid would come to take care of Aakansha and would stay back till Savitha returned from work.

Life as a single mother had not been easy for her but she had still managed to make a success of it. The courage with which she had managed to pick up the pieces after she lost her husband and put both her and Aakansha's lives in order was admirable. Financially she was sound. She had a good job. Rent was not an issue as she owned a two-bedroom apartment in Mumbai. Her entire salary was available to take care of her and her daughter's needs. Mentally she was very tough – tougher than most men at her workplace.

Like everyday, even that day she walked into office at 9.00 a.m. She was very particular about reaching on time. While everything seemed fine, her instinct told her that it was not so. She passed a few desks on her way to her workstation. Heena was already there. Savitha saw her and smiled. It didn't evoke much of a response.

Shrugging her shoulders she walked to her desk and sat down. Heena's desk was right across hers, with only a two feet high wooden partition separating the two.

'Shhh...shhh.' She looked up. It was Heena trying to grab her attention.

'What?' She was a bit annoyed with Heena's response when she had walked into the office in the morning. 'Bitch!' she muttered under her breath.

'Boss is in a foul mood.' Heena didn't seem to mind her hostile looks.

'Is it? What happened?'

'Don't know. But don't go anywhere near him today. He might bite.'

'But why?'

'Am not too sure. But have heard that he was pulled up by his boss for not meeting the target this month.'

'But I thought that was because Deepak and his audit team created an issue. The pipeline was there. We had reviewed it on the morning of 28th before Deepak created chaos.'

'Dunno! Seems like his argument was not taken well. And Ramneek Chahal is extremely unhappy with him. Wealth Management, Insurance, NRI...in fact none of the teams under Ramneek have met their numbers this month. He was counting on mortgages to make it big – and we, too, didn't meet our target. Mortgages as a business would have met country targets, but Mumbai's numbers screwed it up big time. Ramneek apparently called up Karan and blew his top. This is what the grapevine says. I don't know what the true story is.'

'It's ok. In any case my targets were met on 22nd itself. So no one can point a finger at me,' said Savitha and got back to work.

'Savitha,' continued Heena, oblivious to the hostility demonstrated by Savitha, 'did you see Karan's mail this morning? He wants to do a portfolio review this month.'

'What portfolio review?'

'Apparently Bhisham has got back to him saying that the performance of his team is quite skewed. In fact Bhisham has pointed out to Karan that there are a few of his sales guys who are sourcing loans which are so bad that the customers have started bouncing their instalment cheques within a few months of availing the loans.'

'So?'

'So Karan wants to sit with all of us and mull over it. He wants to do it this week. He has just sent a mail this morning giving a heads up on this and wants us to be prepared.'

'Hmm...ok,' said Savitha and got up and walked out of the door to pick up a cup of coffee. That seemed better than listening to Heena's constant chatter. There was another reason for it. She knew that the loans sourced by her team were among the worst performing loans.

That morning again Deepak had laid out devious plans. The fact that Karan had been humiliated and fallen short of his monthly targets by a big margin was not enough to please him.

He walked up to Bhisham's room and knocked on the door.

'Bhisham, do you have a minute?'

'Yes, yes, come in,'

'Bhisham, I just want to emphasize an important issue to you.'

'Yes.' Bhisham was all ears.

'Bhisham, that day you stopped me from carrying out an audit on the month-end. I seriously think the business that we write at month-end is fraught with risks. The way even your credit team turns into file pushers in the last few days of the month defeats the whole purpose of their work. Neither is it advisable nor prudent. You have the entire sales team, led by Karan, sitting on the credit team's heads trying to get their cases approved. Is that a sensible thing to do?'

'Isn't that normal? Sales would push their cases. They have their numbers to meet, Deepak. If the credit folks can't stand up to them and argue their case, they don't deserve to be in credit.' Bhisham took a balanced stance.

Deepak was not the one to be discouraged so easily. 'Bhisham, do you actually think our credit underwriters across the board will be able to stand up to sales bludgeoning?'

'I would guess so. Why? You think differently?'

'Don't know, Bhisham. Maybe it is a good idea to find out. To do a stress-test on our system. I was talking to Sanjit and even he was worried about what goes on at the month-end.' He knew that Bhisham was too scared of the Deputy CEO to go and ask him. Deepak had become adept at name-dropping.

'Why did you speak with Sanjit on this?' There was a tinge of annoyance in Bhisham's tone.

'He had called me to talk about some other issues. This just came up during the discussion.'

'Hmm...ok.' Bhisham didn't have much to say.

'So, Bhisham, I am going to go ahead with my investigations unless you have any reservations. I wish to critically review each and every loan that has been disbursed on the last few days of the previous months. Is that ok with you?' Deepak delivered the final blow.

'It's ok. Go ahead,' is all he could say. If Deepak had Sanjit's approval, there wasn't much he could do about it.

August 2007

Mumbai
GB2 Offices

DEEPAK began to review in earnest the mortgage loans booked during the month-end. He wasn't going to make it any easy for Karan. Deepak was not going to let this opportunity pass without throwing his weight around and getting even with Karan.

A three-member team was put on the job to review all the loan files from end to end. Since Deepak did not have enough capacity within his team, he had arranged staff from the branch-banking side to work on the review project for four weeks. He carefully chose people who were aligned to him. They were given a deadline of three weeks to complete the audit. Deepak himself spent over three hours a day nitpicking with the team, trying to find fault with the entire mortgage process. Deepak was out on a witch-hunt. What started as ordinary corridor banter had now turned into a full-blown battle. Karan could only watch it unfold from the sidelines. (See box on p.38)

As a part of the audit, Deepak's team checked all the application forms. They went through all the verification reports with an intensity never seen before. All loan files were checked for adherence to predefined credit policy. The legal and valuation reports were read

The approval process for mortgage loans is a fairly involved process. Banks normally collect a host of documents from the customers, prior to sanctioning a loan, which include:

1. Income documents like pay slips/Income tax returns, to demonstrate that the customer has the income and employment to pay the instalments every month.

2. Identity proof and address proof – documents like passport copy, driving license, ration card are used as residence proof. Despite taking these documents most banks conduct an independent verification wherein they send agents to the customer's office and residence to verify the veracity of the details provided by the customer. These documents, also referred to as the Know Your Customer (KYC) documents, are mandatory documents as per guidelines laid down by the RBI.

3. Documents related to the property being bought – a housing loan is a loan provided against the collateral of the property being bought. Hence, it is important that banks satisfy themselves that the seller has the right to sell the property. They conduct a title search on the property being funded, for which the documents related to the property are taken. An empanelled lawyer then peruses these documents and gives the bank a legal report on the title of the property. This helps the banks in making sure that the property they are funding is a legally tenable property bereft of any encumbrances and in case the customer defaults, they will be able to knock on the doors of the court of law to recover their dues. They also conduct a valuation on the property which also helps them arrive at the market value of the property. Most banks fund around 70-80 per cent of the market value of the property as arrived at through the valuation process.

again and again to see if there was any laxity in following what the lawyers had asked for and if there were any slips. The legal kits were looked at through a microscope to make sure everything was in order. Not a single thing was left out.

One week went by. Everything seemed to be in good shape. Nothing of significance was identified as a flaw. Deepak was getting frustrated. It was a once in a lifetime chance for him to get even with Karan. But God didn't seem to be favouring him. How could he nail Karan? He had no clue.

While Deepak was spending time on the mortgage audit, his team was busy with the overall implementation of the RBI audit comments. As a part of their BAU (Business as Usual) responsibilities, they also conducted the monthly audit of credit delivery for the credit cards and personal loans businesses. Those two businesses had over the last few months fixed a number of product and process inefficiencies which had been pointed out in the earlier group audit and RBI inspections.

The first report of the monthly audit conducted by Deepak's team came out in the midst of the mortgage chaos. It showed that there had been a tremendous improvement over the last few months. When Deepak presented the same to Bhisham, he was ecstatic.

'So we are getting back on track, at least in cards and personal loans?' a beaming Bhisham asked Deepak when he saw the reports.

'Looks like it, Bhisham. This definitely looks positive. Clearly the processes that we have put in place now seem to be working.'

'Hmm...nice.'

'I think we should send it to Sanjit. Would you like to mail it to him or you want me to do it?'

'I will mail him right now. He will be pleased. I will also mark the mail to you.' Bhisham did not want Deepak to take away the laurels alone. This was an opportunity for him to win some brownie points.

'Sure, Bhisham. This calls for a small celebration, doesn't it?'

'Oh yes, of course,' said Bhisham and then added after a pause, 'in fact, why don't you organise one? Let's have a party this weekend. And we must call Sanjit and other senior management as well. After the last group audit and the RBI audits, the credit and collections teams have not been in the best of spirits. This party will help to boost their morale. Let's work at changing the perception of the credit team.'

'Sure, Bhisham, I will work on this,' Deepak assured him.

The party was planned for Friday evening that week. Raffles – a small idyllic joint in the heart of Bandra-Kurla Complex – was chosen for the party. Key people from the credit and collections teams and most of the sales guys were invited, apart from senior people in the management including Sanjit Banerjee.

An hour to go for the event, Deepak was examining the month-end mortgage files with the team he had assembled. They had yet not been able to dig up anything significant.

'Either all of you are duds, or we run a fabulous credit and sales shop in mortgages!' yelled Deepak. He was quite peeved at the failure of his team to pick out loopholes in the process. 'Three weeks and you are yet to pick out even one issue...and you call yourself auditors! Shame on you!' He was at the end of his tether. 'I am reasonably sure I have a team of incompetent guys who cannot find even a single lapse in a complex business like mortgage,' he hollered as he stomped out of the room.

'This week was supposed to be the last week of the audit and we don't even have one ace up our sleeve. If we do not find something by tonight, those fuckers will go away scot-free. I will have to do something, cannot rely on you losers,' he said before he shut the door on the three auditors sitting inside.

'Jai Ho' was the theme of the party, which was the first one in a long long time for the credit and collections teams. The title symbolised victory and Deepak wanted to make sure that he emerged victorious in the party. He was the 'hero' of the evening. Even though he had joined the credit and risk team just a few months back, he had made sure that everyone saw this success and improvement as his contribution. He walked up to Sanjit standing in a corner and bragged about what all he had done to get the team back on track. Sanjit nodded his head. After all, wasn't Deepak his choice?

Karan was there, too, with his entire team. He was not in a mood to party that night, but not turning up would have been politically incorrect. The senior management would not have viewed it positively. His direct reports were also there in the party.

Savitha and Heena were sitting in a corner, sipping coke and observing others. One after another everyone gave victory speeches and the audience clapped. It was turning out to be a boring chest-thumping event. And then finally it was Deepak's turn to speak. By then almost everyone except Bhisham had given Deepak all the credit for having turned around the process controls in the credit team. Deepak was the star of the evening, much to the chagrin of Karan and his team and even the other seniors in Bhisham's team.

Deepak spoke for a good five minutes. He seemed to have come prepared for the evening. It was a well-articulated performance appraisal speech. He outlined every single thing that he had done and even spoke about the month-end issues and the latest audit that they were doing. And then he dropped the bombshell.

'Some serious improprieties have been discovered, which we are investigating. The mortgage audit earlier scheduled for three weeks has now been extended by a week. I expect to close all my investigations by the end of the fourth week.' And then he looked at Bhisham and asked, 'Bhisham, hope you won't have any issues with that?' In the euphoria and the presence of the big shots of the office, Bhisham, though caught off guard, could not say no.

The moment Deepak uttered this, Karan looked at Bhisham and started protesting, but his voice was drowned in the sea of noise that followed because Deepak had smartly announced that the 'Bar is now open'.

Savitha, too, raised her eyebrows when Deepak spoke about the extension of the audit but let it be because she knew that Karan would do something about it. Anyway she was not too sure if she wanted to continue for long in the mortgage team. She had some other agenda on her mind. Deepak looked like an interesting guy and she needed to know what was going on in his mind. From the turn of events that evening he was an important guy to get to know in the long run.

Savitha tried to go close to Deepak a number of times but he was always surrounded by his team during the course of the evening. She couldn't catch him alone even once. After some time she decided to head back home. Aakansha would be alone with the maid, she thought.

The next day was Saturday and a bank holiday. Deepak was alone at home. His wife had gone to the temple in Matunga and hadn't returned. He was to play an important basketball match for his local team and couldn't go with her. After a quick shower he settled in front of the TV with his laptop. He watched a repeat telecast of India's 1983 cricket World Cup victory on ESPN. It was around the same time twenty-four years ago that the Indian cricket team had brought home the prestigious World Cup.

He logged into his email. His team had sent him some findings from the mortgage investigation which had to be validated and sent back to them. He read through everything and responded with his comments. He was done with it in an hour. Nothing was complex enough to have worried him. Since he had nothing else to do, he waited for his wife to return. Internet provided immediate relief from boredom. He started surfing the net. After checking his personal mails, he logged onto Facebook to kill time.

Many people in his friend's list had posted some weird messages on FB. Friends were turning into philosophers, going by their crazily profound status updates. Some of them were a rather puzzling combination of voyeuristic thoughts and self-pity. A few of them he found interesting and commented on them. Facebook intrigued him. How on earth could something so mundane as this take the world by storm, he often wondered. 'One day this will rule the world,' he said to himself, even as he moved his glance to the pending friend requests.

Ever since he had moved into the audit role and was perceived to be close to the Deputy CEO, a number of unrelated people had started queuing up to be friends with him on social networking sites – a fact confirmed by twelve pending Facebook friend requests. In fact he had logged in the previous night and had cleared most of them. He only accepted requests from people he knew well.

He checked the pending requests. There were three guys from the collections team, whom he summarily ignored. Someone had once told him that if one 'ignored' a friend request on FB, the sender gets to know it and that it could be considered rude if the sender was an acquaintance. It didn't bother him. His answer was, 'Facebook is for personal networking. If people want to network with me on Facebook, they need to know me first.' Fair enough, many would say, except the ones he 'ignored'.

Shankar Kapila – 'don't know him' – Ignore

Bhim Rao Gaikwad – 'hardly know him' – Ignore

Devika Narain – 'yuck! Ugly babe' – ignore

Tuhin Mukherjee – 'Ok' – accept

Akshay Jain – 'too junior' – Ignore

Baljit Singh – 'don't know him too well but Ok...good guy to be in touch with' – accept.

Then he came to the last request.

Savitha – 'Who is she? Do I know her? But wait...nice profile picture. Cute! Let me see more of her...oh yes, I know her. Wasn't she the one at the party yesterday? The mortgages chick.'

Within a matter of seconds numerous thoughts raced through his mind. Savitha's efforts to get closer to him had not gone unnoticed. He had seen her at the party. Someone had told him that she was in the mortgage sales team. He smiled. 'Why didn't I meet her earlier?' He had not really been long enough in his auditing role to have known all the sales guys. Maybe that's why he hadn't come across Savitha earlier.

Showing more interest than necessary, he clicked on to her profile and checked all her photographs and updates. She seemed an interesting person to him. He figured out that she was a single mom, had a seven-year-old daughter and lived in Bandra.

At that very instant the doorbell rang. Hurriedly he clicked on 'accept' and added her as a friend on Facebook. For the first time he had added someone he did not know as a friend on Facebook. But there was always a first time!

Radhika, his wife, came in as he opened the door.

'How was the game?' she asked. 'Won or lost?'

'Can we ever lose? Your husband has always won, baby. Be it a game of sports, career or life itself!'

Radhika smiled. She knew her husband better than anyone else. They were married for seven years now. In those seven years,

Deepak's life was dominated by his love for a few things – basketball was one of them. In his free time he played for a local but extremely popular neighbourhood club called 'Chembur Chargers'. They played in the Division 4 in the Mumbai basketball league. Deepak was the captain of the team.

When they got married Radhika had no knowledge of any sport, let alone basketball. However, after seven years of being with Deepak, she had begun to understand basketball very well – thanks to the overdose of the game she had to endure. She would often go to cheer her husband in the league games. That morning she had gone to the temple to pray for the Chembur Chargers. They were pitted against the strong Bandra Bulls in the semifinals. A win against them would catapult them into the finals and a win in the finals would not only make them the Division 4 champions but also ensure a place for them in the Division 3 league – something that had eluded them for years. And Radhika knew how important it was for Deepak to see his team through to the finals.

That night Deepak and Radhika went out to celebrate their team's win. After a long beer session at the Sports bar in the Phoenix mills complex in Parel, they returned late at night. Radhika was tired and went to sleep almost immediately. Deepak was not feeling sleepy. It was probably the adrenalin of having won an important game that kept him going. He switched on the TV and started surfing the channels. It was just a matter of time before he got bored. He silently tiptoed into the bedroom because Radhika was fast asleep and he didn't want to wake her up. The laptop was on the side rack – where he had left it in the afternoon. He picked it up and walked out of the room.

He connected to the Internet and started surfing. After a few minutes of checking mails, he moved to Facebook.

Shraddha had updated her status – Occupied, Confused, Happy... everything.

He raised his eyebrows and thought for a moment but could not understand what it meant. Six people had 'liked' the comment he was finding difficult to make sense of. 'What is there to like when someone is confused? Strange are the ways of Facebook users,' he said to himself as he moved on.

Suhasini had said, 'Mixed emotions.' What was that? Below that status update there were ten guys asking questions on what or rather who was the reason for her 'mixed emotions'.

Rajesh had said, 'Enjoyed the run in the park...after a long time.'

He was genuinely amused reading those updates. Some day people would write, 'Don't know what I ate, feeling constipated today', or maybe 'third time to the loo, something is definitely wrong...or is the system cleansing itself?' he thought. If Socrates or Aristotle were alive today, they would have had tough competition to face. Facebook philosophers could have given them a run for their money, or at least made them feel inferior. No one would need the former greats!

He was pondering over a few bizarre and meaningless status updates when he suddenly remembered Savitha – his latest friend on Facebook – and clicked on her profile. Her profile picture was amazingly pretty. Flawless skin, innocent face and sharp features – she seemed to be naturally beautiful. Though he had noticed her during the party, his ego had prevented him from indulging her. He clicked on her photo albums and looked through a few of her pictures. The more he looked at them, the more she intrigued him. There was something mysterious and alluring about her and he was not able to figure out what it was. He was lost in his thoughts, admiring Savitha's pictures when suddenly a message box popped up in front of him on the screen.

'Hi!' said the message. For a moment Deepak was confused. Who was this? He carefully looked at the box and smiled. It was Savitha. Was it some kind of telepathy at work?

Instinctively he typed, 'Hi.'

'Do you recognise me?' came the next message.

'Yes, of course.' Deepak was a bit nervous

'I thought you would not know me, so I thought it better to introduce myself.'

'No, no, not required, I remember you. Have seen you so many times at work. Even met you briefly yesterday. How have you been?' The conversation began formally.

'I am doing good. Was just surfing the net. Chatting with a few friends...saw you online, so thought of dropping in and saying "hi".'

'That's so nice of you,' He couldn't think of anything better to type.

The clumsy conversation carried on for a few more minutes after which Savitha signed off.

Sunday was a different story altogether. Early morning after his cup of coffee, Deepak sat with his laptop and logged into Facebook, hoping to see Savitha online. Pretending to be responding to some office mails, he waited for a few hours not doing anything, just logging in and out of Facebook. There was no sign of Savitha. He was beginning to get restless. There was no reason to be and he knew that. But there was something about the girl that interested him and caught his fancy. What was that? Why was he waiting for her to come online? This had never happened to him earlier.

Radhika sensed that something was wrong with Deepak but brushed it off thinking it was work pressure.

Finally Savitha came online at about 3 p.m. The moment he saw her, Deepak pinged her.

'Hi.'

'Hi there,' Savitha responded after a good five minutes and followed it up with a 'sorry, my daughter was around.'

'No probs...so how are you?' Yet again Deepak found himself searching for words – a clumsy beginning of a marathon session that lasted almost four hours. After that chat session, they both knew almost all the significant things that there were to know about each other.

Deepak got to know that Savitha had worked at Standard Chartered Bank (SCB) in credit card sales and had also had a brief stint in marketing before she joined Mortgage sales at GB2. He also got to know that she was a single mother who was working very hard to take care of her daughter who studied in class three at Arya Vidya Mandir. She had been in mortgages for over two years and was looking to move out.

Savitha got to know that Deepak was a career banker, a diehard basketball fan who played Division 4 league and was the captain of the Chembur Chargers. She also got to know that he liked single malt but never drank the night before a game. This she got to know when she asked him why he was not drinking at the 'Jai Ho' party. It was on the night before the semi-final match against Bandra Bulls.

The conversation they had was interesting. It was obviously very difficult to be talking about mortgages and credit for over four hours. The conversation extended beyond that, sometimes bordering on flirting. Whether it was casual, harmless flirting or intentional whether it was initiated by Savitha or pushed by Deepak, no one could say. But it was clearly not a conversation that a senior banker would normally have with a not-so-senior sales person on Facebook.

However, Deepak was besotted with Savitha and was completely in awe of her.

Radhika passed through the room quite a few times but never suspected anything fishy. She thought he was busy with some office work and didn't disturb him. Some vegetables and groceries had to be bought and she went alone because Deepak seemed too busy to be hassled. When she returned Deepak was still on the computer chatting with Savitha.

17 December 2009

Fort, Mumbai

LOCATED in a verdant part of Mumbai city, the imposing RBI building was all about brazen muscular strength and impregnable security. Starting from the Malad stone cladding to the sixty-foot high modern Corinthian columns to the flanking piers and the square-cut frontal section, everything was gigantic in size.

Ronald climbed the steps of the building to enter a large, impressive lobby. At the entrance he was received by Vardarajan, who ushered him into a waiting lift. The lift stopped on the eighteenth floor and both of them stepped out. Vardarajan didn't have to lead the way because Ronald had been there before. He had visited the governor's office many times, but it had always been planned and the agenda of the meeting was never so discreet as it was this time. This visit was unnerving, to say the least. He was there with absolutely no idea of what was in store.

They turned left into a long corridor. A musty smell took over the moment they stepped into the corridor. It smelt as if the carpet had not been cleaned or dusted for ages. But as they moved a little ahead, Ronald could see that it was cleaner and more inviting. The varnish on the wood panelling smelt fresh. Fascinating paintings adorned the walls of the long corridor. Pictures of illustrious former governors hung on the left while the right of the corridor had pictures of past presidents of the country. The framing of the pictures could have been slightly more imposing since this was the office of the Reserve Bank of India – the key and only regulatory body for governing the entire banking system in India.

At the end of the corridor was a door which opened into a large meeting room. Along with plush leather sofas, a carved antique centre table and other accessories the room had a view of the Mumbai harbour and the sea further. The water seemed calm, in stark contrast to the turmoil in Ronald's mind. Vardarajan left him alone in the room and disappeared. 'I will let the governor know that you are here,' he said before moving out.

Ronald's mind recapitulated his first visit to the RBI about a year back when he had come to meet the governor formally before taking over as the CEO of GB2. It was a very cordial meeting; the governor had welcomed him with open arms and sung praises of GB2 and almost acknowledged that no other bank was run in such a controlled manner as GB2. In those days, with banks collapsing like a deck of cards in the belligerent west, GB2 seemed to be as solid as the Rock of Gibraltar.

A lot had happened in the last one year. Many incidents transpired which highlighted the susceptibility, not only of GB2, but the entire banking system to manipulations by a few smart individuals. To a certain extent GB2 had borne the brunt of it. If the incidents of the past week were an indicator to go by, GB2 had reasons to worry. But Ronald was hoping that this meeting was called to address any issue other than that.

At that very instant the door at the far end of the room, which connected the meeting room to the governor's cabin, swung open and the governor walked in.

'Ah Mr McCain, nice to see you. Thank you for making it at such short notice.' The stern look on the governor's face belied any friendly overtures that his speech might have conveyed.

'Good morning, Mr Governor. How have you been?'

'I am fine, Mr McCain. Could have been better though.'

'I am sure.' Ronald was wondering what would come next.

'But you people keep us on our toes all the time. If it was not for the problems which keep cropping up, we would sleep easy.'

So his concerns were right! It was after all about the happenings of the last few days. This was the first time someone from the government or the regulators was talking to him about the chain of events which continued to traumatise him. And now whatever the governor was saying seemed to be confirming his worst fears.

'Mr McCain,' the governor interrupted his thoughts, 'we need to talk. Why don't you make yourself comfortable,' and he pointed towards the plush leather sofa on his right.

Ronald McCain just nodded his head and joined the governor as he sat down. They were hardly at a distance of three feet from each other but the chasm between them was beginning to grow deep. The governor spoke and Ronald McCain listened quietly.

23 August 2007

GB2 Head Office, Mumbai

IT was the middle of the third week of mortgage investigation. The team had not found anything to implicate Karan and his team yet. Deepak's frustration was mounting. He desperately wanted to show Karan down. It is surprising how personal agendas and motives drive businesses rather than propriety and genuine organisational need. Deepak was trying to drive one such agenda and, in all likeliness, was about to fall flat on his face.

The customer loan files seemed to be in order. There was no oversight except a few minor glitches that could pass off as clerical mistakes. He wanted a big catch; something serious that could be attributed to Karan's supervisory failure. He hadn't got anything yet. He didn't want the entire mortgage team to laugh at him. Wasn't he the one who had created a serious issue about the month-end pileup of loan applications and the risks of such a process? A dejected and frustrated Deepak decided to go home. He needed some company and a drink. But he never drank alone. 'Only drunkards drink alone,' he would say.

But who should he call? All his friends had gone back home. Radhika too, was not in town; she had gone to visit her parents in Pune. Suddenly a smile flitted across his face. He remembered his chats with Savitha. She had also given him her phone number. It was quite surprising how in his two-month stint he had never come across Savitha in the credit shop. 'Not surprising, idiot, just unfortunate,' his inner voice said. Maybe he was too busy with the new task at hand. Or maybe she never came there but got her work done on the phone instead. He picked up his mobile and dialed her number.

'Hi Deepak, what a surprise! How come at this hour?' It was well past 9.45 p.m., a bit too late to call a single mother.

'I was driving back home, I thought I will just call you to ask if you are in a mood for a drink?'

'Why? No basketball match tomorrow?' Savitha remembered that Deepak never drank the night before a match.

'Haha...no. I was just feeling a little bored. No one's at home, so I was wondering if we could just catch up for a drink. I can come towards Bandra if it is ok with you.'

'Sure, Aakansha has also gone for a sleepover to a friend's place, so I am game.'

Things were moving a bit too fast. They had hardly known each other for a few days now and they were already heading out for a drink. It seemed more like a date. As Savitha's apartment was located bang on the main road, it was not difficult for Deepak to find the house. It was 10.30 p.m. by the time Deepak parked his car outside Savitha's residence.

Savitha was waiting for him. Dressed in a ravishing, body-hugging black skirt that ended just an inch above the knee, she looked extremely sensuous. One look at her and Deepak was smitten. He had figured out from her Facebook profile that she was about ten years younger to him. 'Gosh! Wish I was born a few years late! At least then I could have given myself an even chance of meeting her before marrying Radhika,' he thought. With an age difference of ten years, there was no hope in hell that he would have met her in office, fallen in love and married her. Unless her parents believed in child marriage! He was deep in thought when Savitha got into his car and sat down next to him.

'Let's go,' she said.

He smiled. 'Looking nice.'

'Thank you. You are being kind.'

'And you modest,' Deepak replied. She just smiled in return.

A pleasant fragrance filled his car the moment Savitha entered. He sniffed to figure out which perfume it was. When he couldn't, he sniffed harder.

'You don't like it?' asked Savitha. Probably he made it too obvious.

'What?'

'The perfume?'

'No, no, it's nice. Why?'

'You have been sniffing very hard ever since I got into the car, so I asked.' She had a naughty smile on her face.

'Oh, not at all. In fact it's really nice. I was just trying to figure out which one it is.'

'It's Carolina Herrera 212. One of my favourites,' she said with a twinkle in her eye.

'Ok, so now it's my favourite too.' He smiled back at her. He was not a natural flirt.

'Are we going to just sit in the car, or will we head somewhere?' Savitha asked. That's when Deepak realised the car was still at a standstill. Shifting the Scorpio into first gear, he drove out of Savitha's building and headed to the Hawaiian Shack on 16th Road in Bandra.

It was a night full of fun, excitement and drinks for the two of them. They were the last ones to leave the Hawaiian Shack and that, too, at 2.00 a.m. In fact they had to be practically thrown out of the pub, as it was well past closing time.

'So where do we go now?' asked Deepak, not in a mood to call it a night as yet.

'Wherever!' Savitha was forthcoming, too.

'Let's go to Bandstand. I have a few beers in my car. We can finish them before we head home.'

'Wow! Car mein bar!' said Savitha. She was a bit high that night. At least it seemed so. But she didn't want to go home. She liked Deepak's company.

The car stopped at Bandstand. Deepak rolled down the windows. They could feel the sea at a distance. It was pitch dark and the sea was not visible. The cool sea breeze was blowing lightly in their direction and the waves were crashing against the shore. It made for a very romantic ambience. Deepak got down and pulled out a few more cans of beer from the boot. His favourite was Kingfisher and he always kept a few cans in the cooler in his car. Savitha, too, got out and they made their way to the seats on the Bandstand Promenade.

They sat down and started reminiscing about their life, career and family. Savitha was the more outspoken of the two. Deepak just listened. It was close to three in the morning. In any other city, it would have been a cause for concern but not in Mumbai. Mumbai was as vibrant in the night as during the day and more safe than most of the other cities. So it did not worry either Deepak or Savitha that they were sitting alone on a dark stretch in the middle of the night. Even the two beat constables who came to harass them backed off after a mere glance.

During the course of the conversation Savitha casually said, 'Too much of chaos today at work.'

'Why, what happened?' Deepak wanted to know.

'Nothing much. Gopal created a ruckus.'

'Who Gopal?'

'He is also a mortgages sales manager. My counterpart.' Savitha informed.

'Oh...yeah, I know him,' Deepak acknowledged.

'He had disbursed a five-crore loan last month. It was the largest loan across the country. It has now come back for cancellation.'

'Why?' Deepak asked curiously.

'The customer has said that he doesn't want the loan now and has asked us to cancel the disbursal cheque.'

'What? He is asking to cancel a five-crore loan? And twenty-odd days after the loan was disbursed! Why?' Deepak was astonished.

'He claims that he never wanted the loan and he was conned into taking it.'

'Bullshit!' Deepak was incredulous. 'How can anyone con you into taking a loan worth five crore? Where is that cheque now?'

'That's what he says, and now he doesn't want the loan. The cheque is still with us. It has not been handed over to the customer or the builder from whom he is buying his property. We just issued the cheque on the thirtieth of last month, at the month-end and kept it with us so the same could reflect in last month's numbers. The sales guys told the credit team that the customer would take the cheque on the second or third and had confirmed the request for issuance of the cheque. The entire legal documentation was also executed by the customer and the cheque was issued thereafter.'

'So what was the chaos about?.

'Gopal, who had sourced the loan, was arguing with Karan on the incentive for that loan. According to Gopal, he and his team had put in the required effort. He did not want to be held responsible for the cancellation and that, too, after the customer agreed to the loan disbursal. He wanted to be paid full incentive.'

'And did Karan agree?'

'No, he didn't. He said that ideally he would have paid but for such a large ticket loan, unless the customer accepted the cheque, he wouldn't agree to the release of the incentive. And incentives are huge. For this loan alone, the incentive would be around three lakh.'

'Wow! That's big money,' exclaimed Deepak. 'But tell me, Savitha, does this happen very often?'

'These days it is happening a bit too often...and that, too, with loans booked in the last few days of the month.'

'Hmm...I can imagine. Gopal would have been disappointed, though.'

'Oh yes. He was arguing with Karan saying he worked on the case and got it approved in four days flat. He spoke with the lawyers and valuers and worked out the entire logistics for the case within four days. So he was adamant that he should get the credit for the loan.'

'Ok, but isn't he supposed to stay away from the valuers and lawyers? Aren't they managed by the credit folks? The sales guys are supposed to not talk to these vendors directly. Isn't that the way it is supposed to be?'

'Yes, Deepak, but practically hota nahin hai. It doesn't happen the way you are saying. If sales doesn't go and interface with these guys, no business will happen. Credit just doesn't have the sense of urgency, you see,' Savitha made her point.

'Hmm...yes. But why are we talking about mortgages and loans in a such a deadly weather! Don't we have better things to talk about?' Deepak said, flirtatiously.

'Of course!' Savitha agreed. 'No more shop talk now.'

Even as they chatted about other things, the revelation by Savitha was constantly playing at the back of Deepak's mind. Something had to be done. What Savitha had just told him had given him the ammunition against Karan. It was up to him how he used it.

By the time Deepak dropped Savitha back home, it was 4 a.m. He went upstairs to leave her till the apartment door. The intent was to kiss her goodbye. But at the last moment, better sense prevailed and he turned back from the door without kissing her. He was not too sure if it was the right thing to do or the right time. In another fifteen minutes he was back in his pad in Chembur. Sleep had deserted him. He was lost in thoughts of Savitha and what she had told him. He had just unearthed something which could turn the world upside down for Karan. Deepak was too excited about the possibility.

The next day was a holiday due to Ganesh Chaturthi and hence the late-night sleep did not impact Savitha's or Deepak's work.

17 December 2009

RBI Headquarters
Mumbai

'So, Mr McCain, this is where we are,' the governor ended his monologue. All along Ronald McCain was just listening to the governor without saying anything.

'So what is the RBI planning to do about it?' Ronald finally asked.

'Mr McCain, you know RBI does not normally tolerate any interference nor does it take instructions from any department of the central or state government. But this is not a normal situation. The finance and the home ministries are after my life. Serious questions have been raised about the policies and procedures followed by foreign banks in general and your bank in particular. And this time I am at the receiving end. It is a serious breach and I can't afford to be seen not acting. I am sure you understand where I am coming from.' The governor was blunt and to the point.

'Yes, Mr Governor, but I am sure you realise these issues could happen in any other bank as well. It's not about Greater Boston Global Bank in particular, but the entire banking system. Why single out my bank for this?'

'It's because these irregularities have been discovered in your bank, Mr McCain,' and after a pause he added, 'all the others are clear as of now. We haven't found anything problematic with any other bank. When we find something, we will take appropriate action against them.'

Ronald couldn't argue further.

'So, Mr McCain, your bank needs to sort things out. Let's see how we can deal with it in the best possible manner.'

'What do you recommend, Mr Governor?'

The RBI governor turned his face towards the door for a brief moment and then left the room saying, 'I will be back in a moment.' He quickly disappeared behind the door that opened into his cabin. Within a few minutes, he was back in the meeting room with an envelope in his hand.

Placing the envelope on the table he looked at a visibly pained Ronald, who was trying to guess what was going on in the governor's mind.

'We have discussed the issue internally and we have no other choice. I will be grateful if you could acknowledge the copy of this letter and hand it over to us. Normally, I would not even have got involved in this, Mr McCain, I would have allowed the Additional Director of Banking affairs to manage this. But given the sensitivity of this case and the possible ramifications, I decided to handle this myself. After this meeting, I have to report to the finance ministry.'

Ronald extended his right hand and accepted the envelope. He pulled out the letter from inside the envelope and began to read it. What he read left him in a state of shock. The letter from the RBI was a warning he had not expected – a warning that could have far-reaching impact on shareholder value back home.

24 August 2007

Anil William's Residence
Bandra, Mumbai

THE entire country was celebrating Raksha Bandhan which coincided with Ganesh Chaturthi that year – a festival when Hindus celebrate the birth of the elephant God Ganesh.

Anil Williams loved Ganesh Chaturthi even though he was not a Hindu. Not that he was particularly fond of Lord Ganesh or was deeply religious. In fact he had not even been to a church for quite a while. Anil and his wife Rimi had high-flying careers and they were seen as iconic professionals in their respective fields. It put tremendous pressure on them, something they enjoyed, but it also kept them out of home for long hours. They would leave early and come back late at least six days in the week. On any working day, the doorman would press the button of the motorised gate to open the barricade for Anil's car to glide into his residence's parking lot well past 10 p.m. If it was a crisis day, well, he would never make it before the early hours of the morning. The doorman would invariably open the door muttering a few obscenities, which Anil would have ignored, had he heard them. In any case, they were never loud enough.

Dhruv, the five-year-old son of Anil and Rimi, would be at home with his grandparents, waiting for his father to be back. After waiting till nine, he would be tucked into bed by his grandmother and patted to sleep, more often than not unwillingly. He would try to keep awake till the time sleep would overcome him.

Holidays like Ganesh Chaturthi gave Anil time to spend with his son. He would take him out to play cricket, go cycling with him, play with him in the Carter Road promenade and shop with him for all the boy stuff. Dhruv liked it, too. The time he spent with his father was quite exciting. He yearned for more such days.

'Dad!' Dhruv called out to Anil innocently. 'Why aren't there more gods like Lord Ganesh?'

'Because one Ganesh is capable of finishing all the modaks in this country,' said Anil and when it didn't elicit a response from Dhruv and instead brought a puzzled look on his face, he shrugged his shoulders innocently and added, 'I guess so.'

'But then we only get one Ganesh Chaturthi in a year. Many more gods will mean many more holidays na, Dad?' Noticing the sad look on Dhruv's face, Anil walked up to him and took him in his arms and cuddled him tightly. 'Dad, why can't you be at home and play with me every day?' Anil had no answer to Dhruv's naive question. He hugged Dhruv even more tightly and the two of them fell on the bed playing with each other.

After a few minutes, Anil affectionately whacked Dhruv on his butt.

'Ouch, Dad! It hurts.'

'You are stinking, my boy. Get up! Time for a shower.'

Anil and Dhruv had just come back from a cycling trip to Carter Road, up and down Union Park, back to Bandstand and then to their house in Bandra. A nine-kilometre bicycle ride was bound to make them sweaty, especially at 4 p.m. when the sun is at its peak. Rimi was away in Bengaluru for a corporate interview and hence Anil was in charge.

Jumping excitedly at the suggestion, Dhruv removed all his clothes and dashed to the bathroom. The water in the jacuzzi came on with a whizz, gushing in from all sides, and Dhruv jumped into the water, squealing joyfully. Anil just smiled. Dhruv loved being with his father, and it was *his* day.

Dhruv was extremely possessive about Anil. He would not let Anil touch his mobile when he was with him. It was futile for Anil to even try. Dhruv would scream so hard whenever he picked up his phone that he would have no choice but to hang up. The phone would be confined to a corner of his work desk in the bedroom till Dhruv went to sleep. Anil gave in to Dhruv's desires simply because he suffered immense guilt at not being able to spend enough time with him.

After an early dinner, Dhruv, tired post a day filled with excitement, went off to sleep. Anil got up from the bed, switched on the television and began watching the replay of the historic India vs Australia test match played at Eden Gardens in 2001. Rahul Dravid and VVS Laxman were launching an attack on the Aussies on the fourth day, and Anil was a huge Dravid fan. As he was sinking into his red automatic recliner, which Rimi had got for him on his thirty-sixth birthday, he remembered something and got up instantly. He walked out of the TV room. Ten steps and two doors later, he was in his bedroom standing by his cherry-hued study table. His eyes scanned the table but couldn't find what he was looking for. He looked around the room and still couldn't find it. Unfazed, he walked into the living room and looked around in vain. He returned to his bedroom, picked up the cordless phone and dialled a number.

A feeble, muzzled noise could be heard from the other room. He walked in the direction of the noise. It was emanating from the vicinity of Dhruv's room. He walked towards the room, cordless in hand. The sound was getting closer. It seemed to be coming from Dhruv's cupboard. Opening the door of the cupboard, he moved around some of Dhruv's clothes and there it was. Dhruv had carefully hidden away his mobile phone, obviously worried that a call would take Anil away from him. He turned to look back at Dhruv, smiled affectionately, walked up to him to give him a peck on his cheek and quietly walked out of the room.

On his way out, as he stretched his left hand to switch off the light in Dhruv's room, he glanced down at the large screen of his mobile phone – six missed calls and eleven unread messages were waiting for him.

Walking back to the confines of his room, he checked the calls he had missed. Two were from Rimi. Manageable. She would understand why he did not pick her calls. If it was urgent, she would have called on the landline or spoken to his parents. One was from Jacqueline, his secretary at work. 'She will call back if it's anything urgent; it is too late to return her call,' he muttered to himself. One was from an unknown number and the other two were from Karan, his boss. He suddenly perked up. Why was Karan calling on a weekend? He normally did not disturb his colleagues on a holiday. But that day there were two calls from him. It had to be urgent. Thankfully the two calls were in the last thirty minutes. He pressed the dial button and lifted the phone to his ear. When he disconnected after five minutes, he was a relieved man. Karan just wanted some information for an early morning meeting the next day. He then went to his inbox to look at the unread messages.

The moment he opened his inbox, he let out a moan. 'What the hell is this? Nine promotional messages. Will the National Do Not Call (NDNC) list ever work?' He had dutifully registered for the NDNC Registry over a year back and despite that got at least eight to ten promotional messages on his mobile everyday. As he was about to keep his phone down, his eyes rolled over to a nondescript message from someone he knew very well. He was quite surprised because the person who had sent him the message was not someone who would usually engage with Anil and his team. He pressed the 'Open' button and the message was on his screen.

Anil read the message once. He did not understand it. He first dismissed it as a prank. Then he read it again. And again. And slowly it sunk in. He slumped back on the sofa, which cushioned his fall. His heart was beating faster. His pulse raced. A few drops of sweat appeared on his forehead despite the chilling impact of the AC.

Why was this sent to him? Had the sender really intended to send the message to him? Worse still, if he was not the intended recipient, who was the message intended for? What should he do? Should he share it with someone? Or should he keep quiet about it? He didn't know the answer. The phone loomed back into his line of sight. He read the message again:

'We must plot some dirty, manipulative stuff on shitface. Savitha hates him, Gopal hates him. We should somehow get Richard, Anil and Ganesh to hate him as well. Kuch kar yaar...we r so close to getting him bumped off!!!'

What worried Anil was that all the four names mentioned in the SMS – Savitha, Gopal, Richard and Ganesh – reported to Karan. So the shitface in the SMS was Karan. Even an idiot could figure that out. Karan was the only common factor that linked all the names in the SMS. What shocked him more was the source of the SMS.

The sender was Deepak Sarup. And it was sent at 4.45 a.m. in the morning. He had missed the message since he was occupied with Dhruv the entire day and had not been able to check his phone.

Why did Deepak send the SMS to him? Was it a mistake? Was it sent to him intentionally? Was there something else behind this? Was there a sinister plan to derail Karan's team? He didn't know.

He picked up his phone and read the message several times. He was shocked. The vicious tone of the SMS was too appalling for his comfort. And, more importantly why was it sent to him? It had to be a mistake. Should he send it to Karan? Should he call back Deepak and ask? He didn't know what to do.

And then as he read it for the umpteenth time he figured it out. Deepak had wanted to send the SMS to Amit Sharma, the credit head for mortgages. And instead of typing 'AMI' on his mobile, he typed 'ANI' and carelessly clicked 'send' on the first name that showed up from his mobile's phone book.

It dawned on Anil that both Deepak and the mortgages credit head were hand in glove. They were conspiring to get rid of Karan, his boss, who was a nice man and a rigorous sales manager.

He kept the phone on the side and decided to think about it the next day.

25 August 2007

GB2 Headquarters, Mumbai

Anil reached office the next day wondering what he should do about the SMS he received on Ganesh Chaturthi. He was a bit confused, not knowing if it was sent to him by mistake, intentionally or if someone was playing a prank. Even if it was a prank, he didn't know if was directed at him or Karan. Not only confused, he was also a bit nervous. Was this a racket he was about to expose?

He was in early that day. Savitha, too, had reached by then. Their seats were quite close by. However, he did not go to her directly. After logging into his laptop, he pinged her, on the intra office chat messenger.

'Hi.'

The message popped up on Savitha's screen. She turned and looked behind. She knew where Anil would normally sit. His eyes were glued to his screen. Wondering why he would ping her when she was sitting right in front of him, she began the chat.

'Hi?'

'What are you doing?'

'Responding to some mails. Some pricing requests. Why?'

'See me in the conference room in the next two minutes. Want to show you something.' She saw Anil get up and walk towards the conference room.

Savitha was in the conference room in the next two minutes where Anil was waiting for her.

'Did you get any SMS from Deepak yesterday?' He seemed to be in a hurry.

'Deepak? Why?' Savitha was surprised. Had someone seen them together? Her guilty mind walked a different track.

'Because I got this SMS from Deepak yesterday. Did you get this, too?' he asked her.

Savitha took the phone from his hands and read through the message. She couldn't understand what was written. Why would Deepak send such a stupid message to Anil? She couldn't understand. 'No, Anil. I didn't get this message. But why would Deepak send this message to you? I am sure there is some kind of misunderstanding here. Why don't you check with Deepak?'

'No, I will talk to Karan first. Let him deal with it the way he thinks appropriate.'

'That might be the right thing to do.' And Savitha walked away from the conference room. The fact that she disliked Karan was known to everyone, including Karan himself. If anything, the sender of the message had got his facts right.

That evening Bhisham called Deepak.

'Deepak, Vikram Solanki just spoke with me.' Vikram was GB2's Head of HR

'Yes, Bhisham. What is it about?'

'Apparently there is an SMS that has gone out from you yesterday to someone in Karan's team, which seems to raise a finger at your personal integrity.'

'What? What SMS are you talking about, Bhisham? I am not aware of any such message' Deepak seemed shocked and surprised at this allegation.

'Look,' said Bhisham and showed him an email. It was written by Karan to the head of HR and copied to the CEO and even to the head of retail banking.

Dear Vikram,

I am extremely disturbed by this incident. This has wider ramifications as we go about building our loans business and that's the reason why I am raising this to you.

Background

On Wednesday (24 August), 'Anil Williams' received a message on his phone from Deepak Sarup, which, I presume, was sent to him erroneously. I would like to believe, looking at the contents, that the message was meant for someone else but was sent to Anil by mistake. Anil too was extremely shaken up and showed it to me this morning. He showed it to me a day late because the day he received the message was a bank holiday. I am reproducing the contents of the SMS below.

We must plot some dirty, manipulative stuff on shitface. Savitha hates him, Gopal hates him. We should somehow get Richard, Anil and Ganesh to hate him as well. Kuch kar yaar. We r so close to getting him bumped off!!

I am concerned about the contents of this message because it speaks about me and I feel reasonably threatened by this malicious effort to plot against me. It also affects my ability to deliver on my job. Such behaviour by the seemingly responsible people of this organisation will be detrimental to organisational goals.

Anil and I can come across and show you the message he received on his phone.

> *Given that the message is manipulative, personal and against the collaborative spirit that all of us are working in, I would request you to take appropriate action.*
>
> *Regards,*
> *Karan*

'Would you like to say anything about this, Deepak?'

Deepak did not know what to say. He definitely seemed to be searching for words in his defense.

'What time was it sent?' Deepak asked.

'Sometime yesterday morning, though the mail doesn't state that. That's what Vikram told me when he called.'

'Hmm, now I understand.' Deepak pretended to have suddenly discovered something

'What?'

'Wait,' said Deepak as he pulled out a phone from his pocket. It was a new Iphone. 'Remember I had a different phone earlier. That one got stolen the night before. I bought this one yesterday. It's not even active. I have asked for a duplicate SIM which will come today. I have been using my Blackberry for making calls all day. If only someone had spoken to me before making it so big, I would have clarified.'

'What exactly do you mean?' Bhisham looked perplexed by Deepak's explanation.

'Obviously someone has found my phone in office, someone who knows about the issues Karan and his team have with my team, and he has exploited the situation. Or maybe someone just wanted to create some nuisance. Or wait a minute...'

'What?' Bhisham was incredulous.

'Could it be that Karan has an inkling of what's coming his way in the audit report? Maybe he is just trying to be aggressive here so that he can blunt the blow of the audit report by diverting attention,' Deepak said, making an attempt at rationalizing Karan not approaching him prior to shooting out a mail to the CEO.

'As in?'

'By using this SMS he will claim that I am vindictive towards him and thus have been deliberately unfair in the audit report. Yes, yes...now I understand his game plan. What a mastermind he is!'

'Hmm...possibly, Deepak. I always thought he was a clean guy. Anyway, now that you speak of this angle...' he paused for a few seconds and then said, 'anything is possible in this world. Listen, why don't you draft a formal message for me to send to Vikram? Since he called me to discuss this, I will have to go back to him formally.' Bhisham was not interested in the Deepak–Karan politics. He just wanted to make sure he responded to Vikram as early as possible and got the matter off his back.

'Right away, Bhisham.'

The moment he got out of Bhisham's room he took out his Blackberry and called on a number. 'Hi.'

'Thanks, baby. Good that you told me about the chaos. Helped me weave a story and they bought into it. I didn't even know that the SMS had gone to Anil till you told me. All this while I was wondering why Amit didn't respond to my message. Thank God I got to know about this on time. And, babes, you are the one because of whom I missed all the calls on my other mobile yesterday. That's what saved me today.' Deepak felt relieved.

'But how? How am I responsible for that?'

'Dumbo, the whole day we were in touch na...on Facebook. And I spoke to you for hours on my Blackberry. I ignored all the calls that came on my other phone. And I never returned those calls because yesterday was a holiday. In case someone checks my phone records, it will show that no calls have been made or received yesterday.' The previous day, Deepak had spoken to Savitha only from his official Blackberry and never on his personal phone so that his wife would not suspect anything fishy. Whenever Radhika saw him on his Blackberry, she would assume that he was on some official call.

'Haha...smart boy. Now Karan has no story to tell.'

'Yes, babes. Now see how I hit back at him. Watch out for the report. It's based on what you told me yesterday. And one more thing before I forget, just be careful this month-end. Even if you don't meet your targets this month, it's fine. You will have enough excuses once the month gets over. But I assure you, there will be no one to whom you will need to make those excuses.' Clearly indicating that Karan would be history soon, Deepak added, 'My SMS might have gone to the wrong person but there is no let down in the intent.'

'Yes, I know that.' Savitha laughed. 'But be careful about what?'

'Just be careful that you don't do anything stupid this month-end. Follow the process. Control your sales force. Targets are secondary. Don't get caught doing anything which is not acceptable from a sales process perspective. After this month-end Karan won't exist.' Deepak was confident of Karan's downfall.

'Be careful, baby.' This was the first time Savitha had called him like that. And Deepak liked it. He wanted to hear it again.

'What, babes? What did you just say?'

'I said be careful, baby. Now go. I have work to finish.'

That was the end of their conversation.

Deepak couldn't wait for the end of that month. He spoke with Bhisham and extended the audit by a few more days so that it would include month-end. Bhisham, too, quietly agreed. He had time and again proved to be a spineless boss who could not take a stance. He had to be pushed at all times. Deepak always had his way with him.

August was turning out to be an extremely bad month for Karan. Against a target of 110 crore of home loan disbursals for the month, he was at 52 crore on the twenty-seventh of August. With four days to go, he had to get another 58 crore of disbursals. The same month-end jinx was catching up. In July, Deepak's histrionics had made them miss their targets. The hangover seemed to continue in August.

In desperation he called for a meeting of all his sales managers. Everyone came in at 9.00 a.m. Karan was already there. The numbers didn't look good. They were not stacking up. The best-case scenario for everyone added up to 115 crore and as anyone in sales would know, the best-case scenarios seldom worked out for everyone at the same time. Someone or the other would screw up. And the final numbers would always fall short of the cumulative best-case scenarios. He was most likely to end the month at around 80-85 crore of home loan disbursals – a shortfall of approximately 20 per cent on his target. For a second month in a row he would be below his target and this made him nervous.

'Get the loans. At any cost! Give whatever pricing the customer wants and make sure we don't lose a single case,' he thundered to his team.

It always paid to take loans from banks on a month-end because suddenly the banks would become a lot more flexible, more willing to take risks and they also offered significant discount on interest rates. A customer always gained in this desperation that banks demonstrated on a month-end.

'Let's meet up in the evening at eight after all your teams return from their respective calls. I want to personally meet every one of your executives. So make sure no one goes home till I have spoken to them.' Karan gave strict orders to his sales managers.

The same evening twenty sales officers of the Mumbai mortgage team assembled in the conference room on the third floor, eagerly awaiting Karan's lashing. They were initially very quiet. The poor numbers were reflecting in their drooping shoulders and weak body language. Their confidence was low and they seemed quite nervous. The nervous silence slowly changed into whispers as they confided their fears to each other, which then transformed into an incessant chatter.

Soon everyone began to laugh and gossip when the door was flung open all of a sudden. Most of them expected Karan to come in and impulsively stood up. But it was not Karan who entered the room.

'Good evening everyone,' thundered Deepak as he walked into the room unannounced. Behind him were three other members of his team. And standing with him was Amit Sharma – the mortgage credit head. All the guys in the room were wondering why Deepak was there, especially when they were expecting Karan.

As if he knew what they were thinking, Deepak began to talk, 'I am sure you must be wondering why I am here.'

'What's going on? Why are you here?' Karan had just walked into the room where he was supposed to do a sales review, only to find Deepak already there.

'I am glad you are also here. We are here to do a quick audit of the sales process. We need to check the bags of all your sales RMs. This is our standard operating procedure and we have a sanction from Bhisham. Hope you will not have no problem with it, Karan?'

'Why wasn't I told earlier? Aren't you supposed to show the basic courtesy of informing me about the audit, investigation or witch-hunt, whatever you call it?' Karan was frustrated with this new development.

'Oh yes, Karan. We would have done it. However, in this case it is supposed to be a surprise check and even the channel heads are not informed about such surprise checks.'

'What??' Karan had an annoyed look on his face. He knew he did not have a choice. His entire team was present in that room and all of them were to be subjected to the random audit. They could be exposed in case something problematic was detected. He prayed everything was in order.

Savitha, too, was in the room. She looked at Deepak and smiled. She knew she was safe. Hadn't Deepak warned her to be careful?

Karan tried to protest but no one listened. He could have asked his team to leave the room immediately but that would have upset his credibility. He could also be held guilty of obstructing an audit which in GB2 was viewed very seriously. He could even be sacked for something like this.

He went out of the room and called his boss, Rajneesh Chatterjee, the business head of mortgages.

'Rajneesh, there seems to be a witch-hunt on,' he said and explained the whole episode.

'You are overreacting, Karan. Let Deepak do his job,' Rajneesh told him firmly. Given that Karan was handling a large part of Rajneesh's business and also was intellectually seen as a competent guy, Rajneesh was perennially insecure of Karan and tried to pull him down whenever he could.

'But this is month-end time, Rajneesh, we will get screwed on our volumes. The asshole screwed up my month-end in the last month too. We cannot afford two bad months in a row,' Karan almost pleaded.

'If you are sensitizing me to the fact that you might miss your targets this month too, the point has been noted with regret,' came the sarcastic retort from Rajneesh. His supervisor did not have the guts to take on the credit folks at a time when GB2 was seen as a bank weak on process control by none other than the RBI.

Karan apologised and hung up. He was probably seeking help from a quarter where none was forthcoming.

Deepak, on the other hand, continued his investigation in earnest. Their checks that day consisted of verbal investigations as well as a physical bag search of all present. Every single document available in the sales guys' bags was checked. The entire process of physical examination took over two hours. Work stood still during that time. Karan paced up and down the corridor outside the conference room but there was nothing that he could do.

The physical scrutiny was followed by a few hours of intense grilling. The sales guys were queried on the process they followed, the lead generation process, the conversion process, the approval process, how they dealt with and convinced the customers and even on the way they managed the logistics between the bank, the customer and the involved agencies like the property valuers and law firms.

After a gruelling five-and-a-half hour session, the entire audit process ended at around 2.30 a.m. in the morning, by which time the entire sales team was mentally and physically exhausted.

Karan, who was outside the conference room all this while, had an uneasy feeling about the entire episode.

'Something is going to go wrong,' his mind alerted him. He had no choice, but to wait.

He went back home late that night, and was in a very disturbed state of mind. Karan was definitely not among those sales guys who slept easy even on the verge of missing their sales targets. This August he was going to miss his numbers again and that, too, for no fault of his. 'Bloody idiot! I will get him one day,' he said to himself as his car entered the basement of his building on Carter Road, Bandra.

That night, he couldn't sleep well. However, he was not at all prepared for what came his way the next morning.

29 August 2007

GB2, Mumbai

KARAN drove into the parking lot of the GB2 processing office in the morning. Despite his disturbed sleep last night, he had managed to reach office on time. He was a stickler for punctuality and he rarely missed his 9.00 a.m. schedule. That day was no different.

As he was driving in, he saw a black Scorpio reverse out. It nearly banged into him but he braked just in time and saved his Honda City from any collateral damage. Not a good omen! He was about to scream at the driver when he saw who it was – the Scorpio had Deepak at the wheels. Karan controlled himself. Was Deepak coming to the office, or was he leaving? If he was leaving, why was he leaving at that time of the day? The look on Deepak's face didn't give him any comfort. He ignored him. 'Focus. Focus. There is a target to be achieved,' he told himself as he removed his laptop bag from the boot of the car.

The day was chaotic. Karan and his team tried their best to meet their targeted volumes but nothing moved at the pace they wanted. Savitha was at her casual best that day. She was not serious about anything. The loan applications she was managing were getting stuck but she didn't seem to be bothered about it. Customers were suddenly not available to sign loan documents and deals were left hanging. Karan was at his wits' end, trying to push her to take her loans to closure. But all his screams, threats, orders were falling on deaf ears.

At around 3.30 p.m., Savitha walked up to him.

'Karan, I need to leave,' she told Karan.

'What? Are your cases under control?'

'Kind of.' She was non-committal.

'What do you mean "kind of"? Where are you going? You are not even at 50 per cent of your monthly target. What's the problem, Savitha?'

'Karan, Aakansha is not keeping too well. I need to take her to a pediatrician. Have to leave now. My maid just called. I have given a handover of my cases to Xerxes. He will see them through. I will be in touch with him on the phone.'

When someone cites illness of their child as a reason there is no way one can ask them to stay back and work. Karan was no different. He just said 'Ok' and walked away from there.

Savitha left office and drove towards Bandra. She reached home in thirty-five minutes. There was no traffic at that time. She parked her car in the parking lot and got off. She did not pull out her laptop bag but picked up her handbag from the car, locked it and walked out of the gate straight into a waiting black Scorpio.

'Hi baby,' she said as soon as she got into the car.

'Babes, I was waiting for you. What took you sooo long?' said Deepak as he moved towards Savitha and kissed her lightly on the lips. He cranked the ignition and the car moved. In no time both of them were cruising towards Manori Bel, a resort on the outskirts of Mumbai.

Somewhere along the way as they were crossing Goregaon, she looked at Deepak and said, 'You were great yesterday. Karan really looked stressed.'

Deepak just smiled.

'I can't work with him any longer. He is becoming such a pain. Even today he literally screamed at me.'

'Don't worry, babes. Soon he will be history.' Deepak assured her.

'But I don't think I want to be here for long. Is there a way to get me into your team, or into credit?'

'You really want to...?'

'Yes, Deepak. That's the place to be in.'

'Hmm...ok. Let me speak to Bhisham. Something may come up.'

She hugged him in return.

'You have earlier been in a product role and a sales role. So I am sure we can use this experience to justify a role in underwriting or policy-making.'

'Wow, baby! That would be great!' And she gave him such a huge hug that the Scorpio wobbled a bit before getting back on track again.

While Deepak and Savitha were in Manori enjoying a wonderful evening, Karan was debating the merits of a loan application which had been turned down by Amit Sharma. His conversation with Amit was interrupted when his phone rang. He looked at his mobile and then back at Amit. 'Boss on line, will come back in a minute,' Karan said and then picked up his phone.

'Hi Rajneesh.'

'What the hell is this, Karan?'

'What, Rajneesh?'

'You haven't seen it?'

'I am not sure I know what you are talking about, sir. Is there a problem?'

'Have you seen the investigation report on the mortgage sales which Deepak has sent this morning to me, Bhisham, Ramneek and Sanjit?'

'No, Rajneesh. It has not been marked to me. When was it sent?'

'It was sent this morning. I have been out whole day and got to see it only now. Anyway, I am sending it to you now. If what has been written in the report is true, you have some serious explanation to do, my friend.' Rajneesh's words sounded ominous.

Karan was left wondering about the report when Rajneesh hung up. 'Isn't it the protocol in any audit that the audited party gets an opportunity to defend all the comments raised before a final report is circulated to everyone?'

He could have taken this up and battled it but in the current scenario, where audit seemed to be everything and with a boss like Rajneesh who would not stand up for him, it was better that he did not go on the front foot. 'Never get into a battle that you are sure to lose,' someone had once told him

Rajneesh's email popped up on the screen in front of him. He clicked open the mail. As he read the contents, he forgot the discussion with Amit Sharma on the contentious loan case.

He checked the time; the mail was sent at 8.52 in the morning. That explained why Deepak was leaving when Karan was coming in. He had in fact stayed up the entire night to prepare the report and get done with it before anyone came in. How vengeful could anyone get?

The mail which Deepak had written to Sanjit didn't really say much. It was a very matter-of-fact mail which just said that the mortgage sales audit report was enclosed. Very unlike Deepak! Deepak was a notorious political monster who always revelled in sensationalizing things. Even during his days in branch banking he would play one against the other and work his way up. He was not known to be straightforward.

Karan quickly clicked on the icon named 'Mortgage audit report – August 2007'. The computer was slow. The attachment took some time in downloading. Karan was getting restless. He wanted to know what were the issues Deepak had highlighted. Eventually, after a long wait, when the word document opened, he found it was a twenty-two page report. Quite a long one for an audit which ended at 2.30 p.m. the previous night.

The Audit Report and Its Aftermath
September 2007 Onwards

GB2, Mumbai

KARAN read through the audit report in a hurry. It was severely scathing about the sales processes followed in the mortgage business in western India. It raised many issues intrinsic to the sales discipline and a few issues related to Karan's leadership and management style. As he read through the report, he was even more shocked. The report was personal. It was not a business audit. It seemed to be an audit which passed value judgements on him as a professional, a leader and on his skills. It was blatantly unfair that such a report was sent to the senior management of GB2 without allowing him a chance to go through it and present his side of the story, which was a norm in the industry.

The report raised certain fundamental issues.

The first big observation was the result of the bag check of all the sales guys. The report revealed that a number of sales guys were carrying blank home loan agreements signed by the customers. Four of the ten sales executives in the room that night had blank but signed loan agreements in their possession, and almost all of those loans had not even been approved. This meant that the customers were made to sign the loan agreements even before the loan was approved. The terms and conditions of the loan were left vacant.

Deepak's had deduced that the sales guys would have got them signed by the customers telling them that the loan had been approved, else no customer would sign a loan agreement...and that too a blank one. According to Deepak this indicated wrong commitments were being made to customers and this would also result in serious customer service issues in case the loans were to be declined later. 'This brought in a significant reputational risk to the GB2 brand, apart from being an incorrect sales practice,' Deepak had said in the report.

'Getting a loan agreement signed by the customer is a tacit acceptance of the fact that the loan has been approved by the bank. If any loans were to get declined later on, the customer would be well within his rights to ask difficult and embarrassing questions from the bank. If 40 per cent of the sales guys had blank signed loan agreements, it only shows this process is rampant and is happening on a large scale,' he had further said in the report.

'In the last two months three large value loans have been cancelled after the loan was disbursed. The investigation team spoke with the concerned credit and sales officers and also with the customers. The customers vehemently pointed that while they had applied for the loan, they had categorically asked the bank to hold back the loan disbursals because they were yet to sort out some issues with the seller of the property they were buying. These three customers also said that they had mentioned this to the sales manager at the time of signing the loan agreements. The sales managers seem to have manipulated the blank loan agreements and got the loans disbursed by filling up the agreements themselves. Once the cheque was disbursed, the only way out was to cancel the cheque and neutralise the loan.' The audit report gave examples of three such cases in the last two months and also transcripts of discussions with the customer where the customer said that he had never agreed to the disbursal of the loan.

A shocking fact identified in the investigation was that the bags of the sales guys contained a few application forms of Standard Chartered Bank (SCB). Complete sets including SCB application form, income documents, identity proofs, etc. were recovered from the bags of the sales guys. This could only happen under two instances. Either the sales guy was parallely working for SCB while he was employed with GB2, or he was buying loan applications from someone in SCB. Both of which were not acceptable sales practices.

What made it worse was that Deepak had categorically mentioned in his report that no one from the leadership (that is, Karan) ever checked their bags or did a spot checking to find out what was going on. In effect, it meant that there was a serious lapse in the monitoring of sales processes.

However, the worst was yet to come.

From the bags of almost all the sales guys the audit team found valuation reports and legal opinions about the properties their customers were buying. This was perceived as a big risk. At GB2, the sales guys were banned from interacting with the valuers and lawyers. The rationale was that the valuation and legal opinion determined the quality of the collateral – offered as security for the loan. Given the sales' vested interest in getting the loan through, there was always the risk that the sales guys would make an attempt to influence the quality and correctness of the valuation and legal opinion. Hence the sales guys talking to valuers and lawyers was a 'strict no' in GB2.

The fact that sales guys were influencing valuers would have been difficult to prove unless the valuer agreed to it. Deepak and his team had interrogated valuers who had confessed to this breach. Deepak had clandestinely done this leg of the investigation by taking Amit into confidence. The two of them had even visited the valuer's office and seized his computer. They made him log into his mails and checked his mails. And there they had discovered mail exchanges between the valuer and the sales staff. This was the 'killer evidence'.

During interrogation, four sales guys, too, had confessed to speaking to the valuers and influencing them to give a higher valuation of the properties being funded. They also told this was a rampant sales practice and was known to almost everyone in the sales teams.

Even though this was a control lapse on the part of the credit team, it pointed to a larger issue – one of personal integrity of the sales teams.

It went on to say that if Karan didn't know of these issues, there was a serious dearth of supervisory control in the team.

There were two other key issues about management practices raised by the audit report. First, that the loans booked in the last three days of the month came at a significantly lower rate than the loans booked during the rest of the month.

The loans in the last three days came in at a rate of interest which was 75bps (0.75 per cent) less than the rates at which the loans were disbursed in the first twenty-seven days of the month. The drop in the last three days was significant and was highlighted by the audit report as a cause of concern. It also tabulated the comparison for the previous six months which was not different.

And secondly, an analysis of the delinquency of the home loan book was also enclosed which showed that loans booked in the last three days of the month performed significantly worse than the loans booked earlier. The audit report thus said that a number of credit norms and sales practices were compromised in the last few days of the month to book incremental business and meet sales targets.

The summary of the audit report severely indicted Karan and lashed out at the fraudulent sales practices.

'Overall the audit of the mortgage practices shows that there is a severe failure of sales control, monitoring and leadership. The sales team has indulged in a number of questionable professional practices which have gone unnoticed or have been wilfully ignored in the quest for achieving monthly targets. The PFS business is advised to seriously relook at the mortgage sales process and leadership in the sales teams.' Thus ended Deepak's audit report with far-reaching consequences.

This was the closest it could come to saying that Karan was a jackass who needed to be moved out immediately. Deepak couldn't have said it directly but he had indirectly hinted at it.

Karan was totally peeved. First Deepak sent an SMS inciting people to plot against him. GB2 didn't do anything about it. In fact they let Deepak go scot-free. And now, he had written an audacious audit report which severely dented his credibility. No one would believe Karan. He knew that.

He called Rajneesh that night. It was a difficult conversation. The audit report couldn't be defended. More importantly, Rajneesh was not willing to listen. He had proven to be a spineless boss.

'You have completely screwed it up, Karan,' he said angrily. Karan wanted to retort but better sense prevailed. For the last twenty-two months he had been delivering on his numbers without fail but just because he faltered one month and some vindictive asshole gave him a poor report, he couldn't overnight turn into a dodo. He knew he was good but Rajneesh was going ballistic. Karan knew that Ramneek Chahal would be putting pressure on Rajneesh but he expected Rajneesh to support him better.

'You know the pressure on growing mortgages. For two months in a row you haven't delivered on your numbers. What do you expect me to do? I have to answer difficult questions. How will you explain this audit? You are not making life easier for me!'

'But, Rajneesh, you know the issues we have had with credit. They just don't seem to share the same sense of urgency. And now with Deepak moving into audit and control, nobody there seems to be bothered about business growth,' Karan tried to explain.

'Karan, I am fed up of listening to excuses. I do not have time to manage these issues. Either you learn to manage stakeholders, or I will get in someone who does. Is that clear? In any case we will now have to respond to these audit comments quickly. I am sure Sanjit and Ramneek will come back very strongly on this. Let's chat after month-end,' and Rajneesh hung up.

Disappointment got the better of Karan. He left work and headed home. He didn't even feel like doing anything. Deepak's behaviour was understandable, given all his grudges against Karan. But he had expected Rajneesh to understand him. Rajneesh should at least have heard him out. Given him a chance to explain his position before condemning him. That's what good leaders normally do. Listen to both sides and then make up their minds. Rajneesh didn't even bother to listen to his side of the story.

Bhisham played his game very smartly. Realising that the only thing which could be traced back to his team was the lack of control on the valuation agencies, he responded very quickly and coerced the poor soul handling the valuation process and the vendors to resign. Even before Karan or Rajneesh could react, he had taken his action and covered himself.

Karan had become a marked man. Someone who was a star till about three months back, was fast becoming a liability, and that too because no one was willing to stick their neck out and back him. It was true that there were flaws in the unit that Karan ran. However, no one tried to find out the root cause or even tried to identify the reasons why those flaws existed in the first place. It was easy to just blame one individual for all the problems and everyone was content doing that as long as it saved their necks.

At the month closing of August, Karan ended at 72 crore of home loan disbursals. A far cry from the target of 110 crore!

The Next Six Months
Q4 2007–Q1 2008

GB2, Mumbai

THE next six months were very momentous in the lives of all the GB2 players.

Karan was totally disillusioned with the way things transpired subsequent to the audit report and two months of below-target performance. He had always held that one or two months of poor performance did not make someone a good or poor performer. No one could be a star for years and a dud the next month or vice-versa. But Rajneesh didn't feel so. And that was beginning to impact Karan.

Looking for a job outside GB2 was a temptation which Karan had never succumbed to, despite extreme pressures. However, this time he gave in. He was very well regarded in the market and it was just a matter of time before Citibank hired him to head their distribution for all loan products in western India. They even offered him a hike of 20 per cent. The day he got the offer letter from Citibank, he quit GB2. He had no motivation to work there any longer. He felt tremendously undervalued. If only Rajneesh had had the spine to help him deal with the politics, he would have stayed. But his boss, the head of mortgages, was so busy cementing his position and protecting his skin in the control-oriented regime that Karan's pleas fell on deaf ears.

On the other side, the romance between Savitha and Deepak was making much headway. They became a lot more open about their relationship. They would take coffee breaks and lunch breaks together and even come and go at the same time. Deepak started leaving office early so that he could spend time with Savitha before he went back home.

This gave fodder to all gossipmongers but that did not deter either Deepak or Savitha. Oblivious of what people around them were saying, they continued bonding with each other.

Savitha's move to credit made life easier for Deepak. In fact it was Deepak who choreographed that move. When Deepak's audit report was released and Bhisham terminated his head of vendor management for the laxity shown in the management of valuation agencies, that position fell vacant.

Deepak met with Bhisham the day he had terminated his resource.

'Bhisham, thanks for taking action on my report. I didn't want to recommend action on the credit folks for obvious reasons. I would rather speak with you than put anything on record about the department I work in. I hope the sales guys also take the cue from you and do something about their people. By the way, have you thought about the replacement?'

'Not yet. Do you have anyone in mind?'

Not really...but now that you ask, what do you think of Savitha?' Deepak casually forwarded her name.

'Who? That girl in mortgage sales?'

'Yes,' nodded Deepak.

'Do you think she will fit into the role?' Bhisham seemed a little skeptical.

'Bhisham, mortgages is going to be our greatest focus area. And she has spent enough time there. She understands the business and the risks. And, in fact, she is the one who tipped me off about sales guys interfering with the valuations. So, she is high on integrity too.'

'Will she be interested?' Bhisham was straightforward; he had no clue of Deepak's intentions.

'I can ask her if you want me to.'

'Fine...ask her. If she is interested, tell her to meet me tomorrow.'

'Sure,' and Deepak left.

The next day, Savitha met Bhisham and had a long discussion with him. At the end Bhisham was convinced that she was a good resource.

After she left, Bhisham called Deepak. 'She is very good, yaar. Knows her stuff. We will take her.'

'How do we do this, Bhisham?'

'The internal job posting is getting released tomorrow. Ask her to apply. While we have a process to follow, tell her that we will select her from the lot of applicants.'

Sixteen people applied for the job the next day. Twelve were shortlisted and interviewed. Of the twelve, Savitha was finally selected.

Within forty-five days, she moved into her new role as 'Head – Vendor Management' for GB2. Though she had to directly report to Bhisham, it was a job at a much lower level as compared to Deepak's or Karan's, despite the fancy designation of 'Head – Vendor Management'.

Savitha was happy. Her gamble on Deepak was paying off. She got to move to the same office as Deepak and hence the two were very close at work, too. Life was beginning to change for the better for her.

Deepak was extremely thrilled with her appointment as he could spend more time with her. Everyone around was envious of him. Despite her age, Savitha looked gorgeous. She didn't, for a moment, look like the mother of an eight-year-old girl. On the other hand, Radhika was blissfully unaware of her husband's escapades and continued to believe that he was a loyal and devoted spouse. How terribly mistaken she was!

Life was one rocking party for Deepak and Savitha, or so he thought, till a fateful day in early January 2008. A shocking piece of news hit Deepak like a bolt from the blue.

He was at his workstation giving finishing touches to an update which Bhisham had requested. Casually, he went to his inbox and clicked on the 'Refresh' button. Four new mails were downloaded. One was an update from his team member. One was a message from Savitha. He quickly opened it. It was a simple message, which just said 'I Love U baby'. He smiled and sent a reply. 'Me2222222222,' it said. The third one was a mail from internal communications which said: 'Protect your password'. He didn't even read it, just clicked 'Delete' and the message was trashed. In MNCs such messages were regularly sent as a part of adherence to global guidelines. GB2 was no different.

It was the last mail, however, that caught his attention. The subject was – 'Organisational announcement'. 'Who is moving now?' he said to himself as he clicked open the mail. It was a mail from the CEO to all employees.

Dear Colleagues,

With great regret I announce to you that Sanjit Banerjee, our Deputy CEO, has expressed his desire to move on and pursue interests outside GB2 in India. Sanjit is a close friend and a wonderful human being. While I am sad to lose him, I wish him good luck in all his future endeavours.

Sanjit's replacement will be announced in due course.

Regards,
Girija Vaswani
CEO

It was a short and crisp message which turned Deepak's world topsy-turvy. He was worried. He dialled Savitha's number.

'Pick up, pick up...pick up...,' he muttered under his breath, waiting for her to pick up the phone.

When she didn't, he got up and walked to her desk. She was not there. He was irritated. 'Where the hell is she?'

He came back to his desk and dialled her mobile.

'I am in the loo. I will call back,' she whispered.

'What the hell! Couldn't she have found a better time to lock herself in the loo?' he grumbled as he made his way back to his cubicle.

Within a couple of minutes Savitha was at his table. 'What happened? Why are you so jumpy?' She had sensed it in his tone.

'Have you seen Girija's mail?'

'What mail?'

'Sanjit's leaving!'

'Oh that one. Yeah, I heard of it yesterday.' Bhisham was telling someone.

'Why didn't you tell me, you idiot?'

'Arre, I didn't get a chance. And how am I to know that it would interest you so much?'

'But you should know how important he is for me.'

'But why? If he is moving, why do you look worried?'

'Babes, I moved in here because Sanjit wanted me to. When he asked me to take up this role last year, he had committed to me that he will move me out of it in twelve months. I have spent a better part of the last ten months trying to put systems and processes in place and ensure all the audit comments are rectified. This is a critical time for me. If he moves now, I will be in deep trouble. No one else knows that he had agreed to move me in twelve months and not eighteen as documented.'

'You are doing exceedingly well here. So what's the worry? Even if you are here, you will do well na?' Savitha didn't see much point in Deepak's fretting.

'No, dumbo! I don't see a career for myself in credit. I am a sales guy. I am a business guy! I need to move back to business. And that's why I am a bit worried with Sanjit moving out. I have no clue what will happen to me now.'

'Try talking to him. I am sure he will work something out. He is not leaving tomorrow morning. He is here at least for some time,' Savitha tried to assure him.

'Yes, I am sure he will do something before he goes.' There was a moment's silence before he spoke again. 'But I worry that he may not have enough clout to do anything now that he is moving out.'

'Yes. That's a worry. Why don't you call him now? Let's see what he says.'

'Yes, yes, come...sit. Let me call him now.' Savitha sat down and Deepak dialled Sanjit's line.

'Sanjit Banerjee's office, how may I help you?'

'Hi Sherlyn, how are you? Deepak this side.'

'Hey Deepak! How are you? You want to speak with Sanjit?'

'Yes, Sherlyn...if possible. "

'Wait, let me check,' and she put him on hold. She came back within ten seconds and said, 'Hold on...connecting you.'

For a couple of seconds, Deepak could hear music play on the intercom as Sherlyn was connecting him to Sanjit.

'Hey, young man! How are you?' Sanjit said as the line connected.

'I am fine, Sanjit. You are leaving the bank? I was shocked when I saw the mail.'

'Haha...young man. Yes, I am leaving the bank. You saw Girija's message, I guess?'

'Yes, sir.'

'At times in life, Deepak, you have to make a choice,' Sanjit said rather philosophically. 'And these choices are not easy. After having spent so many years in GB2, deciding to move out is like moving out of your parents' house and stepping out into the big bad world. I am at that stage in my career where if I don't venture out now, I will never be able to do so. So, even though it was not easy, I took the plunge.'

'Yes, Sanjit. We all look up to you for support and guidance. And all of a sudden you will not be there any longer in the organisation.'

'I will be there for you, young man. I am not moving out of Mumbai.'

'Sanjit, I called to ask something,' Deepak finally decided to pop the question.

'Tell me.'

'When I moved into the audit role at your insistence, you had promised that you will move me out in twelve months. That period will get over in some time now. So I wanted to check with you if it will be possible to move me out of audit before you go. Otherwise I will get stuck here.'

'But why do you want to move? There are issues, but you are doing a reasonably good job.'

'I don't see myself building a career in credit and risk, Sanjit,' said Deepak, at the same time wondering what were the issues he was talking about. 'I am managing right now but the organisation will never see me as the top man for the risk management job.'

'Why do you say that?' Sanjit asked.

'There will be seasoned risk professionals ready to take on Bhisham's role. I will be nowhere in the consideration subset even if I carry on for a few years in this role. I will always be seen as a business guy in a credit role. Always under the microscope,' Deepak explained his apprehensions.

'Hmm...that may not be the right way to look at things but that's the way the world works. Yes, you may have a point there. Ok, let me see what I can do.'

'Thanks, Sanjit. Do keep me on your radar. Please don't forget about me. I am depending on you for this.' Deepak was beginning to realise that he had ruffled quite a few feathers by firing from Sanjit's shoulders. Now without Sanjit, he would himself come into the firing line.

'Yes, Deepak. I am aware. Will surely try and fix up something.'

'Thanks. If I may, I had one last question.'

'Shoot.'

'You just said that despite some issues, I have done reasonably well. What were those issues, Sanjit?'

'Nothing that cannot be fixed, my friend.'

'I would then like to fix it, Sanjit. If you could let me know, I will work on them.'

'Look, Deepak. If you had not asked, I would have called and told you myself but probably at a later date. Now that you ask, I will tell you. See, I have been picking up a lot of noises around you.'

'As in?'

'Deepak, I never spoke to you about this because you were doing a good job. But many people have come and spoken to me… at times bordering on even complaints that you have misused your proximity to me and often played dirty with people. I have also heard that in the team, no one likes you. In fact I did speak to the retail banking head a few weeks back to consider you for a role. He was very hesitant and the only reason he gave me was that it would vitiate the atmosphere in his team. Now that is not a good reputation to have, my friend.'

'But I haven't done anything wrong, Sanjit. I just did my job.'

'Look, Deepak, there is a way one goes about doing one's job. You have done a good job, no doubt, but as you move up in life, managing stakeholders with conflicting objectives becomes extremely critical. You need to know how to get things done without ruffling too many feathers. Our organisation lays a lot of stress on collaboration. People working together. Let me give you an example. When you did the mortgage process audit, it was clear to everyone that you were out on a witch-hunt. You did not even give poor Karan a chance to explain his position before you released the report. Is that the protocol? No. The poor guy was condemned even before he could explain. I just bumped into him at a supermarket the other day and he told me the real reason for his quitting. I am surprised why Rajneesh never took it up. Probably with all the issues that we have had in audits, he was too worried to take up anything with the credit folks.'

'But, Sanjit...,' Deepak began to say something but he was cut short by Sanjit.

'Look, my friend, I will be out of this place. You have to survive here. You can either try and rationalise your behaviour or take this as a learning and move on. If I was you, I would introspect on what went wrong and then make efforts to build bridges which I have burnt. I need to go now. Have a conference call with Singapore. Sherlyn has been standing on my head for a while now. You take care. Will talk in some time...and by the way, please congratulate Sherlyn. She is moving as the CEO's secretary after I leave,' and he hung up, leaving a fuming Deepak holding the phone at the other end.

'Bastard!' muttered Deepak as he kept the phone down.

'What happened?' Savitha could only hear one side of the conversation.

'What did he say?' she asked Deepak.

'Nothing, babes.' He sounded very agitated.

'Come on, tell me. What did he say?' She was persistent.

'He says that I am a political, manipulative asshole...damn!'

'But you are not.'

'I know I am not. But he is saying that the way I handled the mortgage audit, is being held against me. That bastard Karan has squealed to him. Even Rajneesh and Ramneek seem to have said something hostile. He even says that I am a name-dropper and that I flaunt my closeness to him. Though he did not say it clearly, he was implying that he will not be able to do anything for me.'

'Shit! And you were relying on him to take you back into a business role.'

'Yes. So it means that I am seriously screwed. Why did I even believe him and come here?'

'It's ok. Don't worry. Everything will be fine.' She patted his shoulder. That's the best she could do because Deepak's room was in full public view.

Deepak knew that it was not going to be all right. At least for the time being. He knew he was stuck in audit for long.

February 2008

Somewhere in Western Mumbai

IT was a small dingy room, at best 6 ft x 6 ft, dark and damp, with not enough ventilation. In that room was a young lad, who would not have been more than twenty-four years of age. In front of him, on the table, were two computers. One was an old antiquated desktop computer. The wires from it had been unplugged and plugged into a slick laptop, kept close by. The table was small and hence everything on it looked cramped. The graphics on the screen made one infer it was a state-of-the-art and heavily configured system.

Lying on the small table in an agonisingly confusing and cluttered manner were hordes of communication equipment with a mind-numbing number of cables connecting the equipment to a junction box outside the room.

The place resembled a sleazy rundown version of an internet café. The person sitting in the enclosure, which could classify to be called an apology of a room, had been there the entire day and had not come out even for a minute. A bottle of Gatorade and one of water were the only things he had consumed. Even the internet café owner had been given instructions not to allow anyone to come inside. *'There is a little bit of whore in all of us...what's your price?'* Kerry Packer had once said. The whoring price of the Internet café owner was too low and he had happily obliged by keeping the café vacant.

The screen of the laptop was a mish-mash of websites. A crazy number of sites were open, or so it seemed. A few screen shots even showed some source codes, weird combinations of zero and one moving weirdly across the screen. To the layman, this would have looked extremely mind-numbing. But not to the person working in the room. He was at ease with what was transpiring.

After thirty minutes of constant peering into the screen, he took his eyes off. All this while he had been trying not to blink, lest he missed something important. He stretched a bit, slid back in his seat, rested his head against the seat top and then extended his arms to stretch. He was nearly there. The agenda for which he had spent twelve hours on a trot was nearly achieved. Nobody could stop him now.

He picked up a mobile phone lying on the table. Next to it was a voice scrambler, which when attached to any phone converted the sound emanating from the speaker into a string of data which could then be heard by the person at the other end, only if he had an unscrambler. A technique quite common if one wished to escape interception of sensitive conversations.

'I am nearly done. Another fifteen minutes and we will be in,' he said.

'That's great news, comrade. Charu will be happy,' the person on the other end replied

'Yes, the programme is running into its final leg. Once it's done, it will take us straight into the source data of the Indian government's passport office website. I expect this to be completed very soon.'

'Great going, comrade. Which means we will have all the data that we need by tomorrow morning?'

'Yes. I have managed to get into the website. Now I am one firewall away from their data. Before they realise what we have done, we would have gone away with all their important data.'

And then both of them broke into a roguish laughter.

'And the government will be too ashamed to acknowledge this, and will never make this public,' the guy at the internet café bragged further.

'I know...I know. That's how it always works in our country.'

The person in the room then kept the phone down. After carefully disconnecting the scrambler, he packed it up and kept it in a specially designed space in his bag.

As time went by, the grin on his face grew wider. And finally when the words –

Begin download
Press 'Yes' to continue

appeared on his screen, he just clapped his hands in glee. It was a defining moment. What a momentum this would give to their ability to raise funds for their movement!

He pressed *'Yes'* and the download began. He opened the bottle of Gatorade and took a couple of swigs.

At that very instant the owner of the café rushed in.

'What the hell? I have categorically told you not to come in!' screamed the guy on the computer.

'Cops!' the owner said pointing towards the door. He was panting. 'They want me to shut the shop. It's too late.'

'Tell them to wait for another half an hour. I am nearly done,' came the nonchalant response.

'I have tried. I have even offered them money. But they are not going away.'

'How much did you offer them?'

'Five hundred bucks each. There are two of them. Infact they had come some time back. I managed to send them away. Now they have come again.'

'Come on, man. Don't be so greedy. Share what you are making with them too. Give them five thousand each. They will surely go away. It's more than their monthly salary. I will pay you that money. I can't afford to stop now.'

'Ok, let me try. But how long will you take?' The owner didn't seem too convinced.

'Another thirty minutes maximum, after which I will be gone from here.'

'Ok. Let me see if they scoot.' And the owner scurried out to speak to the beat constables.

He could hear muffled noises. The owner was trying to speak to the constables to give them thirty more minutes. The constables were adamant. The voices grew louder. The discussion was escalating into a conflict. 'Damn! What timing!'

'Downloading file. 14 minutes to go' the computer screen showed. If only the cops had come in after fifteen minutes! Even now, with god on his side, he could accomplish what he had set out to achieve.

'13 minutes to go.' He read aloud out the message on the screen.

By now the discussion had grown into a full-blown battle. He could hear some more voices. The battle had spilled on to the street and more had joined in. The shouts were clearly audible. The owner was screaming at the constables, asking them to mind their own business and leave.

'12 minutes to go.'

The guy in the room folded his hands and closed his eyes. His lips started moving as if in a prayer. So close to achieving his goal, yet so far. The street fight was still on. He wanted to get up but couldn't. He didn't want to expose himself to the crowd, especially to the cops.

'*11 minutes to go.*' He didn't see this milestone being crossed as his eyes were closed and he was deep into his prayers. The closed eyes gave him a feeling of darkness all around him. Meditation had taught him how to concentrate on his job.

'*10 minutes to go.*'

'...Beep.'

A beep broke his concentration and he opened his eyes. The darkness persisted. He rubbed his eyes in disbelief and opened them again. The darkness stoically refused to dislodge itself. The only light in the room came from the screen of the laptop, which displayed two words in a box in the centre of the screen.

'*Connection failed.*'

The lights were off. He bent down in desperation and looked at the communication equipment – the equipment he had used to dial into the passport office website failed to respond. The amber light on the face of the equipment was not coming on. There was an eerie silence all around. The noises that had tormented him earlier, had suddenly fallen quiet.

'What the hell?' he screamed. His scream pierced the silence all around, before it fell hauntingly silent once again. He could now clearly hear the conversation outside. Slowly he realized what had happened.

After the conflict had escalated, one of the constables had walked into the café and pulled out the fuse. He was using a laptop and hence even though the power failed, the laptop was functional. The communication equipment that he was using didn't have a battery back up. It was plugged to the power socket. When the constable pulled out the fuse, it disconnected the power to the communications equipment which crashed, in the process disconnecting itself from the laptop, thus thwarting all the efforts of the person in the room.

There was no point fighting with the constables or the café owner, as there was nothing they could now do. The damage had already been done. He quietly packed up all the stuff in the room, disconnected all the communication lines, picked up his bag and left the room through the rear door.

A few minutes after he left, a muted and controlled blast was heard from the room where he was working. The café owner rushed inside only to find that the table and all the equipment on it had been reduced to ashes in the blast, destroying any trace left behind by the person working in that room.

What was his agenda? Why was he working there? No one knew. Everything of relevance in the room was destroyed.

A few miles away a knock on the door woke up the occupant of the house.

'What are you doing here?' the lady asked as she opened the door. 'Is the job done?' she was eager to know.

'No. There was a problem. A power failure disrupted all our plans when we were so close. I was just minutes away from completing the download when a power failure crashed my communication equipment. Anyway, that was not to be. I need to stay here for the night. There might be people on the streets looking out for me.'

'You can't stay here for long. You need to leave before anyone gets up in the morning. No one should see you here.'

'The train to Midnapore leaves from Mumbai Central at 7.30 a.m. I will leave at six. Will that be all right?' asked Kishore.

'Yes, that should be fine. Come in quietly,' she said. She glanced out of the door briefly. Not a soul could be seen on the road at that hour. 'Good,' she said to herself as she banged the door shut.

'The last room on the right. You can rest there. And leave in the morning before anyone else wakes up. And please do not leave anything behind. I don't want any trace of you having stayed here, else I will be in trouble.' she said.

He walked to the last room and kept his bag on the table next to the bed. It was a functional room he and his comrades used when they had work in this part of the country, or when they wanted to hide from the police. He quietly sat down, reflecting on what went wrong. Not connecting the communications equipment to the battery backup was a big, big mistake. They were so close to hacking the passport office website. So close. They desperately needed the passport details so that they could gather the data which would be very useful in fudging identities of individuals. This raw data would have gone a long way in creating forged documents and identities for their comrades and also helped them in raising money for their cause.

And now, the entire government vigilance team would be after them. Everyone would get to know that someone had tried to hack the passport office website. The government would become extremely cautious. It would be almost impossible to make another similar attempt in the short run. Charu would be very upset. Comrade would also not like it at all. Damn! Ten more minutes was all it needed. But now they were back to square one. They had to think of some other plan. And he closed his eyes.

Next morning, when the lady of the house woke up, he was still there.

'What happened? I thought you were leaving at six?' she asked him.

'I spoke with the comrade late last night. He asked me to stay back in Mumbai for a week and await further instructions. They do not need me back in Midnapore. So I am here. Don't worry. I was only waiting for you to wake up. I am leaving now. There is a hostel in the suburbs, which is part sponsored by comrade and our unit. I have been asked to stay there. Didn't want to go there last night.'

'Ok. I will be in touch,' the lady told him.

He then picked up his luggage and walked out of her house. The last she saw of him was when he dumped his bag in the boot of a rickety black-and-yellow cab and got into the back seat.

February 2008

The Next Day Morning
South Block, New Delhi

Partha Thakurta stormed unapologetically into the video conferencing room in the CBI office in South Mumbai. He was accompanied by two of his officers. They were about five minutes late. The home secretary Nicholas Pereira was staring down at him from the video screen, which connected the Mumbai office of CBI to the high profile VC Suite in South Block, New Delhi. It was at his behest that the VC room in South Block was made available to all of them for an hour. They had already lost five minutes. Pereira and his high powered delegation was getting quite restless staring at a blank TV screen in the conference room. The meeting chaired by Pereira was also attended by the secretary in the information technology ministry, the CBI chief and a few other people of the rank of cabinet secretaries.

All of them had been pulled out of their beds early and called upon to attend this emergency meeting. That was partly the reason why all of them were grumpy that Partha Thakurta, the lowest in the official hierarchy, was joining them late. Ideally, Partha should have been the first one to come in and wait for Pereira and the others.

"Sorry, gentlemen. The Mumbai traffic was at its eccentric best today," announced Thakurta as he settled in the chair.

'Gentlemen, can you please let us know all the information that we have? The minister has a press briefing in the next forty-five minutes. He is expecting a download from all of us.' Pereira was trying to gather information for his boss.

'Thakurta, what do we know?' It was the CBI chief.

'Sir, I am afraid, nothing.'

'What?' There was a stunned silence at the other end. More so because of the tone and manner of what Thakurta said.

'Yes, sir, absolutely nothing. I am afraid to say that this has been one of the most stealthily carried out attacks. We have never seen anything like this before. We have analyzed most of the data that we have. The IP address from where the breach was attempted is untraceable. A complex maze of routers and entanglers was used which makes it almost impossible for us to detect the point of origin. Even if we are successful it will take us ages to get to the core of it. We have no idea about the modus operandi, the technology used, or the people behind this attack.'

'But the minister has to say something to the press. They will be waiting.'

'What has been told to the press, sir?' Thakurta asked.

'As of now, nothing.'

'Do they know of this breach?'

'No. I don't think they have been told yet.' Pereira looked at the CBI chief who nodded in acceptance.

'Sir, I would recommend that we do not share anything with the press. Else we will be shamed if the world knows that someone nearly broke into our passport office datacentre and almost stole sensitive citizen information from the Government of India. It would be a matter of even greater shame if we were to go and tell them that we do not know who it was, or how it was done. I would request that we do not speak to the press at all.'

'What are you saying, Thakurta? Do you mean we brush this under the carpet?' Nicholas was appalled at this suggestion.

'I guess to protect our credibility we don't have a choice, sir.'

'If anyone were to find out, we could be lynched,' the CBI chief, too, stepped into the conversation.

'I understand, sir. But if people do find out and we have nothing to tell them, we will be condemned anyway.'

'So?'

'Don't tell the press anything. Put it on hold for some time till we unearth something. We will be at least able to save our face. In any case nothing was stolen. A data theft was just attempted.' Thakurta was very clear in his mind.

The discussion carried on for a few more minutes. Thakurta was very firm and convincing. He had a point. It would have been extremely shameful for a country of the size of India to tell the world that a breach had been attempted on a high security passport office website and that they had no clue if it was the LTTE, the Al-Qaeda or just a plain miscreant. Finally, the Delhi contingent of bureaucrats looked at each other and at the CBI chief. They all nodded. The ministers had to be told.

The entire issue was brushed under the carpet. It was easy to do so because fewer people knew about it and thankfully it got contained before the press could get a wind of it. However, one thing was agreed upon which was logical, too: the investigations would continue discreetly and the guilty would be punished. Thakurta was put in charge of the investigation.

≈

It was in this chaos that Kishore checked into a room in a chawl adjoining the railway track in Chembur. A fifteen-foot high wall separated the chawl from the railway track. Standing outside his room, he could see a few small boys playing cricket beside the track. He stood there for an hour watching the game. It reminded him of his youthful days in his village when he nearly played for his state. His father's death in a police firing changed his life completely. He had to give up studies to provide for his family. Charu had resurrected him and his family had really prospered after Charu came into their lives.

Kishore's younger brother was now attending a school in his village. When his father had died, Kishore had no clue where life would take him and his family but Charu had helped him secure admission for his younger brother and paid his fees. Even his sister had been married off to an educated and well-paid boy based in the nearest city. Charu had yet again lent his support in fixing it up. He had even paid him twenty thousand rupees for the wedding. It was a grand affair and Charu had taken care of the invitees as if it was his own daughter's wedding. His mother had wept and fallen at Charu's feet that night. She was so grateful that he had helped her settle two of her three children. No one else could have done what Charu had done for them.

Kishore owed everything he had to Charu. So indebted he was that he would blindly do anything that Charu would ask him to. About six years back, Charu had even got him admitted into a technical institute run clandestinely, which trained him in computers, softwares, hacking and communications. He had learnt the tricks of the trade extremely fast and was one of the smartest students in that institute. Charu had handpicked him and assigned him the job of breaking into the passport office, showing tremendous faith in him, probably even more than the faith he himself had in Charu.

But now he had failed. The faith that Charu had placed in him lay shattered. How was he going to face Charu now? This was the first major project assigned to him and...and that, too, when he was so close. If only the cops had not come and pulled out the fuse, he would have done Charu proud. He was filled with remorse at having let his mentor down. There was no other choice. He now had to sit back and await the next set of instructions.

17 December 2009

RBI Headquarters
Mumbai

RONALD was shocked when he read the letter the RBI governor handed him. Never before had he seen such a letter from the RBI. He had worked across various countries with GB2 but the tone and contents of this letter were extremely serious and provoking.

Date: 17 December 2009

From
Governor,
Reserve Bank of India,
Mumbai

To
Shri Ronald McCain
Chief Executive Officer,
Greater Boston Global Bank
26, Kalaghoda
Mumbai

Dear Mr McCain,

This is further to our earlier letter dated 24 March 2007 wherein we had highlighted certain serious irregularities in the manner in which Greater Boston Global Bank carries out its business in this country.

It has been brought to the undersigned's notice and as has been reported by the leading media of the country, there has been a severe compromise of processes and overlooking of regulatory norms in your bank. RBI guidelines on various subjects have been flaunted. Regulatory norms have not been respected, indiscriminate lending has been the order of the day, customer complaints have been on the rise and, to cap it all, the recent audit reports have been the worst in a long, long time. We have till date ignored most of these, assuming them to be the cost of doing business in a large and complex nation like India.

However, in the case reported by the press over the last few days, Greater Boston Global Bank can be severely held responsible for waging a war against the nation. Your bank is today being accused of colluding with the lawbreakers and conspiring with them to question the existence of the democratically elected government in India.

Mr CEO, I would like you to investigate the issues that have been raised in the media and give us a satisfactory response within two weeks (see Annexure 1).

In the absence of a satisfactory response, the RBI will take stringent steps that can also include withdrawal of license to conduct banking activities in the country.

I expect to get your response within two weeks from today, and hence this may be given adequate priority.

with regards
Governor Reserve Bank of India

Ronald was so lost absorbing the contents of the letter that he did not realise the governor was waiting for his reaction. When none was forthcoming, the governor took the lead.

'Thanks, Mr McCain, for coming at a short notice. You see, this couldn't wait. We had to move fast. The whole country is watching. We can't be seen as quietly allowing someone to come and screw our system.' If the letter didn't convey the message, the crass language and aggressive tone of the governor to the CEO of a large international bank surely did shock McCain. However, he didn't say much. What could he have? The governor and the entire polity of the country seemed to be up against them. Hadn't they screwed up, and that too big time!!

'I will get back to you,' was all he could muster as he got up to return to the bank.

'I will ask Vardarajan to fix a meeting where we will review the bank's response and decide further action. The meeting will be in or around the first week of January at a time convenient to you, Mr CEO,' and he walked towards his room while McCain dragged his feet towards the door leading to the corridor on his way out.

March–June 2008

Mumbai/Singapore
GB2 Global Results

Early March was result time for most of the banks in the world. Bank after bank started coming out with their 2007 yearly results. GB2, too, prepared to declare its results at a Asia-Pacific level. These would then get consolidated across various regions around the globe for their group results.

Standard Chartered Bank was the first one to declare the results on March 2. GB2 followed suit on 5 March 2008. The grand ballroom of the Raffles hotel in Singapore hosted a glittering ceremony where the Asia-Pacific CEO of GB2, Michael Smith, stood up to announce the results of the group in the region. At the ceremony, media persons from almost all the newspapers and magazines, hordes of analysts and a number of important stakeholders were present. An air of nervousness preceded Michael Smith's walk to the podium. He started his presentation in his usual flamboyant manner.

'Friends, we have had a fabulous year 2007. The results that we have delivered as a bank, and as a financial services conglomerate, have been brilliant to say the least. We have beaten all expectations. While I will share the details of the financials in a while, I would like to list down a few of our key achievements last year,' he began with confidence. His annual results presentations normally began in this fashion. They would be very self-praising, pompous and 'glorifying-the-bank' presentations. Irrespective of whether the bank had a good year or a bad one, the tone of the presentations would be the same. Only the degree of bravado displayed would vary depending on the profits reported by the bank in that year. Given his flair to speak to the media and to communicate a positive intent, invariably it would be Michael who made the presentation to the media and stakeholders. This had been the case at least for the last three years.

Michael spoke for about twenty minutes. Many in the audience were reminded of Steve Jobs when Michael spoke. He briefly mentioned the group's foray into new businesses in India and Indonesia, their leadership position in wealth management in Singapore and Hong Kong, their growth in the corporate banking business in developed markets like Australia, Hong Kong, Singapore and also the joint ventures they had formed with local banks in China. It was a fairly impressive presentation. He wrapped it up with the financial update for 2007.

GB2 had made a profit of $ 2.3 billion in the region as against $ 1.3 billion the year before. On the face of it, all the numbers and the ratios looked very good. GB2 seemed to have built a highly profitable business. The year 2007 seemed to have gone off very well for GB2.

When he finished his 'rockstar' presentation, all the stakeholders gave him a standing ovation. Hadn't he led the bank admirably and made it one of the hottest emerging market banks in the world? The numbers pleased almost everybody, or so it seemed going by the smiles all around.

Most of the analysts had predicted a profit of $1.9 billion for the region but Michael Smith's GB2 beat it to record over $400 million better than what the analysts had expected. There was celebration all over.

'We have thirty minutes for questions,' the moderator announced and the floor was thrown open to the audience.

Quite a few hands were raised.

'The gentleman in a pale yellow shirt on the far right,' the moderator pointed a finger towards the reporter and singled him out.

'Sir,' he began, 'the performance of GB2 in 2007 has been truly admirable. What's your outlook for 2008? Do you think this is a performance you would be able to repeat in the coming years, or is it a flash in the pan?'

'Interesting question, my friend. This growth in numbers has come as a result of a disciplined effort and cogent strategy backed by excellent execution at the grassroot level. In fact this year we have laid all the building blocks for growth in 2008/9. We don't need any significant investments in technology, infrastructure or new businesses. All that is done. We just need to sit back and reap the benefits.' And after a pause Smith added, 'I am reasonably confident that we will better these results in the next twelve months.'

'Thank you, sir.' The reporter sat down. The question seemed rigged considering the way the reporter was singled out to ask the question and Michael had probably rehearsed the answer well.

A few more questions were raised by the audience. All were answered with equal panache and ease. There were questions about strategy, resources, new businesses, possible obstacles to growth. Michael answered all of them brilliantly. He had fixed almost everything. Everything was going as planned.

The session was nearing the end. 'Next question, please. We have time for two more questions only, gentlemen,' the moderator boomed. Again a few hands were raised. 'The gentleman in the third row from front...red tie.'

The reporter immediately got up.

'Sir. I represent....' Hardly had he begun speaking when he was cut short by a person sitting in the fifth row. He seemed to be an Indian reporter who had travelled all the way to Singapore to cover the AGM.

'This is absolutely ridiculous. Rubbish!' he screamed. The room fell silent.

'I have been for the last twenty-five minutes diligently trying to follow the procedure and protocol to ask my question but every time the gentleman on the podium picks out someone who has already been identified. In fact I have seen the moderator nod at the reporter in the crowd at least thirty seconds before the call for next question, and invariably the question is asked by the person at whom the moderator nodded. If this is not nonsense, what is?'

Fearing that this might cause collateral damage to the brand GB2, the moderator quickly stepped in. 'I am sorry, sir. There was no such intent. May I request you to go ahead and ask your question to Mr Michael Smith?' And then he looked at the reporter who had just begun his question and apologised, 'My apologies, sir. Will it be fine if you ask your question after this gentleman?' He just nodded and sat down.

'Honourable CEO,' began the Indian reporter. Indians were still very respectful when it came to dealing with white skin. 'My name is Chaitanya Kumar and I represent the leading financial daily in India. I have a query on your strategy in the emerging markets, particularly with reference to your strategy in India. Why is it that in India, your retail bank continues to make a loss? This year your bank in India made a loss of over $245 million in their retail banking business.

The results have been camouflaged by the excellent performance in Singapore and Hong Kong. The losses in your credit cards and personal loans business have just begun to impact you. In 2008 the impact of these losses will be significant.'

He continued, 'Now look at the Standard Chartered Bank. They have reported significantly higher profits in their retail business not only in India but across the globe. How do you explain that, sir? How can one foreign bank operating in a market like India deliver results year after year, and another makes significant losses every year? Something seems to be going wrong. What is it? Our information shows there is a fair bit of confusion in your leadership team in India. Your bank today has double the headcount that Standard Chartered has in India while they have twice your number of branches. Despite your having double staff strength, they generate more business than you across all product lines. Doesn't it point to a warped and confused way of running the business, Mr CEO?'

Michael Smith was stumped. He did not expect this question. The meeting till then had gone very well...and now, out of the blue, there was this question which clouded his credibility. All the glory, the aura he had created was thrashed. Everything he said thus far suddenly seemed to be untrue.

He thought for a moment before he answered the question. The first time in the evening when he had to think through an answer. Maybe this was the first question that was not fixed beforehand.

The response was quite unconvincing. Michael did not have an answer to why SCB made double the profits as GB2 in India. He had no answers to why they were losing millions of dollars in their cards and personal loans business. He had no answer to explain the lower productivity per employee in India. What he managed to do instead was to create enough doubts in the minds of the press reporters and stakeholders that everything he said that evening may not be the truth.

The evening ended on a low note. Newspapers next morning were extremely caustic about GB2's strategy in emerging markets. Some even questioned GB2's claim to be an emerging markets' bank. Even the stock markets reacted negatively to the entire press conference. The stocks of GB2 fell by 4 per cent in the morning trade.

A peeved Michael Smith ordered a detailed review of the India business. It was a knee-jerk reaction to the stock fall and the press conference debacle. India of late had been a stressed business and had received quite a bit of attention from the region on account of losses, but for the first time it received sponsorship at such a high level. Michael Smith himself drove the review.

A number of sanctions were imposed on India pending the completion of this review. Costs were frozen. Foreign travel was stopped except at the CEO's level. Recruitment was completely frozen. Hiring wasn't allowed, even as a replacement hire for someone who quit the bank. Organisation structures and span of control were revisited. A strategic planning team from Singapore descended on Mumbai, to review the end-to-end process. Standard Chartered Bank became the buzzword. Everyone was obsessed with comparing GB2's performance with SCB.

≈

In this chaos, there was only one person who benefitted.

When Karan moved to Citibank in December 2007, the organisation advertised that position and filled it internally with Govind K, who was the head of cards sales. Manish Bhalla, the India head of cards business, was extremely upset that Govind had left him and moved to another business. He held on to him for two months on some pretext or the other and released him to take over his new role only in February 2008. When he couldn't find a replacement for him either internally or from competition, Manish decided to look at the FMCG (Fast Moving Consumer Goods) sector. After an intense search he narrowed down on one candidate.

'Let's do one last reference check before we make him the offer,' Manish Bhalla told Joel Wilkins, the HR Head.

'Bhelllaa,' said Wilkins with his trademark drag. 'We have done three reference checks already. Why do you want to do one more?'

'Don't know, Joel. My instinct tells me that we should play safe and do our homework. Give me a day's time. I will revert to you by tomorrow.'

'Look, Bhellaa, we have the offer ready. We are ok to roll. Once you get back to us, we will make him the offer.'

'Great. I will get back to you latest by tomorrow.'

'It's ok, pal. It's your business. You take your time. Today is Monday, the third of March. You have time till Thursday. If you do not get back to me by Thursday, I will ask my team to press the button on Friday. We will release the offer. Else we will get you some more CVs for prospective candidates. Will that be ok?'

'Oh, Friday is too far. I will revert by tomorrow, maximum by Wednesday.'

'Great. Just give me a call if you need any help from us,' and the discussion ended.

Bhalla called up a few industry contacts who had worked with the external candidate and did a quick and discreet reference check. Everybody gave him a roaring feedback about the guy. 'I don't believe in interviews,' Bhalla had once told Wilkins. 'For me the most critical thing is reference checks. It's extremely easy to fake a forty-five minute interview but it is almost impossible to doctor a good reference check. That's why I would rather do ten reference checks than do four rounds of interview.'

On Wednesday, 5 March 2008, at 6.45 in the evening, Bhalla called Wilkins at his desk, only to be greeted by his answering machine. 'You have reached the voicemail of extension 6468. To leave a message please record after the beep, else hang up.'

I will just drop him a mail, Bhalla thought, and he began typing out a note. 'Let's go ahead with the west guy.' He had put one issue to rest.

Next morning when he reached office, there was a message from Joel waiting for him.

'Bhalla, please call me when you see this.'

Bhalla immediately called him.

'Joel, what happened? Just saw your message. I called you last evening, too. But, you lazy bum, you had left by then.'

"Every day of the week, I come in two hours before you, my friend.'

'Hmm...ok. Tell me. You left a message for me – to call. '

'We have a problem.'

'What problem? Has someone else made an offer to Srinivas?' Srinivas was the guy they were planning to hire in the regional cards sales role for west.

'No no. No one has hired him. In fact we haven't even spoken to him.'

'Then?'

'We have a bigger problem, my friend'

'Will you tell me, Joel? Or will you keep running around in circles?'

'Bhellaa, we cannot hire the guy!'

'But why?'

'In the AGM in Singapore, there was some discussion around the headcount in India. Apparently it was quite acrimonious. Serious questions were raised about the retail banking business in India.'

'What questions?' Bhalla wanted to know

'Pretty much the same stuff which keeps cropping up every time. Which everyone talks about. GB2 not doing well. SCB doing much better. Productivities, costs, business volumes, profitability! You know all that goes around, Bhellaa, don't you?'

'Yes, I know. But what has that got to do with the price of coffee in Brazil?'

'Pardon me?' Jeol couldn't get the sarcasm.

'What does that have to do with the hiring of Srinivas?'

'It has, my friend. It has. Michael Smith is mighty pissed. And when he is pissed the way he is, no one argues with him. He has put a blanket ban on any hiring in India. This morning I have received a detailed note from Singapore. It calls for a complete review and overhaul of our retail business in India. It calls for a complete freeze on the headcount in India till this entire review is over. It may take three months or even six months. I really don't know.'

'Which means we cannot hire anyone in the retail business? What if someone leaves?'

'The note from Singapore prohibits even replacement hires. So you can't hire from outside. Period.'

'When did this mail come?'

'This morning.'

'Joel, then I have an easy solution.'

'What?'

'Issue Srinivas a backdated letter. Issue the appointment letter dated yesterday. We will be home,' Bhalla smartly suggested.

'Bhellaa, are you sure what you are saying is appropriate, especially in front of the head of HR?' Joel suddenly took on the trademark moral and ethical high-ground stance that most international secondees project when they take on a role in India.

Bhalla suddenly realised that what he was asking Joel to do may not be appropriate and quickly backtracked.

'Haha, Joel, I was just kidding,' the nervousness in his laughter could reach Joel. 'But what do we do now?'

'Speak to Sanjit. Maybe he will be able to help. I am sorry, it is out of my control now.' Joel was quite upset with Bhalla's suggestion to backdate an appointment letter.

'Ok. Let me try.'

The next call that Bhalla made was to Sanjit. HR came under Sanjit's direct line of control. If there was something which could be done now, Sanjit was the one who could do it. Thankfully Sanjit was in office and his secretary put the call through.

'Good morning, Sanjit.'

'Hey Bhalla, how are you, my friend? How come so early in the morning?'

'Sanjit, I am facing a small problem...,' Bhalla made Sanjit aware of the hiring issue.

'Hmm...I am aware of this direction from regional office. But you know what, Bhalla, when Michael Smith passes a directive, no one messes around with it. We cannot issue a backdated letter to Srinivas.'

How the hell did Sanjit know about this? What an ass Joel was! Even before Bhalla could call him, Joel had called up Sanjit and briefed him about the entire predicament.

'I was just kidding with Joel. Of course you know that I was not serious,' Bhalla tried to save face.

'Yes, yes...I know. I have worked with you long enough, Bhalla.'

'Anyway, let's see what can be done. Let me think about it and come back to you.' Sanjit hung up.

That evening Sanjit called back Bhalla.

'Bhalla, I have thought about the options in front of us. I have even sent feelers to the regional office and they have come back strongly on it. I seriously do not believe we have any hope in hell to hire anyone from outside. You will have to sell this job internally, to someone within the bank. But that might also be a tough job because no one will be willing to let go of people at a time when hiring replacements has become so tough.'

'Ohhhh gawwwd!' Bhalla was clearly disappointed.

'It's ok, Bhalla. We have been through worse times. And this is just a matter of three to six months. You can do your hirings after that.'

'I will get screwed in the bargain.'

'Why don't you try to hire some internal candidate? I will give you a waiver on the mandatory internal job-ad process. Identify a candidate, and if he wants to move and his boss is supportive, I will allow you to move him without advertising the job internally. This is purely on an exceptional basis.'

'Which boss will be supportive and release his team member... especially in these times? You only said that a moment ago.' Bhalla didn't seem to be encouraged.

'Yes, I know. But I also know of one such candidate, who I will be able to convince and also his boss.'

'Who?'

'Deepak Sarup. Interested?'

Sanjit dropped the bait and Bhalla fell for it. He thought for a moment and said, 'Will you talk to him? Or do you want me to do it?'

'Let me do this for you. I will speak to Deepak, Bhisham and even to Ramneek and revert to you.'

'Thanks Sanjit,' and Bhalla hung up. He felt that he had swung a deal. Sanjit smiled to himself. He had kept the last bit of the commitment that he had made to Deepak. His conscience was clear now. He could leave in peace.

Within three weeks Deepak moved as the Regional Head – Credit Card Sales for GB2 for western India.

May 2008 was his first month in his new role in GB2. Isn't life all about being in the right place at the right time and the universe conspiring in your favour? The reporter, who asked the aggressive question from Michael Smith at the AGM, had done a big favour to Deepak, who wanted to desperately move out of audit and control into a line function.

June 2008

Jhargram, West Midnapore
West Bengal

U MAKANT Mahato owed his allegiance to the Maoists. He lived in the Jhargram area of west Midnapore in West Bengal a town 150 kilometres west of Kolkata. That day he had come to Kolkata, all alone, by a state transport bus from his small dusty town. In Kolkata he went to Ultadanga, near the Salt Lake area seeking a shop, whose address had been hastily scribbled on a small piece of paper.

Not many people knew where it existed. Half the people he spoke to looked at him as if he was some other-worldly creature. I could possibly have been due to his attire. He was dressed in a dirty dhoti and a vest, considered quite unusual in that area of town.

Finally he met someone who didn't know the exact location of the shop but knew the topography and guided him to a narrow lane at the far end of the road connecting the local branch of Magma Finance to Salt Lake. He entered the lane. It was crowded. It looked like a wholesale market. There were many small shops selling everything from clothes, groceries, household goods, rice, etc. Once he entered the lane, he did not have to struggle to find the address on the slip. This shop that he was looking for was on his left. It was a large ration shop dealing in wholesale quantities of rice, pulses, wheat. 'Ultadanga Kirana and General Store' announced a large board hung precariously above the narrow shutter of the shop.

From the outside he could see some activity. There were in all about six workers and four customers already in, and it wasn't even noon yet. A number of large bags of rice were stacked outside and the workers were arranging them on the steps leading to the main store. Inside the store there were over a dozen sealed and stitched bags, presumably of rice and wheat, a weighing scale and large weights indicating it was a wholesale shop. A Shopping and Establishments Act approval certificate hung on one of the walls. It looked fake but one couldn't be sure. A large picture of Goddess Lakshmi hung on the wall just behind the main counter. A fat, pot-bellied middle-aged man, josstick in hand, was making a very devoted attempt at bribing Goddess Lakshmi to endow him with some of her everlasting and never-ending wealth. By the looks of it, Goddess Lakshmi had relented.

Umakant Mahato stood outside the shop, looking at the activity inside, trying to decide whether to go in or not. He stood there staring intently at the store when one of the shop boys came to him and asked, 'Do you want something?'

'No, nothing. I want to see Shri Jagan Mohapatra. Is he there?' Mahato asked the boy.

'Bada sahib?' Then the boy pointed towards the person sitting behind the counter doing pooja. 'He is there. You see that gentleman at the counter, that's Bada sahib. Do you want to meet him now?'

'Yes. Please tell him that Uma from Jhargram is here.'

'Ok.' The boy nodded. 'I will let him know.' He walked up to the Bada sahib and told him about Uma waiting outside.

'Send him in,' Jagan roared in Bengali.

The timid shop boy immediately disappeared and came in with Umakant Mahato. After ushering him in, he quietly vanished.

'Bolo!' Jagan thundered.

'I have come from Jhargram. I was asked to see you.'

'Who sent you?'

'Sunil Mahato. He asked me to see you and give this to you. He said you will understand.' He pulled out a torn half piece of a ten rupee note. Umakant had only one half piece, which he showed to Jagan. The note was torn almost through the centre.

Jagan looked at it. He read out the currency note number on the torn half note and walked up to his table. From the bottom-most drawer, he pulled out a bundle of notes. All of them were torn. In fact it was a bundle of torn half notes. He looked through the bundle as if searching for something. After rummaging through about fifteen notes, he stopped. He pulled out a half note from his bundle and stepped back towards Umakant. For the first time he smiled at him.

He held up the torn note which Umakant had given him alongside the half note that he pulled out from his bundle. The two parts of the notes fitted against each other. They were two halves of the same ten rupee note. Jagan was satisfied. Umakant was genuine. Not a decoy.

'Ok, tell me. What do you want?' Jagan asked.

Umakant took out a slip of paper from the hidden pocket in his vest and handed it over to Jagan.

Jagan took the slip, walked up to his desk again, took out his spectacles and started reading the note. When he finished, he looked up at Umakant and said, 'I may not have all of these. Stock is yet to arrive. I will give you whatever I have.'

'Hmm...ok,' said Umakant. 'Just write on the piece of paper so that I can take it back to them.'

'Don't worry. We will do all the paper work. Now come in.' He started walking towards a door at the back of the store. He had a small key in his hand. The door was locked. It seemed as if it was rarely opened.

A few workers gathered around him when he stood next to the door, opening it. 'What are you doing here?' Jagan barked and all of them scurried back to their jobs. He looked at Umakant and smiled, 'I don't want people around me when I go into this room. You never know who will open his mouth to the outside world. So the only person who enters this room is me.'

Umakant had a look of ignorance on his face as he entered the room with Jagan. He did not know what Bada sahib was talking about. It was a large, dingy room which looked like a godown. It was dark, too, and a damp smell emanated from inside. It was a restricted zone. There was, however, nothing suspicious about the stuff lying in the room. There were about twenty sacks full of what looked like rice and wheat. Pulses occupied one corner of the room. It looked like any other godown of a wholesale shop.

With his left hand Jagan fumbled for the switch board behind the door and switched on the solitary bulb in the room. It was not enough to light up the entire room which still looked very dark. He walked ahead to the farthest corner of the room where four large sacks were stacked.

'Come here. Help me to move them,' he said. Together they moved the four sacks from their positions. On the floor below the sacks was a latch. Jagan bent down and opened the latch. It was in fact a secret door, well hidden from the eyes of everyone by sacks of rice. Jagan lifted the secret door and sat down next to it. He pulled out the list from his pocket and looked at it intently, as if he was memorizing the contents of the list. He kept the list back in his pocket and bent down and started pulling out certain objects from the secret closet.

It took him five minutes to take out most of what Umakant wanted. He put the stuff on the small table adjacent to the secret compartment and then packed it neatly into two boxes and sealed them.

'How are you going to pay for it?' he suddenly asked Umakant. Umakant was empty-handed; he didn't look like he was carrying cash with him. Umakant heard him and again rummaged through the secret pocket in his vest and pulled out something. It was a credit card. Jagan looked at it and smiled.

'Wait. I will now have to account for this money.' He thought for a minute and said, 'Ok. I will show it as purchase of rice. Let me give you a bill for the same. Otherwise, how will I justify this payment?' And he set about making a real bill.

After making the bill, he swiped the credit card given by Umakant and then looked at him.

'I have swiped 46,000 rupees. You have that much available in the card na?'

'Don't know, Jaganji. I was just given this and told to give it to you when you asked for payment.'

'Hmm...ok. What's your name?'

'Umakant Mahato.'

'The card is in the name of Ankush Tandon. How did it come to you?' Jagan asked him.

'They gave it, sir. They came home and gave me this card and the list and asked me to get this material from you.'

'Hmm...all right. Not for me to ask,' Jagan said to himself as the screen on the card swiping machine displayed – 'Approved' and printed the charge slip for Umakant's signature.

When Umakant began to sign, Jagan stopped him. 'Sign as Ankush, not as Umakant.' The latter who had just begun to sign his name stopped and signed as Ankush.

Within a few minutes, Jagan led him to the back door. 'Go straight, take the first right. It will lead you to the main road, which will bring you to the front of the shop. And come back in August for the balance material mentioned in the list. I will get another consignment in forty-five days' time.'

Umakant thanked him and made his way out of the godown towards the main road. In his hands were two large boxes, containing three INSAS rifles, four countrymade revolvers, gelatin sticks and improvised explosive devices. All this had to be delivered back to some people in his village. They were the same people who forced him to grow opium in his maize field. They had paid him enough to keep him and his family happy. He earned some extra income by running some errands for these guys the way he ran it for them today. It was not much of a work for him, and the money offered was good, too. To hand over this entire booty to them he would get ₹5,000. To him that was as much as he would make by two months of working in his field. So he happily did what he was told.

Umakant returned to Jhargram. The same night a man covering his face with a muffler came to their hut. He paid him ₹5,000 in cash and picked up the two boxes from him. He turned to leave the house, took a few steps and then stopped.

'Where is the credit card that I gave you?' He had nearly forgotten to take it back. Umakant got up, went towards the wall where his vest hung on a nail hurriedly forced into the brick. He pulled out the card from the secret pocket of the vest and handed it back to the person who had come to collect it. That was the last he saw of him. He did not see his face. If he ever met him on the road by chance, he would not be able to recognise him.

After the visitor had left, Umakant entered the kitchen, which was nothing but a corner in the same room, opened the sugar-box and stuffed the entire cash into it. It was to be used at an appropriate time. Not immediately.

In the first week of August 2008, Umakant made another trip to Ultadanga Kirana and General Store to get the second lot of the consignment and again paid with the card in the name of Ankush Tandon.

June–August 2008

GB2, Mumbai

The first few months in card sales department gave Deepak a sense of *déjà vu*. In his earlier stint in branch banking he had played a number of sales roles and had come out on top in almost all of them. He had been topping the branch league tables with amazing regularity. In those days, if Karan was a superstar, Deepak, too, was not far behind. In the eyes of people who mattered, Deepak was also up there.

In the initial phase in cards sales, his reputation and the halo around him carried him through. His boss, too, gave him the benefit of his stellar background and allowed him to learn on the job. Deepak's experience in managing sales force, different channels of distribution was a bit dated. He was now shaking the dust off by slogging it in the field. He went out with his sales guys on calls, did daily reviews with his channel managers, spent time with all the other stakeholders like credit, operations and others to understand the business. He did all that it took to polish his knowledge and understanding of the product. 'Once I understand the product, I will be able to push my sales guys to do a good job,' he told himself. It was just a matter of time for Deepak to start rocking yet again.

However, things did not exactly shape up the way they were supposed to. In the second month of Deepak's stint with cards, he fell short of targets by over 40 per cent. Cards had been identified as a strategic product by the management of GB2 and hence everyone in the senior management had their eyes on this business. Bhalla was not too pleased with the progress. He called Deepak to his cabin one day.

A worried Deepak reached five minutes before the meeting and was ushered into Bhalla's presence.

'Hi, Deepak,' Bhalla began.

'Morning, sir. How are you?'

'I am good, my friend. But I am not too sure if you are doing good. If your team in west starts meeting their monthly numbers, both of us can surely be better,' he came to the point pretty quick.

'Yes, sir. I know we have let you down last month but rest assured we will surely make up this month,' Deepak tried to assure him.

'Deepak, I have full confidence in you. Sanjit, too, has recommended you strongly. As you are aware, we have chosen you over many other external candidates with relevant work experience. You will have to justify your selection. And in sales, there is no other way of doing that than meeting your numbers. I am sure you understand that. I know that you have a history of great performance in branch banking. But this is a different ballgame.'

'Yes, sir. You will not have any reason to complain. I assure you that.'

'As long as you understand the issue, my friend, I am fine. Please make sure there is no screw-up this month.'

'Yes, sir.'

'Son, the entire world is watching my ass which is dependent on the numbers you deliver...and if someone tickles my backside...I will take his, keep that in mind.' And he looked away from Deepak, into his laptop. Deepak turned and walked away from him. 'Bastard,' he muttered as he walked away from him, making sure that he wasn't loud enough for Manish to hear him.

This was the first time Manish Bhalla had had a conversation with him on the numbers. It was short and crisp – and surely did not go Deepak's way. And he did not like it. He had never been in such a situation in his professional life. This was the first time he was responsible for non-delivery. He knew that Manish was giving him the benefit of his past performance and Sanjit's recommendation. He also knew that he would not be able to rest on his past laurels for long. One thing was clear after this meeting – Deepak's resolve to succeed in his new role.

That night when he met Savitha at her residence, he replayed the entire conversation between him and Manish Bhalla.

'What can I do if the approval rates are low? I am getting in the required applications, but most of them are declined. Credit is too tight these days. What more can the sales guys do?' He was frustrated with the way Bhalla treated him.

'Hmm...,' Savitha was listening quietly.

'You know, na, what the current approval rates are. Twenty fucking per cent. Out of every five applications my sales guys bring, one gets approved. Citibank runs at 45-50 per cent approval rates, ICICI is at 65 per cent. How on earth will I compete with them? My sales guys are leaving me because they are not able to make decent incentives. I am at my wits' end. No one will understand what I am going through.'

'I do, Deepak. I do.' Savitha hugged Deepak, who was beginning to get a little worked up. None of his bosses had ever spoken to him the way Manish had today. More so after the stint in audit, where he enjoyed much authority due to Sanjit's backing. He, somehow, had to get himself back there in the eyes of people. He was a performer. And performers never gave up.

The month of August was slightly better than July. The login for card applications was tracking well. By the fifteenth, the cards sales team had logged in almost 80 per cent of the total applications they had in the previous month. Deepak was thrilled. Things seemed to be under control. The team was beginning to pull its weight.

'Retail works on energy,' he would keep telling his team, and in August his team had started to demonstrate tremendous energy. All his efforts seemed to be delivering results.

'Why don't you make a song and dance of this? Bhalla should at least know what you have done in August was practically inconceivable in July,' Savitha told him when they went out for dinner on Independence day.

'I know, but I don't want to sell myself. He should himself come and say that I have done well this month, especially after last month's conversation I don't want to go and tom-tom myself more so after he degraded me so much,' Deepak replied.

'You are right. But at least subtly you should let Manish Bhalla know that there has been a tremendous increase in volumes in August. I am not too sure he even looks at the daily MIS.'

'But how?'

'Maybe organise a team activity and call Bhalla to be the guest of honour. He will automatically get the right messages,' Savitha suggested.

'Not a bad idea. But what kind of event should I organise?'

'Why don't you organise a game of basketball for your team? It will be interesting. You also like the game. Bhalla can come in as the chief guest.'

'Hmm...not a bad idea. Let's quickly look for a court to organise the event. Even if Bhalla doesn't get the hint, it's still ok. We will at least have some fun.' Deepak was brightened up by the idea.

Savitha knew that anything to do with basketball would perk Deepak up. 'You in any case are a member at Chembur Sports Club. Don't they let out their courts for such events?'

'Yes, they do. I will find out. That's what I had in my mind, too.'

Thus was conceived a strategy to organise an event for the entire cards sales team at Chembur Sports Club. The date was fixed for 23 August 2008, a Saturday, when the entire sales team would have an off. Chembur Sports Club was to provide the court, officials to manage the event, balls and light non-alcoholic refreshments. GB2 was to arrange for music and beer. The club rules did not allow serving of hard drinks on the sports field.

On the day of the event, Deepak landed up at the sports complex a couple of hours before time. He wanted to brief the organising team and also make sure that all arrangements had been properly made. A few team members had also been singled out for their good performance. He wanted to give out a few certificates to them. 'It would be nice if Bhalla gives out some certificates,' Savitha had told him. After all, Bhalla had to go back pleased with the cohesiveness and the energy of the team. There couldn't be any slip-ups.

At the Chembur Sports Club, Deepak met with the event managers, members of his team who were working with the event managers and the club officials. The incharge for the basketball court knew Deepak very well, as he often played there in the local league. He also got introduced to the two umpires who were to see them through the evening. He spoke to them for about five minutes and then headed back to the confines of the AC office with the incharge of the basketball section.

'Sir, why these two umpires? Where are your regulars? I don't see Srivastav around,' Deepak asked the incharge. Srivastav was the usual old time basketball coach at Chembur Sports Club. He often moonlighted as the umpire during these matches.

'Oh, you don't know...?' the incharge paused.

'Know what?'

'Srivastav had a major accident early this week. His bike was run over by a truck on Eastern Express highway near Vikhroli. For hours he was lying on the roadside. No one even noticed him. The truck hit him in a dark stretch of the road. The blinding rains made it worse.'

'How is he now?' Deepak was getting a bit irritated with the unnecessary details.

'He is in a coma. Doctors say that the next seventy-two hours are critical. If he pulls through, he will be fine. Else it will be difficult for him to come out of the hospital alive.'

'Sad,' Deepak said.

'Yes. He has been with us for over fifteen years.'

'Hmm.'

'But you don't worry. One of the guys we have here is new. Joined us only three days back as an emergency replacement for Srivastav. But I have seen him. He is good. In any case you are only having a fun game, not a league. So these guys should be able to manage.'

Deepak nodded and came out of the office. Srivastav's plight had made him uncomfortable. He was the umpire in almost all the matches Deepak had played there. A pleasing personality, whenever Srivastav sent someone off the field, he would do so with a smile. None of the players ever contested his ruling. 'I just hope the new guy is at least half as good as Srivastav,' he said to himself and walked towards the court where the tournament was to be played.

Manish Bhalla arrived on time. It was a high octane event with almost all the teams battling hard for the trophy. Deepak strategically placed himself right next to Bhalla and kept whispering something into his ears all along. Obviously, it was not about the game. Bhalla kept nodding to demonstrate his interest in Deepak's talks. Savitha and a few others from the credit team had also come. In fact to display camaraderie between sales and credit, Deepak had invited a number of people from credit department but only a handful had turned up. Bhisham was not in town.

From where she was seated, Savitha could clearly see what Deepak was trying to do. It was her idea. Wasn't it? And it was working for Deepak. She smiled at her own success.

The trophy was lifted by the sales team representing South Mumbai. In the short final match they defeated the Chembur sales team. The event ended on a high note. A number of awards were doled out on the court that evening. The Bandra sales team made a clean sweep of the performance awards. Of the sixteen awards given out that night, eleven went to the Bandra team. The leader of the Bandra team, Rakesh Godhwani, was a proud man. He led one of the largest yet the most productive team in Mumbai for GB2 in cards. He was also the most important guy for Deepak in Mumbai.

After the event, Deepak escorted Bhalla out of the Chembur Club and walked him to his car. Bhalla seemed extremely happy.

'I am glad you are getting a grip on the team. The energy that I could sense here today is positively infectious. I hope this will result in August being a turnaround month for cards in western India. It's all in your hands.'

'Yes, Manish, you will see a resurgent West this month. Our login numbers look very good. I hope to meet our targets this month,' Deepak almost promised Bhalla.

'Hmm...let's wait and see. I will be happy to see you succeed. Thanks for a great evening,' said Bhalla as he got into his car.

Deepak quickly got back to the basketball court where half his team was dancing with joy, some of them already drunk. He looked towards Savitha who was also looking at him. Winking at her, he raised his right hand and made a 'thumbs up' sign. She smiled. It was *'Mission Successful'* for them.

It was time to celebrate. Deepak hit the dance floor with a vengeance. Beer was guzzled as if it was going to go out of stock soon. He had never got drunk on beer. That day he wanted to. For the first time Manish Bhalla had said something nice to him, and he was happy about it.

The party lasted till 11.30 that night. The club rules did not permit them to play loud music or party in the open beyond that. Deepak was the last one to leave the floor. Savitha was with him, matching him, move for move, shake for shake. They looked like an item together. Everyone noticed but they didn't bother.

'My baby wanted some whisky today, na?' Savitha cooed in his ears.

Yes, love. Wish we were allowed to serve whiskey. It would have been so much fun. I really wanted to get drunk today,' Deepak replied.

'Hmm...I know, but rules are rules. And the club won't change them for my baby,' she said and hugged him tight. She was a bit high, too. Thankfully no one could see them. Or so they thought!

'Next time we will do such an event only if we are allowed to bring in whiskey. Not fair!' Deepak was cribbing. He was in no mood to go home. 'Is there any place where we can get some whiskey now?'

'Almost all the bars would be shut,' Savitha answered.

'I can help you get some.' Startled, both of them turned around to see who it was. It was the referee who had temporarily stepped in place of Srivastav.

'Oh, hi.' Savitha frowned when Deepak acknowledged his interference. How could someone overhear their conversation and that, too, so unabashedly?

'My apologies. I was walking close by and couldn't help overhear you guys. It was not by intent but by accident.' Probably Savitha's frown was so apparent that the referee immediately apologised.

'Oh, it's ok...it's fine,' laughed Deepak.

'I am serious. I stay close by and I have a decent stock of whisky. If it is ok with the two of you, you can have a drink with me before you head home,' the referee offered.

'Oh, no. But thank you for the offer.' Savitha was quick to decline.

'It will indeed be my privilege if the captain of Chembur Chargers shares a drink with me. You are the captain of my dream team. You are my idol, sir.' When the referee flattered him, Deepak couldn't refuse. This was his weakness. People could get away with even murder with Deepak as long as they praised his game of basketball. And after the referee touched his vulnerable nerve, there was no going back.

The three of them headed to the referee's house, which was close to the club. The referee opened a new bottle of Chivas Regal in Deepak's honour and Deepak was extremely touched. He hadn't realised that he had such a fan following in the suburb.

So, Mr Referee, are you new to Chembur?' asked Deepak.

'No, I have been here for some time now. I have just joined the club on a temporary basis. The full-time coach was injured in a bus accident. A bus hit his scooter and disappeared in the blinding rain,' he answered.

'Yes, yes, the game incharge told me back at the office. But how do you know it was a bus?'

'Just a guess. That's what people say.' The referee felt a bit discomforted by this question from Deepak

'Hmm...he was a nice guy,' said Deepak.

'He *is* a nice guy, Deepak. Remember he is still alive.'

'Oh yes. Thanks...,' and then he suddenly remembered that he didn't know the name of the referee. 'By the way, I don't even know your name,' Deepak asked him.

'Haha...yes...my name is Anakadundubi Venkula....'

Deepak cut him short. 'Hold, hold...I didn't follow a word of it. Actually, I like calling you "Referee". You ok with that?'

'Yes, sure.'

'So where do you work? I am sure you do something more than being a basketball referee.' Deepak wanted to know more about him.

'I am looking for a job...attending job interviews at the moment. Recession is killing my opportunities. No one wants to hire. Almost everyone I know is laying off. I have just taken up this club job so that I can make ends meet.' The referee's answer made Deepak think for a while.

'Hmm...club job to make ends meet...and serving Chivas Regal at home. Interesting combo.' Deepak looked at the referee with raised eyebrows and asked, 'What's the story, mate?'

'This is a very old bottle. I got it as a gift from my previous employer when I did a project for them in half the time. I don't drink alone at home. So it's just been lying around.' The referee poured out one large drink for Deepak. Savitha, who was listening to the conversation patiently, declined the drink. She wanted to make sure that Deepak was driven back home safely and her expressions indicated that there was something about the referee that she didn't like.

The conversation that night centred around the game; the interesting aspects of basketball, NBA, the various basketball leagues in the US, the players, the sponsors, etc. The referee seemed very well informed and was able to engage Deepak in a conversation. For Deepak, it was a feeling of association, joy, pride and, to a certain extent, intellectual stimulation. He had met many basketball fans in his life but here was one who knew the game well. He liked talking to the referee and found him very interesting. Time flew by. Neither of them had a clue about what time it was. Radhika had gone to Delhi and hence Deepak was in no hurry to reach home. Savitha had asked her maid to stay over and take care of Aakansha that night because she knew that the post-match party would last long.

Savitha was not a sports person. She didn't quite understand basketball. The never-ending discussions between the referee and Deepak bored her but she sat there quietly listening to them. For the first time she was seeing Deepak discuss basketball so animatedly with someone. It was about 4 a.m. when the discussion ended. Savitha, by then, had crashed on the couch in the one-bedroom tenement of the referee.

By the time the referee shook her awake, Deepak was sloshed and not in his senses. Savitha took him to the car and dragged him to her house. The maid helped her support him and took him to the guest bedroom and dumped him on the bed there. He had no clue where he was till he woke up at four in the afternoon. It didn't matter because it was a Sunday.

Aakansha had gone out to play and the maid had gone back home. It was just the two of them. Savitha went to wake him up with a cup of tea. Deepak was lazing in bed. He had vague memories of being carted up the stairs by Savitha and her maid. Memories of the basketball discussion with the referee and the many pegs of Chivas Regal came back to him. Savitha knocked on the door. Deepak turned around to see her and smiled.

'Time to get up,' she announced as she kept the cup of tea on the bedside table.

'Or maybe time to get you into bed,' said Deepak naughtily as he extended his arms and pulled her into bed and kissed her passionately.

'Deepak, control...control. Aakansha will be back any time,' Savitha tried to dissuade him.

'Where is she?'

'She is out with her friends, playing.'

'Does she have a spare key to the house?' Deepak's eyes betrayed a tinge of mischief as he asked her the question.

'Chup, Deepak. How would she have the keys? She is barely eight.'

'Then what is the problem?' And Deepak hugged her and rolled her into the bed. 'We will see what to do if she comes back,' he said before he held her in his arms. His lips sought hers and she began to melt in the warmth of his love. She responded with lesser intensity initially. She hadn't yet completely shed her inhibitions. Deepak's loving embrace made her discover her latent desire but not before something pricked her conscience. She suddenly remembered she hadn't been with a man since her husband passed away a few years ago. Maybe it was time for her to shed her ice-maiden image and allow her feelings to overwhelm her. However, the closeness, the attraction for Deepak, the desire was too much for Savitha to handle. She succumbed to his wishes and what followed was a love-making so intense that they were lost in the ocean of ecstasy. There was also a fear that Aakansha could return any time and Deepak did not want to be left high and dry. By the time they finished, they were both exhausted and lay inseparable in each other's arms. Deepak smiled at her and kissed her lips. 'You are amazing. Why didn't we do this earlier?' he told her. She just smiled and got up.

'Sexy!' he called out to her.

She turned back.

'Come back, sexy woman,' he said mischievously.

'Come on, don't be greedy. Get up now.'

'Sexyy...you are too hot!'

'...and?' Savitha began fishing for compliments.

'Sexy...hot and sweet.' Deepak knew how to please her.

'...and?' she asked again.

'Interesting, nice and intoxicating.,' Deepak was ready with more compliments.

'Enough, enough! Chup now.' She smiled at him. The smile was not easy to understand. It was hiding a maze of thoughts, a web of emotions. Savitha felt that what had happened was probably not right. It should not have happened, not because Deepak was a married man. She hadn't forgotten that in the path that she had decided to tread in life, she had no space for love, for commitment. Aakansha had to be brought up. She was her first priority..

Deepak, on the other hand, lay on his back, contended. He always made Savitha go weak in her knees. His friendship with her was the talk of the town. While the gossip mill worked overtime and people had predicted that they were sleeping with each other, this was the first time they had made love. Despite it being a hurried one, he enjoyed it while it lasted. She was good in bed. He closed his eyes and thought about Savitha, her warm naked body next to his and their high energy love-making a few minutes back. He shook his head, smiled and got up. 'Why did it have to end?' he thought as he walked to the loo.

On his way back home, he called the referee and thanked him for a wonderful drinking session the last evening.

'Thanks, buddy, you were the only one I have met who knows so much about basketball. Otherwise this country is pathetic when it comes to discussing sports.'

'I have the same problem. People behave as if they really like this game but hardly know anything about it. I am happy, Deepak, there is someone with whom I can talk basketball,' the referee said.

'Yes, yes. We must meet more often,' Deepak suggested.

'Why not this evening? I am headed to the club. If you reach there in time, we can also head out for a drink before we pack up.'

After a moment's silence, Deepak responded. 'Done! In any case I am alone and do not know what to do.' He turned his black Scorpio towards the Chembur Sports Club. Thus began a friendship which, they didn't know, would redefine both their lives one day.

August 2008

Somewhere in Dantewada Chhattisgarh

Raj Kumar aka Tiger was sitting in his room staring intently at a sheet of paper. His office was on the outskirts of Dantewada district and was reasonably well stocked. Proximity to the district headquarters had helped Tiger make sure his office was always connected with the rest of the world through mobiles and internet.

On the sheet that had caught Tiger's attention were a few telephone numbers and some names with monetary amounts written against them. He looked at the list that ran into pages. There would have been over a thousand names in the list. Flipping through the pages, he checked if there were any errors. He was particularly concerned about the last column. The heading on that column said 'Amount to be paid'.

'Binayak! Where the hell are you?' He screamed. A few guys scampered around to find Binayak. Some even banged at the toilet door wondering if he was there. Binayak was nowhere to be seen.

Tiger was getting impatient. The list was important. He couldn't afford any screw-up. This was the most critical cog in their wheel. And stupid Binayak had made a blunder! 'Binayak...Binayak!' he screamed. No one knew where he was. There were two other men in the room. 'What are you doing here, staring at my face? Go and find that incompetent fellow!' He howled in Oriya. Tiger's temper was legendary.

Finally someone found Binayak. He was standing outside the thatched hut, at a tea stall, gossiping with some villagers. He was told that Tiger was looking for him and he came running inside.

'Sir, you called me?'

'Idiot. You made this list?' Tiger flung the list at his face. Thankfully one of the sheets landed in Binayak's hand and he looked at it. Nodding in acceptance, he looked at Tiger sorrowfully, 'Is there a mistake, sir?'

'How many times have I told you that the amount can't exceed ₹50,000?' Tiger barked.

'Sir, I checked, none of the figures listed here is more than 50,000.'

'Check again, you fool. I found out three mistakes in the five pages I saw. This can completely derail us. I don't know if you understand how critical this is.' He was beginning to lose his patience. Binayak scuttled to his table to re-check. Tiger turned to his left, tapped on the switch that powered his paper shredder and shredded all the pages that Binayak had given him. He had to wait for the new set of papers. He needed to be very careful with the information that was mentioned on the papers. It could not fall in wrong hands, especially the law enforcers. It had the potential to jeopardise their entire mission. It could expose everyone.

Binayak was back in twenty minutes with a fresh set of papers. Tiger looked at them very carefully and then handed them over to Uttam, his right hand man. This time they were in order.

'You know what to do,' he told him. Uttam nodded, took the list and disappeared.

Around the same time, in Somajiguda, a wealthy suburb in distant Hyderabad, Ashok Ghandy was relaxing in his palatial house. It was well past ten at night and he was beginning to feel a bit tired and sleepy. He had an early morning flight to catch, too. The Union Minister for Rural Development and Tribal Welfare had called for a meeting in Delhi and Ashok was representing the cause of the tribals of Andhra Pradesh in that meeting. He put down his working papers, and got up. He poured himself a glass of water from a jug kept on the table and gulped it down slowly, lost in thought, possibly thinking about the next day's meeting. He kept the glass down and was about to retire to his bedroom when the phone rang.

'Hello?'

'Hello, am I speaking to Ashok garu?'

'Speaking.' Ashok Ghandy nodded subconsciously.

'Saar, I am calling from Comrade Tiger's unit?'

'Yes, yes, tell me.'

'Sir, he asked me to give you some numbers.'

"Hmm...ok.'

'Sir, can you please note these numbers down.'

'Wait...wait,' exclaimed Ashok as if suddenly shaken out of his stupor. 'Wait, let me get a pen and paper.' There was a pause for about half a minute before Ashok got back.

'Yes, tell me.'

'Card number 5143 6345 2347 6289. Amount to be paid – ₹48,000.'

'Ok.' Ashok noted down the numbers.

'Card number 5143...7890 – ₹42,000, card number 5143...7430 – ₹49,800, ...card number 5234...5467 – ₹39,000,' the person on the phone rattled off more numbers.

'Ok, let me repeat the numbers,' Ashok repeated the numbers to check if he had noted correctly.

Yes, sir. It's correct. Thank you.'

'Ok. The needful will be done.'

'Thank you, sir. Please SMS at the other telephone number that you have once the job is done.' And the caller hung up. He was about to dial the next number when he felt a hand on his shoulder. He turned back. It was Uttam.

'How many to go?' asked Uttam.

'Sir, twenty more calls to be made...I should be done in an hour.'

'Good. We have to finish all the 200 names by tonight.'

The caller returned to making calls. Uttam turned back and headed outside. He had to report the progress to Comrade Tiger.

By then, Ashok Ghandy had peacefully retired to his room and switched off the lights. Lying in his bed, he was thinking of the plight of the tribals and the things the government was doing to alleviate their misery. This also helped him to revise the points he was going to raise in the meeting next day. He was not attending the meeting with any political agenda in mind. He really felt for the cause of the tribals and was supporting them whole-heartedly. His thoughts went back to the previous year when he had successfully led a march from Hyderabad to Delhi garnering both support and contributions for the development of the people residing in far-flung tribal areas. Even though he was from the opposition party in Andhra Pradesh, almost all political parties had put their differences behind and supported him. Such was his persuasive ability and integrity.

Ashok woke up very early the next day. He had a 7 a.m. flight to Delhi and he was at the airport by 5.50 a.m. Just as he was about to get down from the car, he took out a bundle from his bag and gave it to the driver.

'Here, take this.' The driver looked at him and extended his left hand to receive the bundle.

'Uhhh...not this hand,' Ashok reprimanded him.

'Oh...sorry, sir.' The driver then hastily retracted his left hand and stretched his right hand to accept the bundle from Ashok. He opened the glove compartment and shoved the bundle into it. Ashok then dug into his shirt pocket and took out the piece of paper on which he had written the numbers the night before. The driver pocketed that slip and drove away. No words were exchanged. The driver knew what to do. It was a regular practice, which would take place at least once a fortnight.

That afternoon the driver went to the local branch of Citibank and filled out six deposit slips. He went to the teller counter and deposited the cash given by Ashok into the six credit cards whose numbers the caller had given to Ashok the previous night. The amount to be deposited was also mentioned on the slip given by Ashok.

On his return from Delhi late night, Ashok SMSed 'Done' to the other number that he had. He had done this for months together and knew the process.

Late in the night, Binayak logged into internet banking across various banks and checked all the 200 cards whose numbers had been given to a number of people like Ashok Ghandy across the country. Cash had been deposited into 188 of them. Approximately seventy-five lakh of cash had been paid into the 188 cards by people who sympathised with their cause. One of those cards was in the name of Ankush Tandon. The purchase of arms from Ultadanga Kirana and General Store façade in Kolkata had now been fully paid for.

17 December 2009

Mumbai

RONALD was waiting in the porch at the bottom of the stairs leading up to the towering gates of RBI when the chauffer drove in to pick him up. The chauffer got out and opened the back door of the car and a baffled CEO of GB2 plunked into the back seat of the BMW 7 series. The interiors of the car were soft, the design complex. His mind was buzzing with iterations which were even more intricate than the mechanics of the new 7 series Beamer.

He picked up his phone and dialled Sherlyn.

'Yes, Ronald,' she answered.

'Sherlyn, you there?'

'Yes, it's me. What can I do for you?'

'Sherlyn, can you please call Saurabh and ask him to be in my room along with the fraud team in the next thirty minutes. Also tell him to call me on my mobile. I need to talk to him.'

'Sure, Ronald.'

'And tell Saurabh, it's urgent.'

'Sure.' She did sense the urgency in Ronald's voice.

Ronald hung up. How would he explain to his higher-ups that this was not a problem created by him? How was he going to weave a story which was coherent and believable enough for the shareholders? It was not going to be easy. This was a difficult phase. The stance aken by the RBI was not at all comforting. During his years of work with the bank in various countries and over decades of dealing with the regulators, he had not encountered such a tricky situation. Did the governor of the RBI have some other agenda? He didn't know for sure. Ronald was confident that if the system was fair, they would come out of it unscathed. He was worried about the vested agendas that various people in the government and the regulators were driving. He was lost in thoughts when his phone rang.

'Yes, Saurabh,' Ronald spoke into the phone.

'Ronald, you wanted me to call you? How was the meeting with the Governor?'

'It's the same story but this time the RBI is taking a very strong stance.'

'What does that mean?'

'They have issued us a show cause notice and have just stopped short of accusing us of waging a war against the nation. This is serious. It can even threaten our licence if we don't do anything about it right now.'

'Hmm...does not sound good.'

'Yes, It doesn't. See me in my room in the next thirty minutes? I also want to meet Inder, Bhisham and Ramneek. Tell them to be in my room by the time I get in. Tell them to drop everything they are doing and focus on this. We cannot afford to screw it up. Do you understand, Saurabh? Tell Bhalla to be there, too.'

'Yes, Ronald.' Saurabh could not say anything else.

Ronald was already thinking of how to sort out the issues raised by the RBI. How was he going to convince them that he ran a controlled business and that what had happened was a strange tryst of fate?

However, the damage had been done. Unwinding the same was long and tedious process. It would take time but there was no alternative. A blunder had happened and it had to be managed.

Chembur, Mumbai

Life at GB2 was getting tough for everyone. Michael Smith' tirade against the Indian management had impacted the structure of the country team. August 2008 saw a new leadership take over GB2. Ronald McCain was brought in to replace Girija Vaswani as the CEO for the group in India. In times of a crisis, the regional office of GB2 felt it appropriate to bring in an expat CEO who would be more aligned to their strategic directives. The pressure on the management to deliver extraordinary results had risen and Micheal Smith had no time for debates.

Michael Smith wanted huge commitments from Ronald on the profitability and growth for 2009. 'It's now or never, Ronald,' Michael Smith had told him. And when Michael Smith said something, it was cast in stone.

Everyone in the leadership position in GB2, all those who reported to Girija, were on tenterhooks. A new boss in tough times was always a challenge to deal with. Especially people who had a good relationship with Girija were worried that Ronald would surgically take them out. They were paranoid if they would keep their jobs. And when such paranoia strikes large teams it impacts people down the line, too.

On the other hand, what started off as a one-off drinking session at the end of the intra-office basketball tournament had transformed into a budding friendship. It is said of friends that either sports or women get men to bond together. In this case it was the former. A common love for sport – basketball. The referee's knowledge of the game really impressed Deepak while the referee was bowled over by Deepak's humility. The latter had been warm and friendly with someone not from the same economic strata – and that was an exception for Deepak. He was not known to be humble or unpretentious. At work he had always been hard-nosed, arrogant and rude. Maybe it was *basketball* which softened him.

The two of them hit off very well. They started meeting almost everyday at the club. Deepak used to visit the club regularly for his practice sessions. The referee would also be there. They didn't have to make too much of an effort to hook up. Occasionally Savitha would also accompany him. On those rare occasions, she would stay aloof from the referee. She was not too comfortable with him. But she never said anything to Deepak. After all, it was his life and he was free to choose his friends.

The referee was looking for a job and Deepak was in a position to at least guide him, if not arrange a job for him. He fixed up a few interviews for the referee in some companies where he had contacts, but nothing really worked. Recession had started to prevent friends from obliging each other. Almost every organisation where he tried to get the referee a job was retrenching. Jobs were being cut across the industry which was making it tough for the referee. People did oblige Deepak by interviewing the referee but nothing was reaching a closure. The referee, on his part, was happy that Deepak was trying to get him a job and Deepak was happy that he found a good friend in him; someone he could relate to outside the office.

At work, things were not all that great for Deepak. August had turned out to be a better month than July...only marginally. Despite all the hectic lobbying in August, they ended the month short of target by 16 per cent. Deepak had to undergo one more round of depressing conversation with Bhalla on sales targets.

'Look, Deepak, I genuinely do not have the patience or the time. I agree August was a better month than July. However, you not only fell short of the August numbers but also failed to cover up for the shortfall in July. Where will I get those incremental credit cards from? You are really pushing me to a stage where I am beginning to wonder if you are the right guy for the job.' Bhalla sounded nasty and ominous.

Deepak had no answer. What could he say? His numbers had let him down big time. 'Yes, Manish. We will surely make an attempt to do better and meet target in September.'

'That you will, my friend. I need you to cover up for the shortfall in July and August in the remaining four months of the year. Also, remember that since the festival season begins from October, targets go up sharply in the last quarter of the year. You have to gear up for that.'

'Yes, Manish. We will not give you a chance to complain,' Deepak assured him.

'There won't be another chance, Deepak. Remember that,' he paused for some time. 'Look, Deepak. You are a good guy. Good pedigree. You have done well thus far. But...' and there was a threatening pause again. Deepak's heart sank. What was he going to say?

'But I have a target to deliver. A business to run. You are today managing what is the most critical part of my business. And I can't afford my biggest region to miss its numbers every month. September is your only chance. And here is a deal. I know it is going to be difficult to cover up the July–August shortfall in September. Go all out and meet the planned September numbers. We will spread the shortfall equally in the last three months of the year. I will be fine as long as you deliver the numbers in September. Else, my friend, I will have to look for someone else. I hired you on Sanjit's recommendation. Please make sure that you live up to it.' The threat was very obvious. Deepak again fumed but there was little he could do. He also knew that the embargo on hiring had been lifted and the India business could again hire from the open market. Even Sanjit, his saviour, was no longer with the bank.

That night Deepak and the referee went out for drinking. Savitha didn't go along as her maid had ditched her and she had to be at home, baby-sitting.

After a few drinks, Deepak poured out all his woes in front of the referee. Deepak was not the one to get into emotional ranting after drinking. Normally, he would camouflage his thoughts well. 'If the other person gets a wind of your emotions, he can control you,' he believed. But that day was different. It showed how emotionally dependent he had become on the referee in the last three weeks. Deepak, spurred by the fact that the referee wasn't linked with the GB2 in any way, behaved in a manner which was very unlike him. He would never have opened up in front of a person who, not so long ago, was only a stranger for him.

'Do not worry, Deepak. It is a transient phase. It will pass...and you had a better August. I am sure you will have an even better September"

Deepak smiled and said, 'I hope so...by the way, what's happening with your job hunt? Any luck?' Referee told him that he had started trying in software companies who were also hiring graduates. Deepak agreed that it was a good idea and they said 'Cheers' to another round of Chivas. The referee's influence on Deepak's life was growing fast. Good or bad, only time could tell.

The morning prayers in the second week of September was an informal review of the performance of the various businesses in August. In that session it clearly came out that GB2 had not grown the loans book in the same manner that they had grown the other businesses of the bank. The pressure was on retail banking to grow the loans book again. Ronald Maccain himself was a retail banker at one point in time and hence his fondness for cards and mortgages was not hidden from anybody. As expected, credit cards and mortgages were the two areas behind which the bank decided to put its might.

This meant that Manish Bhalla was in the hot seat. He couldn't wait to download his stress to the entire team and sent out a mail the same evening asking all his reporters to join him on a conference call.

Five minutes before the call was to begin, Manish Bhalla was prancing up and down in his small cabin. Ramneek Chahal, his boss, had put the ball squarely in his court. He had been asked to increase new credit cards acquisition by 25 per cent in the last three months of the year. At a time when he was already running short on targets, growing his acquisition was out of question. But it was a diktat from his boss, who in turn wanted to impress the new CEO – and he didn't have too much of a choice.

The call began at 5.30 p.m. sharp. 'Hello guys,' Bhalla's voice cracked on the speaker phone. He got six 'Hi's' in return.

'Who all are on the call?' he asked. The introduction lasted a few minutes. And then Bhalla came to the point.

'Folks, in today's morning prayers it was decided that we will have to step up our cards acquisition. They have asked us to acquire 25 per cent more customers than the planned numbers for the last quarter of the year. The CEO has challenged us with these numbers. Do you think it is possible to push ourselves to deliver this number?'

No one answered.

'Guys, come on!! Wake up. Do you think it is possible to deliver these numbers?' Bhalla asked again.

There was silence again. Finally someone spoke. 'Manish?' It was Deepak. 'We are already running behind our current month's targets. Our target for the last quarter is really steep. It's at least 20 per cent more than what we are delivering in September. Then how will we accomplish 25 per cent above that? In effect, it means we have to acquire 50 per cent more cards than what we are acquiring now. I don't see us getting there.'

'See, this is the problem with you, Deepak. Absolutely zero on aspiration! If you don't aspire for bigger targets in life, how will you even get there?' Manish was too caustic. 'and if I go and tell the new CEO that I cant meet his first demand of me, then neither will I be in this job, nor will you guys be. We better figure out a way, folks'. He continued. After Manish lashed out at Deepak, no one opened their mouth. What was the point in saying something and then getting beaten up publicly? What Deepak had said was right. It made sense. Growing by over 50 per cent of the current month's numbers was not a joke. New channels had to be built, new people had to be hired and new sales promotions had to be launched. All this required time. Even Manish knew it. But since the diktat came from the top, he was equally helpless.

The monologue continued, 'Face it, folks. This year has not been a good year for the India business. We are nowhere close to our targets. The CEO feels that we stand no chance of meeting our targeted profit numbers. He would rather push initiatives which will give us results next year. The agenda is to invest and grow this year, so that the results come the next year.'

Deepak, for once, smiled. Wasn't this common with a mid-year management change? The CEO Ronald McCain was new and had taken over in the middle of the year. He would not be accountable for the profit for that year. It was extremely easy for him to get away by putting the blame on his predecessor for the year bygone. It made more sense for him to rather pack the rest of the year with money-draining initiatives which would give returns in 2009, when he would be accountable for the full-year profitability. The CEO wanted to increase cards acquisitions in 2008 so that he could take the costs linked to the cards acquisition within the year, and the revenue from those cards could start coming in 2009. 'Smart CEO,' he said to himself.

By the time the call ended, it was agreed that the new targets would apply for the October–December quarter. Deepak who was struggling to meet his numbers for the month knew that his problems were only going to be compounded by this.

It was decided to form a task force under Deepak to figure out a list of initiatives to ensure that October turned out to be a bumper month. Manish had figured out that even though Deepak had not delivered in sales volumes, he was brighter than many others in his team.

Over the next three days Deepak and the members of the task force met a number of times and came up with three recommendations to take the volumes to 25 per cent higher than the planned numbers, as Ronald had wanted.

Firstly, they recommended to launch a sales contest in October to push sales volumes. If they managed to increase the run-rate in October, all of them knew that the momentum could be sustained in November and December. People who met the highest slab stood to go overseas on a paid holiday. The winners of the highest slab would spend three days in Switzerland at the company's expense.

The second recommendation was to increase payouts for the DSAs (Direct Sales Agents) so that they go all out after the bloated targets. The third recommendation was Deepak's masterstroke. He wanted the credit and the operations teams to be a part of this sales contest so that they could also swing into action and contribute towards it. Deepak was smart enough to understand that without the support of the credit team there was no way they could meet the targeted volumes.

All his recommendations were accepted and a new campaign – 'Chariots of Fire' – was born. It was an interesting theme aimed to push the team to ride the chariots of fire to reach an unachievable goal.

September was an average month for Deepak. He just about met his monthly numbers. Bhalla was not ecstatic but he was not as caustic as he had been with Deepak initially. Deepak had shown some traction in generating volumes and had also exhibited good abilities in managing the growth strategy for October. More importantly, Bhalla needed him more than ever. He couldn't afford a demotivated sales team in his largest region.

For Deepak, as with any sales guy, the joy of meeting targets was short-lived. It lasted only for a day, after which the reality of the next month and its targets hit him. With September fading out of memory and October approaching, Deepak was faced with a bigger challenge. The Mumbai team had acquired 4,000 new credit cards for GB2 in September. That number was initially supposed to go up to 5,000 in October. But with the new diktat, it went up to 6,200 cards a month in the last quarter. He had struggled to get to 4000 in September. How on earth was he going to deliver 6,200 cards in October? He had no clue. He was happy that Bhalla hadn't made any noise about covering the July–August shortfall in the last quarter. Had he done that, the target of 6,200 would have gone up even more.

On the night of 1st October, when the 'Chariots of Fire' contest was announced to the entire credit cards team, Deepak was on a high. Deep down he considered it to be his plan, and it was. He was happy to see it launched with so much fanfare. Even Manish Bhalla, who was normally meagre when it came to praising someone, was generous in singing Deepak's glory. Finally, the targets were put up on the screen. Deepak's heart sank when he saw them. Though he already knew the numbers, seeing them put up in black and white made his heart beat faster. The three pegs of whisky that he had downed by then suddenly lost their impact. It was the first time Bhalla had praised him publicly. He couldn't afford not to accomplish his target for October. 'Chariots of Fire' could go to no one else. It had to be him. He had to win the contest. And for that, he had to get to 6,200 cards, at any cost.

The drive back that day was mired in introspection. How was he going to achieve the target? It was already the first of October. The next day was a holiday. He had already lost two days of the month, not knowing what to do. Savitha was with him that night. Realising that Deepak was in a thoughtful mood, she did not strike up a conversation with him. Deepak stopped the car when he reached the parking lot of the Chembur Club. He hadn't spoken a word since they left the banquet hall where they had all assembled for the launch of 'Chariots of Fire'. The ignition was still on, and Deepak was staring into the blank wall ahead of the car.

'Deepak, are you ok?' she asked.

'Yes, babes, I am fine.'

'You haven't spoken a word in the last twenty-five minutes. What happened? What are you thinking so much?'

'Nothing, baby. I am just worried about the October numbers... thinking how to get closer to them. I can't let anyone else win this contest. I have to prove to Bhalla that I can do it. That I am the most capable guy in his team.'

'You are, Deepak. No one in the team is more intelligent or competent than you. Come, let's get ourselves a drink. The referee will be waiting for you. You missed the game tonight.'

'Yes, let's go,' Deepak said and stepped out of the car. The car was locked with a beep as they walked towards the bar where the referee was waiting for them.

The discussion that night centred around the bank; the cards business, 'Chariots of fire' and the targets. The referee understood bits and pieces of the entire story but not being a banker, he found it difficult to relate to.

'Arre, what is the problem, Deepak, I am sure you will find hundreds of people willing to take cards. Who doesn't want money? Give me one, I will take it. In this bar alone you will find thirty people willing to take your card. Then why are you getting stressed?' the referee tried to calm him down.

'You stick to basketball, you idiot. Everyone will want to take money. But finding a guy who will return it to you on time is difficult. It's not a gift cheque, it's the cards business,' Deepak rubbished him.

'Hmm...right. Now I am beginning to understand.'

'From 4,000 cards in September to 6,200 in October is almost impossible', said Deepak

'Unless we get some bulk deals', added Savitha. Deepak looked at her and nodded.

'What do you mean by "bulk deals"?' The referee was inquisitive.

'Corporate deals...large companies signing up bulk cards for their employees. In such deals we get 100 or 200 cards in one go. Deals like these will make life easy.' Deepak responded to the referee's query. 'But they take time', he added.

'What kind of companies do you look at for these deals?' the referee asked.

'Companies which have around 400-500 employees, multinational organisations, companies with established offices and the reputation for paying good salaries and attracting good talent...companies which are the target market for our corporate bank relationships,' Deepak answered. And after a pause he added, 'Actually even if they are not target market for corporate relationships, that's also acceptable.'

'Hmm...ok.'

Deepak continued, 'Actually, with these companies it is important to be in their line of sight, in their consideration subset, when they are thinking of doing such deals. Otherwise you can keep going and banging your head against their walls and they will not indulge you.'

'You mean to say that you should be there when the company wants to cut the deal, right?' The referee saw Deepak's point.

'Yes.'

'I think I can help you here. But I don't know if at all you would consider this as a help since I don't know much about this.' When the referee said this, Deepak gave him a perplexed look.

'What do you mean?'

'Deepak, I might know of one such company. I don't know how big this opportunity is for you, or if at all you would see this as one.'

'Stop caveating and tell me what you want to say.' Deepak was getting impatient.

'Symbiotic Technologies,' the referee said.

'What about them?'

'Heard the name?'

'No.' Deepak shook his head.

'It's a company based in Kalina. The office is close to Raheja Centre Point. It's a software development firm. I had gone there for an interview a few days ago.'

'So?'

'Deepak, the company has over 500-600 employees, many of them based overseas. They pay well. Sad that they rejected me. But now that you are looking for large companies with a number of well-paid employees, it struck me that this could be a potential opportunity for you.'

'Hmm...keep talking. I am listening.' Now Deepak was interested.

'That's not all. That day I had gone for an interview I saw a guy with a Citibank ID card around his neck. Maybe he was there to sell cards or loans or something like that.'

'That's interesting.' Deepak looked at Savitha who nodded in return. 'Do you have any contact there...someone I can speak to?' he asked the referee.

'I will give you the number of the person I met there. He works for their HR department. You can either speak to him directly or get someone to call him.'

'Great, my friend. Sounds good.' Deepak was excited at the prospect.

'If this works, I will give you all my contacts in companies I have interviewed with and you can talk to them and see if they are interested in your offer,' the referee suggested.

'Thanks, buddy. I just can't tell you how much of a help this is.'

'If this works, what do I get in return, apart from "thanks"?' the referee asked smilingly.

'Anything you say, my friend. I will give you whatever you want,' Deepak promised.

The referee smiled again. He pointed to the Titan watch that Deepak was wearing and said, 'Give me that.'

'What? This watch?' Deepak sounded surprised. 'I will get you something far better than this. What do you say?' He looked at Savitha.

'Hmm...yes. Why Titan? You should buy him an Omega,' Savitha chipped in. And they all laughed.

'Waiter!' screamed the referee and the next round of drinks followed.

October 2008
GB2 Telecalling Centre
Mumbai

T RING! Tring! Tring! The phone was picked up by the person at the other end after three rings. Swati was thrilled. Firstly Deepak sir had given a referral and a number to be called. The call to the HR Manager of Symbiotic Technologies was her first call in the morning and someone had picked it up in the third ring. Third of October has begun in an ominous fashion, she thought, even as a gruff voice came on line.

'Hello.'

'Good morning, sir, main Greater Boston Global Bank ki taraf se bol rahi hoon,' she began the introduction.

'What? What are you saying, young lady?'

'Sir, main Greater Boston Global Bank ki taraf se bol rahi hoon.' she parroted.

'Hold on! Hold on!' the person at the other end was beginning to get irritated. The girl held on. There was some activity at the other end. The man she had spoken to was calling out to someone else. It was taking time. Swati's patience was running out. She was beginning to get restless to get onto the next call. Setting an outer limit, she said to herself, 'Thirty seconds, and I will hang up if no one comes on line.' This was despite the fact that they had been specially trained not to hang up till the person at the other end had hung up.

'Haanji bolo,' finally someone responded.

'Sir, main Greater Boston Global Bank ki taraf se bol rahin hoon.Hamare paas aapke liye ek bahut badhiya credit card ka offer hai.' Swati struggled to convey to him that she had a great credit card offer for him.

'Hmm...,' the speaker on the other side barely acknowledged. He probably did not understand what she had just said.

'If it interests you, I tell you,' Swati managed to quickly switch over to broken English from her speedy Hindi.

'Toh aap credit card ki sales kar rahin hain. We don't need it now. Thank you.'

'Sir, please take it. It is very cheap. And with every card we are giving four flight tickets free to anywhere in India on Kingfisher airlines. Very good offer, sir. You will like it,' she tried to convince him.

'Dekhiye, we do not need it now. If we need credit cards, we will call you. Why don't you give me your number? Kya naam bataya aapne?'

'Sir, Swati. Myself Swati. My phone number 9999999999. If you ever need cards, please call me only. I will give you your card in one week, sir.'

'Ok, ok. We will call you.'

Swati hung up. The first call in the morning had gone waste. She wondered how the day would go.

Hundred calls to make, fifteen appointments to fix for the sales guys – life was getting monotonous and dreary in her job as a telecaller at an agency which was selling cards for GB2. How was she going to motivate herself to get through the day?

'God, please help me,' her eyes automatically reached towards the ceiling as she instinctively picked up the telephone and started dialling the next number on the list.

It was her routine every day. She would come in by 9.30 in the morning and almost immediately get down to calling prospective credit card customers from some lists compiled by the agency owners clandestinely. Some of those lists would have been acquired from some unscrupulous database dealers who, in turn, would have acquired the lists from companies by paying off someone at the lowest level.

Expected to call a hundred prospects every day, Swati would even skip lunch breaks to ensure that she finished her work to head back home in time and cook dinner for her ailing mother. She hated this job, but the measly ₹6,500 she was paid was worth its weight in gold. Add to it the incentive she made which was around ₹200 per card sold to leads generated by her. It added up to make quite a decent sum. She needed the money to run the house, for her mother and to pay for her ever-increasing lifestyle needs.

By the end of the day, Swati was in a depressed frame of mind. That day was particularly disastrous. She managed to secure only six leads for the sales guys against a target of fifteen. She was wondering how she would escape ridicule and being pulled up for under-performance. Worried about the consequences, her mind was adrift even as she was packing up to leave.

Deepak was furious when he heard the update on the call made to Symbiotic Technologies. He called Gautam Bajaj, the telecalling shop head, and blasted him

'Bloody idiot, pata bhi hai yeh call kiske liye tha? Do you even have a clue?' The telecalling head just hung his head quietly.

'This was a fucking corporate deal and not a deal for a single card. I had given you this lead to see if we could close it in our favour, and you passed it on to a fucking telecaller. Are you out of your mind? I give you a 500-card deal and you handle it like a one card transaction. Fucking asshole. Teri toh chutti kar deni chahiye! Give me one reason why you should be here? Nikamma kahin ka! Just go and call the telecaller who made the call to Symbiotic.' Deepak was enraged.

Gautam quickly went to get Swati. She had left for the day. If he told that to Deepak, he was sure to lose his job. He was scared to come back. He hung around the telecalling shop for ten minutes wondering what to tell Deepak. Finally, he walked back to Deepak's cabin and opened the door. He was literally shivering in his pants. He had never heard Deepak scream like that. When the door opened, Gautam was greeted by a pleasant sight. Deepak was not in his room. He looked around but Deepak was nowhere to be seen. He turned around and looked at Deepak's assistant.

'He's gone to see Bhalla. Something urgent has come up,' she said without being asked.

'When will he be back?' Gautam asked, hoping that he didn't come any time soon.

'I don't think he will be back now. Bhalla's secretary told me that he has called for a review meeting and that might take time.'

Gautam couldn't hide his joy. This sudden call from Bhalla gave him some time to plan his response. Maybe he could call that customer again and speak to him on the corporate deal. In any case he had left a word with Swati's team leader asking her to call him back.

Swati was at that time making her way to the railway station. She was feeling quite low that evening. She climbed the stairs at the railway station in Malad, walked a few feet and took a few steps and got down at platform No. 3 from where she always boarded the Malad–Dombivli fast train which left Malad at 6.45p.m.

She had hardly got into the train and settled down when her phone rang. Digging into her bag, she took out her phone. It was a number she didn't recognise. Dumping her phone into her bag, she looked out of the window. She was not in the mood to talk.

The train started moving. Hardly had the train moved a little when her phone rang again. It was the same number. Someone was trying to reach her desperately.

'Hello, kaun?' she picked up her phone and spoke.

'Hello, is this Ms Swati?'

'Ji, Swati bol rahi hoon.'

'I am Rajib Sen…from Symbiotic Technologies. You had called us in the morning.' It suddenly struck her. Of course she remembered. This was the first call of the day. She had left her mobile number with Mr Sen. Normally she would only give her office number. She had no clue why she gave him her mobile number.

'Yes, sir. Tell me, tell me.' She was very excited that Rajib had called back.

'You had said in the morning that you have an offer on your credit cards. Can you tell me more about it?'

'Sir, we have an offer going on wherein if someone takes a full fee paid platinum credit card we will give that person four tickets on Kingfisher airlines, absolutely free. You want it, sir? Should I send someone?'

'Look, Swati, we are looking for a corporate deal for all our employees. We want to give credit cards to all our staff. We have over 1,200 employees in Mumbai, Chennai and Delhi offices. We want to give cards to everyone. I don't know if you are the right person. Can you ask the concerned person to meet me and close this out?'

'No problem, sir. I am the right person.' Swati had started salivating. 1,200 cards in one go. Seemed very exciting. She thought that even if 700 of the 1,200 cards got issued she would make an incentive of 200 per card which meant...which meant...a lot of money. She was poor in making mental calculations.

'When do you want someone to come and see you, sir?'

'Can someone come tomorrow?'

'Sir, I will ask my manager to come. When you want him to come? Please tell.'

'Any time after six p.m. tomorrow. You can give him my mobile number. He can coordinate with me. What is his name?'

'Sure, sir. I will ask him to call you in the morning and see you tomorrow.'

'Great! Thanks.'

Swati was super excited when she disconnected the phone. For the first time in her life, she had come in the vicinity of such a large deal. She was cribbing as she got out of the office and God answered her prayers almost immediately. She tried calling Gautam's number, but it was switched off. He had probably switched it off due to the fear of Deepak calling him back, but Swati didn't know that.

When she couldn't speak with Gautam, she sent him an SMS and headed home. In any case Rajib had to be met in the evening. She could pass on the information to Gautam in the morning, too.

That night sleep deserted her. By this time she had got her math right that if she managed to get 700 cards out of the 1,200 employees that Rajib was mentioning, it would make her an incentive close to a lakh-and-a-half; an amount which she had not earned the whole of last year. Wide awake, she began wondering what to do with the money she would get. Three pairs of Lee jeans, two shoes from Catwalk, a new bag, and if she had money left, she would buy a second-hand Maruti. Wow! So many things in one go. What had she done to deserve this? And by the time she finally did go to sleep, she was dreaming of an apartment in a Goregaon high-rise. Money makes people hallucinate, that's what Swati was doing.

The next day morning was full of excitement. A 1,200 card deal at one go was a big one by any standard. The moment Swati told her boss about it, all hell broke loose. Gautam was very thrilled. He could now go to Deepak and tell him that the lead had been handled properly and that he was just overreacting the previous day. However, better sense prevailed and he didn't do that. He just called up Deepak and told him that the deal was under control and that he was meeting the customer that evening.

'Fix up the meeting this evening. I will come with you,' Deepak told him. After the previous day's confusion, he was not too sure if Gautam would be able to handle such a large deal all by himself.

'Deepak, would you want to come right for the first call? Let me take the first call alone. You can come in for the next one. The customer will also be happy that we have got along someone senior for the next call,' Gautam suggested.

'It's ok. We do not have the luxury of time. We have to close the deal as soon as possible. I will come.'

That evening, Deepak and Gautam walked into Symbiotic Technologies. It was a swanky office in Kalina, which was an erstwhile down-market community dominated area that had suddenly shot to prominence due to its closeness to the Bandra Kurla Complex (BKC). Kalina, a poor neighbour of BKC, had benefited most from the opulence and grandeur of BKC.

The sixth floor office of Symbiotic Technologies was extremely well done-up. If the building was impressive, the interiors left Deepak and Gautam spell-bound. The reception was immaculate, the sofas looked rich, the painting on the wall seemed expensive and the furniture stylish. They were lost in admiring the ambience when a pretty face looked up from beyond the counter.

'May I help you, sir?' she asked them.

'Oh yes!' Deepak was stunned when he saw the receptionist. She was also a piece of art. For a moment he was dumbstruck by her beauty. He stood there with mouth agape as if he wanted to say something but words deserted him.

'Sir, is there anything I can do for you?'

Seeing the regional head struggling for words, Gautam took the lead. 'We are here to see Mr Rajib Sen.'

'Oh, sure. Who should I say has come for him?'

'Deepak and Gautam from Greater Boston Global Bank.'

'Thanks, could you please take a seat. I will inform him,' she said and left to inform Rajib.

Within five minutes, Rajib was at the reception. He ushered them into a conference room right next to the reception. A few pleasantries later they got down to the crux of the meeting.

'Sir, Swati mentioned that you were interested in a corporate deal for credit cards for your employees,' Gautam asked Rajib.

'Oh, yes. See, we are a large software export firm. We have over 1,200 people working on our rolls. We hire the best of talent and pay them well to stay with us. A number of our employees spend money on office work, hotel, travel, etc. We don't want them to use their own funds. We would rather help them with credit cards from a bank like yours and make them spend on those cards. Once done, they can then claim it from us through the regular expense reimbursement process. Is something like this doable?'

'Mr Sen,' Gautam began only to be cut short by a fidgety Deepak. 'It's possible, Mr Sen.' He butted in. 'It's definitely workable. How would you want us to do this? Would you want these cards to be corporate cards, in which case the liability on the card use will be on Symbiotic Technologies, or would you want your employees to be issued individual credit cards where we will appraise the credit-worthiness of each employee and then issue cards? If it is the former, we will appraise your company and then give limits to all your employees. The call will be yours. You can choose the type of card and credit limit for your employees as long as it falls within the overall cap we set for your company. In the latter case we will collect individual documentation from all your employees and then appraise them individually. We will also run a check on the credit bureau for every employee of yours. There might be some rejections, too. What is it that you are looking for?' Deepak said with his typical multinational arrogance.

'I would rather have them take a credit card on their own names and not a corporate one. Would you have an extensive documentation for this? If it is too difficult to get one, I would rather let it be. I don't want too much headache, or for that matter make it too complex for my staff.'

Rajib had delivered a subtle threat – either do it in a comfortable and convenient manner or lose the deal. This sudden threat worried Deepak. The prospect of losing a deal of 1,200 cards loomed large. It softened him greatly.

'Mr Sen, please do not worry. We will work out the best deal for you. In fact I will come back to you with a proposal which will make it very attractive for you and your employees. Sir, we today have one of the best products in the market. Good travel offers, excellent reward points on card usage, twenty-four hour helpline, access to airport lounges, etc., are just a few of the benefits that we offer on our cards. We will give you the best product at best rates, sir.' Deepak's voice betrayed his desperation.

'Good sales pitch, Mr Deepak Sarup. Almost everyone offers these facilities now. What I want from you is an easy and painless processing for my staff. Also, I can't have your people roaming around my office for the next thirty days, collecting documents and application forms from my staff. So if you have an easy solution, come back to me by tomorrow.' Rajib got up. 'Thank you for coming, gentlemen.' Deepak and Gautam, too, had to get up. Their host had pulled the curtain on the meeting.

On the way out Deepak looked at the office one more time. Sexy office! Wonderful décor, he thought. He could see about thirty people furiously working on their computers as if their lives depended on how soon they finished what they were doing.

'And, Mr Sarup,' Rajib's call made Deepak stop and turn back.

'One more thing...Citibank has already made me an excellent offer. They will pick up all documents from me and deliver the cards here in office. See what you can do better than them. I have almost closed the deal with Citibank. Swati called me yesterday morning and I felt that she was quite convincing. That's why I decided to speak to you. Think about it and get back to me quickly. I do not have much time.'

Sure, sir,' nodded Deepak. 'Can you please tell me a little more about the Citibank offer? What are they doing for you?'

'They will collect all employee data from me. I will collect the forms from my employees and hand over the documents to Citibank. Symbiotic Technologies will confirm the employee residence and office address that we have in our records. On that basis Citibank will issue the card to the employees. For employees who have been with us for less than six months, Citibank will do their regular verifications and issue a card. But for employees who have been with us for more than six months there will be no verifications.'

'That sounds interesting. However, I think we will be able to better that,' said Deepak, even as he turned and headed towards the main door.

As soon as they stepped out of the office, Gautam looked at Deepak and asked, 'What is your view, sir?'

'Arre, this is a brilliant deal. Sure shot hai yeh toh. We must not let this go out of our hands. Let's screw Citibank this time around. Let's talk to Bhalla and the credit department when we get back.'

But he knew it was not going to be easy. Citibank was known to be a real pain in the back when it came to letting go of a deal. They would chase it as if their life depended on it. Deepak had crossed paths with them many a time in the past. Even in his previous roles in branch banking and wealth management he had seen that they were very aggressive and undercut for every big deal. In lending they were known to approve loans that GB2 would never even dream of approving. They would lend to customers whose profiles were suspect and whom every other bank would hesitate in giving out cash. Deepak knew that Symbiotic was not going to be an easy deal. But he needed it. And needed it very badly at that. 'Chariots of Fire' depended on it. Didn't it?

Back in office, he called the referee. 'Hey, referee, how are you, my friend?'

'I am good...waiting in the lobby of Global Infocom for an interview. I have been sitting here for the last forty minutes, waiting. I seriously wonder why these guys take so much time in meeting with candidates!'

'Best of luck, my friend. Achcha listen, I wanted to tell you something. We met with Symbiotic today. Met that Rajib Sen.'

'Oh, you did? Good, good. It's a nice company. I was very disappointed when they didn't hire me.'

'How well do you know their background? They are asking for the moon. I was wondering if it would be worth putting up a fight to get this approved.'

'Oh, I am sure it is! And Citibank would not be chasing this deal for nothing. They are normally smart in these things,' the referee reminded Deepak.

'You mean we are not? Thank you for the compliment, my friend.'

'Haha...that's not what I meant. You know what I meant, you idiot.'

'How do I get to know more about their background?' As soon as Deepak asked the question, he heard some commotion in the background. Something was going on at the referee's end.

'Listen, Deepak. I have got to go. They have called me inside. Why don't you Google on the company? You will find some details. I am sure they have a website too.'

'Oh, yes. Best of luck.' Deepak hung up wondering how stupid it was of him to not have thought that earlier.

He quickly logged into his laptop and googled on Symbiotic Technologies. It showed up a number of links. Many of them were just news articles and press releases. He clicked on the link which was the home page of Symbiotic Technologies. It was a brilliant, hi-tech website. The jazz blinded him. He was very impressed – completely sold on the company. The history part talked about the company's twenty-year legacy. The list of clients seemed impressive. The geographical spread was large. They had operations all over the world. He had to do this deal – there was no way they were going to lose this to Citibank.

Later that evening when he met Savitha and they were driving back together, Savitha brought up the topic.

'How did Symbiotic go?'

'Arre, yes. I wanted to tell you about it. There was too much chaos today...just slipped my mind,' Deepak replied to her.

'Growing old, baby?' she asked with a naughty smile playing on her face.

'Shut up now. I am sure you don't need evidence to prove that your baby is not growing old?'

'Haha...kidding, love.' She quickly made amends.

'Hmm...I know. Symbiotic was chaotic. The guy wants the earth and the moon. He wants us to issue cards to his employees on the basis of his confirmation. He will give us their application forms and supporting documents along with income details. He wants us to issue a card to them on that basis alone.'

'How many cards?'

'He claims over 1,200 cards but my guess is around 600-800 cards.'

'Which is big.'

'Well, it is,' Deepak agreed.

'Will he give us the KYC documents?' Know Your Customer documents were collected from customers for all new relationships by every bank. It was a regulatory requirement and was prescribed by the RBI.

'You mean address and ID proof?'

'Hmm...,' Savitha nodded.

'We can ask him. We can tell him to give us the application forms, a confirmation from the company on their address in the company records, salary details and KYC. He would ideally have all of these with himself and wouldn't need to harass the employees.'

'Sounds good.'

'You think this will fly internally?' Deepak asked.

'You mean within credit?' asked Savitha.

'Yeah.'

'Let's try. The only hitch for you here is the verification which is under my control. And if we strongly believe in this deal, the same can be waived.' The unit which Savitha was handling managed the entire verification process. GB2 would send agents to the customer's residence and office usually to confirm if the applicant's office address and residence were authentic. These also served as a verification of the applicant's living standards and hence were a critical input into the lending approval process. However, the vendors doing the same were controlled by Savitha's team.

'How should we position it to Bhisham?'

'Deepak, Bhisham will ask his team. If we are waiving verifications for the employees, he will ask me. I will strongly recommend, given the employee profile and the company background. He should agree.'

Deepak smiled. 'It helps to know people in credit, doesn't it?'

The plan was made. Deepak would put the proposal up to Bhisham, who in turn was expected to refer it to Savitha. It happened exactly as they had planned. Deepak gave a glossy proposal to Bhisham, which was liberally littered with literature lifted directly from the company's website.

Bhisham glossed over the proposal. Seeing the link in the proposal, he clicked on it and checked the website. It was impressive. 'Finally we seem to have got our act right in the credit cards business,' he said to himself. As expected he forwarded the proposal to Savitha with a request to get back to him by the end of the day.

Savitha saw the mail from Bhisham and smiled to herself. Wasn't she too smart? She had predicted it just the way it was unfolding.

She didn't need to spend time doing any research. In fact even before Bhisham sent it to her, she had drafted a response for him. All she did was to retrieve the mail from her drafts folder and press 'send' on her mailbox. She also marked a bcc on the mail to Deepak. If there was a time lag of four hours between Bhisham's mail to her and her response, it was only to make sure that Bhisham got the impression that all the required diligence was done and nothing was short-circuited.

Dear Bhisham,

This is with reference to the proposal received from the cards team on issuing credit cards to employees of Symbiotic Technologies in Delhi, Mumbai, Chennai and Bangalore.

I would like to confirm that I am comfortable with what is being recommended subject to the following:

a) *These offices have to be visited by senior members of my team and visit report to be filed.*

b) *KYC documents should be provided. Exceptions to this have to be approved by either you or me.*

c) *Credit Bureau check should be done on applicants prior to issuing any credit card. If any applicant does not have any record on the bureau which indicates that he has not taken any loan/credit card from any other lender, we will do a complete set of verification on him.*

d) *Any employee with less than six months vintage in the company will not be issued cards under this program.*

e) *These cards should be tracked on a monthly basis and any adverse performance needs to be highlighted immediately.*

Subject to these, I am fine with what has been recommended.

Regards,
Savitha

On the basis of this mail, Bhisham responded to Deepak with a confirmation of the proposal, subject to the conditions laid out by Savitha. Deepak was only too pleased because the mail sent to Bhisham was in fact drafted jointly by Deepak and Savitha. Only Bhisham didn't know about it.

The same evening Deepak sought a meeting with Rajib Sen. And the same day the deal was clinched. Symbiotic Technologies tied up with GB2 for issue of credit cards to over 1,200 of its employees. Deepak agreed that Symbiotic would hand over all the application forms, KYC documents and salary details to GB2 in consolidated lots, instead of GB2 collecting them from individual customers. In return GB2 would process them within three working days and deliver the cards in bulk to the office of Symbiotic Technologies, to a designated individual in the Human Resources team. The HR team would then hand it over to the employees and get an acknowledgement from the customer to GB2 within a week, failing which the cards would be cancelled.

As a part of Symbiotic Technologies' green initiatives worldwide, the statements were all e-statements, that is, no physical paper would ever go to the customer. They would all be sent to the designated email ID of the individual card holder.

This was a big win for GB2 as a result of which Deepak scraped through his targets. In October he managed to issue 6,342 credit cards of which 900 were from Symbiotic. More than 10 per cent of his card acquisitions that month came from Symbiotic. None of the other regions came even close to their targets. It was a big win for Deepak and he owed it almost entirely to his friend – the referee.

Deepak won the 'Chariots of Fire' contest, and that too by a wide margin. No other region even qualified for it. In the eyes of Manish Bhalla, Deepak was a star. A rising star who held the potential to help him meet all his aspirations!

In November too, aided by a couple of similar leads from the referee, Deepak was able to meet all his targets. He was the only regional head to come out on top. Everyone else was struggling.

Deepak owed a lot to the referee for his success. Without his leads Deepak would have fallen short of his numbers. The friendship between them blossomed to the extent that they became inseparable. Savitha was the third cog in their wheel of life. Blissfully unaware of the referee or the presence of Savitha, Radhika was going about her life under the impression that Deepak, her hardworking husband, was a dutiful family man.

After the starry performance in October and sweeping the 'Chariots of Fire' contest, Deepak had manfully walked up to Bhalla and told him that instead of enjoying the prize-winning foreign trip in November he would rather do it in January, at the end of the stressful quarter. Bhalla had agreed.

In January of 2009, the 'Chariots of Fire' jamboree headed west to the pristine slopes of the Alps in Switzerland. Deepak was a part of the team as a winner. Thirty-two people from the cards team, including people from sales, credit and operations went on that trip. Deepak had cleverly manipulated it in a way that Savitha was also a part of the group. Wasn't she the one who helped him clinch Symbiotic along with a few others?

Interlaken was the chosen location for the four-day offsite, as it was the most Indian of all the Swiss sites. While the entire team returned after four days, Deepak and Savitha stayed back. They decided to head to the south of Switzerland and spend some time together before they returned to India. They had stopped bothering about what everyone else would say or think long back. They were extremely open about their relationship. For the public eye, they did not share the same room. Otherwise, they were as much together as they could be.

The referee was waiting for them at the airport when they landed back in the wee hours of a Monday morning in January. Both were surprised to see him. He did not look good. The creases on his forehead were quite a far cry for his carefree self. Deepak was quite amazed to see him like that. It looked as if he had not slept in a long while. The stubble on his face had grown long. Both of them realised that something was wrong.

'Arre, referee, what are you doing here?' Deepak asked him.

'I came to pick you guys...haven't seen you in, like, ten days... was beginning to miss you folks.'

'Shut up! Tell me what happened. You look so weird.' Deepak then added with a touch of concern, 'Is everything ok?'

'Yes...kind of. Come, let's go.' He picked up one of Savitha's bags and led them to a waiting taxi. Referee didn't own a car, so he had hired a taxi to take them back home.

They first went to drop off Savitha at her Bandra residence and then headed towards Chembur where both of them stayed. Along the way Deepak kept asking him what the problem was but he did not tell him anything. He kept deflecting the issue. Finally, they reached Deepak's apartment complex.

Deepak got down. The referee, too, got down to help him with his luggage. The building watchman came running, too. The referee helped him off-load the luggage from the boot and stood there waiting for Deepak to finish giving instructions to the watchman. 'Take it up carefully. There is lot of breakable stuff in the bags,' Deepak instructed him. Once the watchman moved out of the scene, Deepak turned towards the referee.

'So you will not tell me what happened.'

'Nothing, Deepak. It's ok. I will manage.'

'Hmm...whatever. Do tell me whenever you feel like. I hope it is not serious.' Deepak started digging into his hand bag which he had

ept with himself, presumably because it had his passport, foreign
urrency, etc. After rummaging through it for a few seconds, he pulled
ut a small box. He closed the bag and gave the box to the referee.

'Referee, my friend, this is for you. A small token for all that
ou have done for me,' Deepak said.

'What's this?'

'Open and see. Tell me if you like it.'

Both of them moved to the building lobby even as the referee
ried to carefully remove the wrapping paper.

'It's ok, you can tear it. I am not too sentimental about it like
nany others.'

'I was just being nice since you brought it all the way from
witzerland.' The referee tore open the wrapping paper.

'Wow!!' he screamed in delight as he saw what was inside the
ox. His eyes nearly popped out. 'What? Why did you buy this,
Deepak? You are mad...this would be very expensive, isn't it? Idiot!
ou didn't have to do it,' he rattled off without waiting for Deepak
o respond. Deepak just stood quietly, smiling.

'Expensive...yes but not if you go Dutch. It's a gift for you from
ne and Savitha.'

'But why?'

'Referee, you helped me a lot in the last three months. You have
o idea what you have done for me. If I am where I am today, it's
ecause of you. My Switzerland trip was because of you. The 'Chariots
f Fire' victory was because of you. This is just a small token to tell
ou that we love you and value what you have done for us. Thanks,
uddy. You mean a lot to us.' Deepak put his arms around the referee
nd hugged him. There were tears in his eyes.

Once Deepak released him from his embrace, the referee stepped
ack and slowly opened the box and took out the nice brand new

Omega watch. 'Wonderful!' he squealed in joy like a child. H remembered the discussion with Deepak and Savitha not so lor ago about the watch. He would have settled for the Titan watcl but Savitha had said, 'Why Titan? We will buy you an Omega.'

Probably because Omega was his favourite. Even in his one roo tenement, he had three posters of Omega watches. Maybe that's wh Deepak bought it for him. He knew his fetish for Omegas. He ha never had enough money to buy an Omega. But whether he woul have bought an Omega even if he had enough money, he wasn't to sure. There were other pressing needs.

'Thanks, Deepak. I will call Savitha and thank her too. Th means a lot to me. My first Omega watch in my life. And I owe to you.'

'Hmm...enough of melodrama now, my friend. Tell me wh. was wrong with you. Why were you looking as if your house w. struck by lightning?'

'In fact it has been almost struck by lightning, Deepak. Rememb(I told you about my family in the tribal village a hundred miles fro Midnapore? My sister, who got married last year, has come bac home. Her husband's family has sent her back. They have made demand of three lakh rupees. I don't know how I will manage tha I need to go back and settle her.'

'When did this happen?' Deepak was shocked.

'The day you left. I was in fact waiting for you guys to com back so that I could tell you and then leave.'

'You could have called us and told us. Waiting for us was n(that important, idiot. We would have come back and called you.'

'Yes, but there is no mobile signal at the place where my paren stay. There are very few land lines which don't work half the tim If you think of roadside villages as rural India, you should con here to see. That's real tribal land. If one phone conks out, it does not work for months. You have to walk miles to get to another phone. No roads, no facilities. It's a chaotic life there. And no one in our government is even bothered about their welfare...about doing something to resurrect their lives, to bring up their standard of living and to give them the basic amenities.' His eyes had become red while speaking. He was very emotional about the issue.

'Well, I am not the government, dear referee. I am Deepak...a banker,' he said with a slight smile. 'Chill, buddy. Do not worry. It will be all fine. When do you plan to leave?'

'I am taking a flight to Kolkata tomorrow morning. It will take me close to two days to reach my village,' the referee replied.

'Hmm...ok. Give us a call whenever you can. We will be waiting to hear from you.'

'Sure, Deepak. You guys have been my only support in Mumbai. Can I leave this laptop with you? It is not safe at my house. I'll collect it when I come back.'

'Shut up now,' said Deepak as he extended his hand and accepted the laptop bag. '...please go home and get some sleep before the morning flight.' The two of them hugged each other and Deepak turned towards his apartment and the referee got into the waiting cab to head home. That was the last Deepak was seeing of the referee for some time.

Just as he was walking up to his house he picked up the phone and dialled Savitha. The call was on waiting. She was talking to someone else. At this hour? Who could it be? Normally she spoke to him at that time.

He stopped at the stairs. He didn't want to climb up to his second floor apartment. He would rather speak with Savitha before he went up. He waited for a minute and called again. Again the call

was on waiting. Pangs of jealousy overcame him. He didn't like he
talking to anyone at 3 a.m. He sat down on the stairs and waited. Sh
would normally call the moment she finished the call. As expected
she called within three minutes.

'Hi. You had called?' she asked him.

'Yes, who were you speaking to?'

'My boyfriend.'

'What?' Deepak was irritated by her casual answer.

'Dumbo! What sort of question is this? I was talking to th
referee. He had called to thank me for the watch that you gave him
He seemed to be thrilled.'

'He is facing some problems. Did he tell you about that?'

'Yes, he did.'

'Poor guy. Chal, I will call you later. I called only to tell yo
about the trauma he is going through but you already know. Goo
night now. Sleep well, baby, and miss me,' Deepak crooned int
the phone.

'Of course, I will. Goodnight, baby.'

And they hung up.

Mumbai GB2 Headquarters

Ronald McCain's car drove into the impressive and sturdy building of GB2. Behind his façade of strength, he was a nervous man. A man who genuinely felt that something that had happened in GB2 could have happened in any organisation. However, due to the overall outrage over the rampant growth of foreign banks and the collapse of almost all the banking majors in the developed economies, these very foreign banks had now been singled out for rough treatment by the RBI. In any economy, the regulators were protective of their home-grown institutions and India was no different.

McCain stepped out of his car. A few guys standing outside the office, smoking, suddenly dropped their cigarettes and stood erect and wished him a good day. He didn't even notice. He was lost in his thoughts. If the Ahmedabad issue, which happened before he took over the reins of GB2 in India, pushed the organisation into the watch list, this episode could signal a 'Control + Alt + Del' for the future of the organisation.

Save a solitary issue in Ahmedabad wherein the bank had got embroiled in an ugly spat with the regulators on the issue of opening and transacting on Demat accounts, GB2, thus far in India, was a clean organisation. The Ahmedabad episode was over a decade old and was more or less forgotten as a transactional and control lapse. However, this instance was about to turn their dream-run into a PR nightmare and he was right there in the centre of the tornado. He was made aware of all this and more as he walked into the room to a waiting audience of the compliance head and a few other colleagues.

He looked at Saurabh with disgust. How could he not manage relationships with the RBI effectively? At the same time his heart told him that he was not being fair. Saurabh could not have predicted this, in fact no one could have.

October 2009

Chhattisgarh

I N the Dhauli forest, deep in Chhattisgarh, after the black-top tar roads broke into potholes, transformed into brown and mellowed dirt tracks and even way beyond the point where the dirt roads crumbled into winding mud paths, after the last semblance of a civilisation ended with the last of the streetlights disappearing in a distance and after the last ray of sunlight was blocked by the dense jungles, a tall, red monument suddenly appeared at the edge of a clearing. Twenty-five feet in height, it was topped by a hammer and sickle and was built in the honour of a fallen warrior. White letters were scribbled across the base: 'Every drop of martyrs blood will make the new generation prosper.'

Though it looked like a memorial, it was nothing but a caution. A warning that one was entering a liberated area – a zone where Marx was revered and Mao was alive. In this region, an army of guerrillas, owing allegiance to the leftist thought process, commonly known as Naxalites, controlled and ran a shadow state. Amidst the dense jungles, isolated villages and crippling poverty, the Naxalites ruled the roost. The Indian Government was a distant, inconsequential and a hated idea.

These regions had been a mute witness to India's spectacular growth in the nineties and beyond and had been woefully left behind in terms of wealth and progress. This had helped the Maoist army to feed off the anger of the country's poor and helped them take root and grow strong in these areas.

The Naxalites consider state power as a weapon in the hands of the rich and the ruling classes which are against their movement and they hold them accountable for failing miserably in uplifting the standard of living of these tribals. So their prime target is to destroy government property and the democratically elected government representatives. They try and destroy the power of the state and act uncontrolled in their own domain. They go after the state police and paramilitary with the sole aim of paralyzing the ability of the state in containing their atrocities.

To enable and empower the tribals to fight the Naxalites and the ever increasing fear to life and property, the government started encouraging local uprisings by the tribals against the Naxalites. In a movement which saw bipartisan support from the government and the opposition in Chhattisgarh, scores of tribals were trained in the use of arms and ammunition for self defence. These tribals were given the status of SPOs (Special Police Officers) and paid a small retainership per month.

The SPOs consisted of young village men recruited, trained and armed by the state government to combat the Red army. Since they had joined the government in its battle against the Naxals, they were the most vulnerable to being targeted. Targeting the SPOs also sent a signal to people fed up of the Naxals and wanting some semblance of sanity to be restored in their lives.

On a fateful night in October 2009, a battalion of over forty SPOs and fifteen members of the CAF (Chhattisgarh Armed Forces) was resting in an ashram in Ranibodli, about 520 km south-west of the Chhattisgarh capital in Dantewada district. The ashram school had been converted into a training camp for SPOs.

Babulal, one of the SPOs, had just returned to his temporary bed, a mat, on which a blanket was hurriedly laid out, after relieving himself in the forest adjoining the ashram school. A small distance away, in a single story building, about fifty students, all in the age group of nine to thirteen, slept blissfully, unaware of the stress in the lives of Babulal and the fifty-odd remaining guys. The entire battalion was armed with assault rifles and a few AK-47s. The stock of ammunition was enough to last them for five to six hours, time enough to requisition and get back up forces in case of any emergency.

Something in the dal that was served that night in the school didn't suit Babulal's appetite. He was feeling very uneasy. He had already relieved himself thrice in an hour. He had just returned to his bed when he started feeling uneasy again. There were no toilets in the block that the security forces were occupying. The only toilet was in the children's area and access to that was shut after ten at night. It would be opened only at 5.45 the next morning. If anyone had to attend the call of nature at night, they had to trek 100 meters into the dense jungles and run the risk of getting bitten by slithering snakes or insects. Babulal didn't have a choice. He got up, walked to a hand pump in the compound, filled up a small brass lota with water and began the trek for the fourth time that night. He was feeling very weak.

After he exited the gate of the school compound, he suddenly stopped. He heard the sound of footsteps on the dry leaves amidst the dense forest. Instinctively he hid beyond a large tree which dwarfed the school gate. He couldn't see anything suspicious. A stray dog passed his way. 'False alarm,' he said to himself and went his way. Hurriedly he relieved himself and walked at a feverish pace back to the school camp. As he neared the camp, he heard some whispers.

He froze. They had company. Who were they? From where he was standing, he was well hidden by the bushes. He didn't move. He tried very hard to hear the voices. Though he couldn't hear very clearly, one thing was sure. Whosoever it was, was planning an attack on the camp.

Instantly he thought about the kids in the neighbouring building. How could someone be so merciless? He inched closer to them. They were waiting in ambush. Waiting for the night to get pitch dark. Waiting for the camp to fall silent before they attacked. The Naxals had no scruples. They were happy attacking the enemy when it slept, without giving it any time to defend. His hands and feet were beginning to get cold. He could not have gone to the camp without being noticed. If they saw him, he would be dead. He decided to quietly wait and see. The dal and related problems were forgotten.

The clock ticked by. It had been an hour since he moved. If there was one of them, he could have handled it himself. But he could hear four different voices. If there were more, they didn't speak. He was outnumbered.

By around 1 a.m. a few more arrived. And then a few more. The numbers kept intensifying. They all followed the same modus operandi. Every group would come in led by a commander. He would be given a task and some ammunition and he would lead his team to a designated area surrounding the camp. By 2 a.m. there were over 250 of them. Babulal had lost their count long back. It was pitch dark. The only light in the entire area was the one glowing in the verandah of the dormitory occupied by the SPOs and CAF. A lone gunman sat there, below the light, keeping guard over fifty-odd sleeping SPOs.

Babulal could see because he had been in darkness for over two hours now. The Naxals were trained to see in the dark because they invariably operated at night. Babulal didn't know what to do. From where he was, he could see the back of the commander. The chief whom everyone referred to as 'Comrade'. He was the one giving out instructions to everyone.

And then it happened. After patiently waiting for over two hours the Naxals struck. The Comrade signalled the attack by raising two torches in the air and waving them fervently across each other. He seemed to be possessed. He was jumping up and down, waving his hands, pumping his fists and screaming. About thirty Naxalites rushed towards the camp and attacked the dorm where the SPOs had retired for the day. Mercifully they spared the children's area. As they neared the windows, they lit crude petrol bombs and threw them into the camp. The bombs landed in the midst of the sleeping paratroopers and exploded. Some of the jawans were killed instantaneously while some woke up and ran to save their lives. In the melee they opened the door and ran into the open, towards the forest. The moment they came out in the open, they were greeted by a hail of fire from the Naxals' newly acquired AK-47s. It was instant death for almost all of them. Some of the jawans caught hold of their weapons and returned the fire. It was futile. Too little to save them from the onslaught of 300 charged and possessed Naxals!

Babulal watched all this unfolding in front of his eyes and couldn't believe what he was seeing. His own men, his friends, his brethren were being killed ruthlessly.. The comrade was still jumping up and down, egging his team and screaming his guts out. Babulal was furious. In an inspired moment, when he noticed that the comrade was alone, and his back was towards Babulal, he rushed to him. The comrade didn't quite hear Babulal approaching in the melee of bombs exploding and people screaming. Babulal lunged at him from the back and pushed him down. The comrade fell. No one was around. No one could hear. Babulal kicked him incessantly. Not enough. His blood was boiling. Something had to be done. He picked up the flaming torch which had fallen from the comrade's hands and went closer to the fallen comrade. He kicked him one last time in his back and dropped the torch on him. The comrade's clothes caught fire. He squealed in pain. The anguish was similar to the one felt by the scores of SPOs dying in pain. Babulal kept kicking him, screaming out obscenities. He didn't realise what he was doing but he was in pain, in grief. The comrade screamed as fire engulfed him. His clothes, his hair, his body was on fire and his followers were busy mounting the attack, unaware that the comrade was injured. Babulal, who seemed to be traumatised by this attack, didn't stop his verbal and physical volleys despite the comrade shouting in pain. And then suddenly Babulal collapsed. He fell on the ground, and his face crashed into an AK-47 which was lying on the ground, presumably of the comrade whom he had just set on fire. He clutched the back of his head and felt blood oozing out of his scalp. From the corner of his eyes he could see someone bending over and trying to shake the lifeless body of the comrade, in vain.

The death of the comrade had spoiled what was a 'near-perfect victory' for the naxals. Over fifty policemen killed, a huge haul of arms and ammunition and a big moral victory. The celebrations were cut short as 150 Naxals crowded around the burnt body of their comrade. Suddenly, they heard the rumbling of police trucks in the distance. A helicopter providing cover could also be heard. It was clear. The troops were headed their way. It would be dangerous to stay where they were. Within minutes they cleared the site. Almost everyone disappeared into the thick jungles. By the time the police party arrived, there was no one at the site. Only the dead bodies of the SPOs, Babulal, and the burnt body of the comrade could be seen amidst the heart-wrenching wails of the children locked up in the dorm next door.

The Naxals had left behind the body of their comrade. He was dead and thus useless now. Rather than waste any resources on him, they would rather focus on people who were alive and served their cause. Such was the mercenary approach of the Naxals.

The next morning the sight at the ashram school was very tragic. The bodies of all the SPOs were identified and handed over to their kin. There was only one body which was neither identified, nor had a claimant. Police were baffled. They were supposed to know every individual who stayed at the dorm. Here was one who did not appear to be a policeman but whose body was found at the place from where the Naxals attacked the dorm. Which would mean that he was a Naxal. Even if he was a Naxal, who was he?

13 December 2009

Mumbai

IT was the ninth anniversary of the attack on the symbol o democracy. The day when terrorists from across the border hac made a daring attempt to break into Parliament! The entire nation watched the episode replaying in front of their eyes as channel after channel hyped the attack on the TV screen throughout the day.

Deepak was at home watching the drama on TV. He had nothing better to do. He would normally be on a Facebook chat with Savitha on a Sunday morning but that day Savitha had to be away for a sports day celebration at Arya Vidya Mandir, her daughter's school.

Dressed in his shorts, seated on a sofa, he was bored. Radhika too, had just stepped out to the local Chembur temple. He callec out to the maid and asked for a fresh cup of filter coffee – his thirc since the morning. Deepak had become addicted to filter coffee after his marriage to a South Indian.

The last one year had been momentous for him. After the Switzerland trip, his image in Manish Bhalla's eyes had undergone a sea change. He was a star and could do no wrong. Every single month in 2009 had been rocking – each month being better than the previous one. The high point came in the festive season of October and November, when he clocked 18,000 credit cards a month, a volume which was unimaginable when he had taken over in 2008. His stars

vere on the ascent, so much so that in the succession planning for
etail banking, he was the first choice to succeed Manish Bhalla if
nd when the latter moved from his role as Head of Credit Cards
ousiness. The demons of the past, the biases created on account of
.is political relationship with Karan, had all been exorcised.

He was lost in thoughts of the year almost gone by when a ring
n the doorbell disturbed the trance that he had got into.

'Mangala, dekhna kaun hai (Mangala, just see who is at the door)?'
.e called out to the maid. No response. After making coffee for him,
he maid had stepped out to get some vegetables for lunch. Radhika
lways insisted that Sunday lunch be made from fresh vegetables and
.ot from the old and stale ones stocked in the refrigerator.

He had to get up himself and open the door. Cursing the maid
.e got out of the chaise lounge in the living room and walked to
he main door, barely eight steps away. While Deepak was very agile
nd quick at work, and extremely athletic at play, at home he was
lower than a snail. It was very difficult to push him out of the couch.
However, that day was different. There was no one else at home.

Outside the main door stood four unknown men. He had never
een them. Three of them were smartly dressed in jackets while
ne had not even worn a tie. Probably, he was an apprentice of the
ther three.

The questioning look in his eyes didn't encourage the four men
o volunteer any introductions.

'Mr Sarup?' One of them broke the silence.

'Yes.' The quizzical look persisted.

'Mr Sarup, do you mind if we just step in and talk to you.'

Deepak was irritated. 'What the hell? These guys come to my
ouse, want to talk to me and won't tell me who they are?' he
vondered.

'Sure, but I would appreciate if you gentlemen first introduce yourselves, tell me what you want and then come inside.'

'Oh, I am so sorry, Mr Sarup.' When one of the four men said this, Deepak smiled. So this was not intentional. They genuinely forgot to introduce themselves.

'Mr Sarup, my name is Thakurta...Partha Thakurta,' one of the men introduced himself.

'Ok,' said Deepak, still confused. That name didn't mean anything to him.

'I am from the special projects cell of the CBI.' The word 'CBI' slightly shocked Deepak. Why would CBI come to his doorstep? He was suddenly worked up but kept his calm.

'Can I see your IDs please?' he asked the men.

The four men patiently showed their IDs to Deepak and waited till he finished checking them. The three men in jackets were from the CBI while the fourth was an inspector with the local police who had just accompanied them in case they needed any help. Why would the CBI come looking for him? Why would a senior cop accompany them? Sounded a bit eerie. He was now sure that they would have backup outside the building, on the road. But why would they do this? He was no criminal. In any case he was about to find out.

He stepped away from the door, and led them inside. 'Please come in.' All of them came inside and made themselves comfortable on the living-room couch.

'What can I do for you, Mr Thakurta?' asked Deepak.

'Mr Sarup, we are here to talk to you about a case we have been investigating.'

'Ok...,' the drag in Deepak's voice gave an impression that he had no clue what they were talking about. 'So?'

'We believe that you may have all the information, Mr Sarup,' this oxymoronic statement from Thakurta stumped Deepak.

'Sorry?' Deepak didn't like his tone. The look on Deepak's face turned aggressive. 'I will give you whatever information I have. But as of now I am completely clueless on what you are referring to.'

'Do you know somebody by the name "Francis"?' asked Thakurta, with a straight face.

Deepak thought for a while and responded, 'No, I do not know anybody by this name. In fact, I don't know anyone you might have an interest in.'

'Mr Sarup, it will be nice if you just give us the answers to the questions we ask. If there is any interpretation that we need you to do, we will tell you. I am asking you again if you know anyone who goes by the name Francis,' Thakurta paused in his sarcastic rebuttal for a couple of seconds before he added, 'irrespective of whether we might have an interest in him or not.'

'No,' Deepak swiftly replied.

'Are you sure, Mr Sarup?'

'Yes, absolutely!' Deepak didn't have any friend named Francis and he had never worked with any such person.

'Ok, then maybe you would tell us what this is about.' Thakurta took out a plastic cover and showed it to him.

'What are we trying to dig out here, Mr Thakurta?' Deepak was confused, wondering what was going on. Deepak took the plastic bag from him and looked at it. He did not know what to say, nor did he understand the relevance. What Thakurta showed him was a unique piece. The colour was so distinct. So different from the rest. There was no way he was going to forget that exquisite piece.

The look on his face gave it all away.

'Hmm...so I can safely assume that you know what this is? Maybe you could explain?' Thakurta continued.

'I will, Mr Thakurta. But how did this come to you? And why is it sealed the way it is?'

In response, Thakurta just rolled his eyes once and then fixed his sight directly on Deepak. 'Out with it Mr Sarup,' he said, a bit firmly this time.

'I will tell you the entire story. But before that you need to tell me what this is all about. How did you get this?'

Thakurta was a CBI inspector. He had dealt with criminals all his life. When criminals think they can outsmart the cops, invariably they crumble. There was no need for pressure tactics or torture. It was just a mind game.

'Ok, Mr Sarup. But remember, today I have all the time in the world. I will leave from here only after I have gathered all the information that I want.'

'Hmm....'

'Have you heard of Ranibodli...the massacre which took place a few months ago...in October?' Thakurta began his story with another question.

'The same one where over fifty policemen were ambushed. I read about it in the papers,' Deepak answered.

'Not ambushed, Mr Sarup,' suddenly Thakurta raised his voice. 'Murder! It was cold-blooded murder of fifty-five policemen in a school compound. It was a heinous crime committed by a bunch of jerks supported by well-educated people in big cities.'

'Yes, I remember,' said Deepak, though he didn't understand the relevance of the last part about 'well-educated people in big cities'.

'In that attack, all the bodies except one were identified. The identified bodies were all of policemen. Fifty-five bodies at last count. They were all buried with full state honours. However, what people don't know is that there was a fifth-sixth body, which has not been identified till now. It's kept in the Sambalpur state morgue, pending identification.'

'What does it have to do with me?' Deepak was getting nervous now. Till now Deepak was under the impression that it was something routine. It was now becoming clear to him that this was a serious investigation, something which he had no clue about. Thakurta talking about killings and dead bodies scared him.

'It has, Mr Sarup…it has. Else we would not be wasting our time here. The person whose body has been recovered we suspect to be the one against whom there are a number of cases in Chhattisgarh and he might be one of the most wanted Maoist leaders in Dantewade. The right hand man of Charu, the founder of the Maoist movement in the forests bordering Maharashtra and Andhra. No one has seen him before.'

'What?' Deepak was extremely shocked. Words eluded him.

'A body search conducted on him revealed a few things. We found a wallet on him, and in the wallet was a credit card.'

'All right…'

'In the name of Francis.'

'What? Credit card in the name of Francis?' It suddenly struck Deepak. The events that had happened a few weeks flashed in front of his eyes.

The mail from Saurabh Bhambani had hit him as he was running for a LRO (Long Range Outlook) presentation. LRO was a name given to strategic plan presentations. Prompted by the success of Standard Chartered Bank, GB2 was drawing up a three-year plan for all their businesses in India. This was Ronald's initiative and people at all levels in every team were involved. As it was an exercise driven at the senior-most level, it was very critical even from a personal growth perspective. Managers were being judged by their contribution to the LRO exercise. As Deepak was getting late for the LRO discussion, he did not wait to read it on his laptop, and instead decided to read it on his way to the conference room on his Blackberry.

It was a mail which Saurabh had forwarded to him with a note saying 'please respond'. In fact the mail was a request from the law enforcers asking for some details of a particular credit card and Saurabh had diligently forwarded the same to Deepak, as it was a Mumbai-based card.

'Doesn't Saurabh know that these mails are responded to by the operations team,' he said to himself as he pressed the 'forward' button and sent it to the operations team based out of Chennai. The police had asked for a number of details which included a copy of application form, the photograph given by the customer while applying for the credit card, address on record, statements for the past twelve months, payment record for the last twelve months, details of cash transactions made in the account, etc. They had even asked for details of the sales agent who had sourced the application and who had approved the card. It was a fairly exhaustive request, not a routine questionaire. However, he was in the LRO frame of mind and had quietly forwarded the mail to his operations unit.

And now, sitting in front of CBI officer Mr Thakurta, he recalled that the mail related to one Mr Francis. Probably it was the same Francis – Francis D'Silva. What was the connection? Why was the CBI at his doorstep? Had he knowingly or inadvertently done something which had brought him under the scanner? What should he do? Should he call up the bank and ask for help, or should he play along and see how he could get out of this spot? There was no point hiding information. As far as he knew, he had done no wrong.

A maze of thoughts engulfed him when the booming voice of Thakurta brought him back to reality. 'So, Mr Sarup, are you listening to me?'

'Yes, of course....'

'As I was telling you, we found the card during the search of the unidentified body. A platinum credit card in the name of Francis D'Silva. The card has been issued by your bank.'

'Yes. Wasn't this the same card about which CBI had sought some information from us some time back? I remember the mail with the information request.'

'Mr Sarup, you are right. This is the same card.'

'I remember I had asked our operations team to provide all the information to you. Hope they did?'

'Yes, yes. Your bank responded extremely promptly. When we saw the information provided by your bank, we discovered some inconsistencies in the entire data.'

'Inconsistencies? What kind of inconsistencies? If you so require, we can provide all the clarifications that you might need,' Deepak offered.

'Francis's platinum card had a credit limit of three lakh,' said Thakurta and paused. 'Mr Sarup, a person is killed in a gun battle in RaniBodli in Dantewada...and guess what? We find a three lakh limit credit card on him. It is very unlikely, Mr Sarup, that anyone within miles of Dantewada will have the income to justify a credit limit of three lakh rupees.'

'I understand. One needs to have an income of around a-lakh-and-half a month to justify a limit of three lakh.'

'Yes, so you better have an explanation of how a person living in RaniBodli has a credit limit of three lakh,' Thakurta said.

'I am not too sure I would be able to tell you anything right away. I do not keep track of all credit card customers. It is physically impossible for me to do so.'

'But Francis D'Silva is not 'anyone', Mr Sarup.' The drag where he said 'anyone' was quite evident. 'You know him personally.' He added.

'What do you mean?'

'After what I showed you just now, I was hoping you would not be as surprised as you are feigning to be. However, I must say I am bit amazed at your stance. But that's fine. Hold your comments till you hear the entire story.'

'Please believe me...I will tell you whatever I know about this. As of now I have absolutely no idea. If you give me some time, I will even check out all the application details and come back to you with a solid reason behind how a three-lakh credit limit was given, if that's all that you want.' Not that Sarup had much choice.

Thakurta was not interested in his appeals. He continued, 'Even though we recovered a credit card with the name Francis from his wallet, we were quite surprised to see that this gentleman had a sacred thread around his chest. A sacred thread is what the Hindus wear – "the janeu". Was the deceased a Christian named Francis? Or was he a Hindu with the credit card in a Christian name? Either of which is concerning. The former indicates the growing clout of Christian separatists taking advantage of the Maoist insurgency and creating chaos in the region while the latter indicates serious fraud percolating into the Maoist camps, which is a larger cause of worry. In either case, it is important to know the identity of the killed person. Is he Francis or is he someone else? We need to quickly find out.'

'And how do I come into the picture?'

'Hold on Mr Sarup. Let me finish,' and Thakurta stopped, allowing Deepak time to wipe the sweat from his forehead. 'And now on to the packet that you are holding in your hand. It is very unlikely that something like that would be found with someone living and working in the jungles of Dhauli. Do you recognize that, Mr Sarup?' He waited

'Not too sure. I have seen pieces like this before'

'Mr Sarup. On investigating, we found that this is something which has been bought by and paid for using your personal credit card.'

'How can you be so sure of that? There could be multiple pieces of the same model,' argued Deepak.

'Deepak, do we all look like idiots to you? Three of us will not come to you on a hunch.' This was the first sign of aggression from Thakurta, who had kept his cool till then.

'We have evidence to prove that this was something you had bought on 13 January 2009, in Interlaken. I am sure you know that every Omega watch has a unique number engraved below its left strap hinge. The same number is mentioned in your purchase receipt and in the information held with the company. This unique number helps in settling warranty claims and issues related to servicing. It's a standard practice followed by Omega. When we found this watch on the body, it surprised us no end. We thought we had hit a dead end until we figured this bit about the serial number. With support from the Swiss authorities we found out that this watch was sold at the store at Interlaken. We sent our officers to Interlaken who were able to establish that this watch with the corresponding serial number was bought by you,' and then he paused. 'Mr Sarup, you had bought this watch from Time Out International in Interlaken. We have foolproof evidence. This is not a hunch.'

'What? Is this the same watch?' Deepak could not believe what he was hearing. The referee, the guy who he thought was a close friend, the person whom he and Savitha had gifted an Omega watch, for all his help, was a Naxalite. A Maoist leader. A rebel. His heart sank. It seemed as if someone had pulled the rug from under his feet. 'It can't be. This cannot be true...this cannot be true,' he muttered.

'Mr Sarup, this is true. You paid for this purchase through your credit card. We even have a copy of the charge slip. Would you want to see it?'

'No, it's fine.'

'Now would you want to tell us more about it, Mr Sarup? What do you know and how much do you know about this guy? What is your part in this entire movement? How are you involved in this?' This time Thakurta's voice was even more threatening. Deepak got worried.

'Couldn't it be that someone stole the watch from him, or possibly he sold it to someone? I know he was in some kind of financial trouble. His family was going through stress. His sister had come back from her husband's house because they could not pay the dowry that was demanded. Maybe to make ends meet, he sold it. And your Francis could be the guy he sold it to.'

'Maybe...,' Thakurta looked at the other investigator. 'File please.' He then turned to Deepak and said, 'Mr Sarup, I take your point. We have considered this aspect too.' And he handed a sheet to Deepak. 'This has pictures of the deceased. While these are not clear, it's is not too difficult to identify the person. You may want to take a closer look.'

Deepak took the pictures from Thakurta. Without taking his eyes off Thakurta, he pulled out the document from the envelope. The moment he took it out, his face went pale as if blood had drained from his cheeks. Sweat broke out on his forehead and started streaming down from his eyebrows to the corner of his eyes.

Was it because he was seeing a badly mutilated body for the first time, or was it because he knew the person in the picture? He did not say. Was this some set-up? And finally when words escaped his mouth, Thakurta heard him whisper, 'This is Anaka...my friend Anakadundhubi...the referee.'

The Morning After Mumbai

MONDAY morning, at 5.30 a.m. Ronald's phone rang. He had just got out of bed. Whenever the phone rang at that hour, it always made him nervous. He believed a call at an unearthly hour invariably meant bad news.

'Mansi, what happened? Is everything ok?' he asked the caller.

'Ronald, I just got a call from *The Times of India*. They are carrying a very sensitive news item. I am shocked that they didn't even bother to inform us earlier. Now after today's edition has been printed and dispatched, they called me to let me know.' Mansi, the head of public affairs for GB2, was nervous as hell. The shiver in her voice made Ronald even more worried.

'What is it about, Mansi?'

'Ronald, do you have access to the internet at home?'

'Yes, I thought we left the Stone Age way behind,' Ronald was being sarcastic in the face of a crisis.

'Why can't this idiot reply straight and keep his smart comments to himself,' thought Mansi. 'Can you log in to *The Times of India* website? This is front page news in the national edition.'

'What is it about, Mansi? You are making me nervous.'

'Ronald, I would rather have you see it first.'

'Ok, wait,' said Ronald as he went to his table and opened the laptop. 'Tell me the URL.'

'*www.timesofindia.com*,' Mansi replied.

And there it was...'DANGEROUS NAXALITE HELD IN MUMBAI – sensitive data recovered from residence of the senior executive of Greater Boston Global Bank.'

Ronald's eyes popped out when he saw that. He didn't know what hit him. He started reading through the article.

'What the fuck?' muttered Ronald as he moved from the first paragraph to the second.

'In a clear pointer to growing urbanisation of the Naxalite movement, early Sunday afternoon Deepak Sarup, a senior manager with the Greater Boston Global Bank (GB2), was arrested from his Chembur residence. Deepak has been accused of assisting the Naxalite movement in Central India spread its tentacles in Mumbai. Sensitive data regarding possible terror attacks by the Naxals in Mumbai were recovered from a laptop seized from his residence.

'What stated off as a rural uprising in 1967 in a distant village of Naxalbari (from where the term Naxalite movement derives its name) resonated on Sunday in Chembur, an up-market suburb in Mumbai. It is now clear that this movement is no longer restricted to the tribal villages of West Bengal, Orissa, Chhattisgarh and Andhra Pradesh. It's now made its way to the up-market towns and holds in its talons the rich and the famous. Naxal sympathisers are no longer based in villages. Now they are educated, sophisticated and city-bred.

'The accused, Deepak, works with GB2 as a credit cards sales head and has been found to have deep-rooted links into the Naxal movement in Dantewada district of Chhattisgarh. "We suspect him to be one of the masterminds of the October 2009 massacre of over fifty-five police personnel in RaniBodli in Dantewada district. He has been arrested under the special provisions of POTA" (Prevention of Terrorism Act), said a source in the CBI on conditions of anonymity... the article went on.

'What the hell is this, Mansi?' screamed Ronald on the phone.

'We were not aware that he was involved in this, Ronald.'

'I don't expect you to know what Deepak is up to. I expect you to know what the press is up to. How could the biggest story of your life get published without you knowing it? It's your damn job. You are paid to keep a tab on the press and manage it, Mansi.' Ronald was furious.

'Yes, Ronald, I understand. But such news cannot be prevented from getting published.'

'Mansi, for God's sake spare me this crap early in the morning. I am not an idiot. I know these news items cannot be prevented or managed. But I expect you to know that such a story is about to break, so that it gives us enough time to manage these things internally. Now the guys from Singapore will be on our head within the next thirty minutes. Anyway, we will do this performance evaluation later. Let's first manage the issue on our hands. Can you please find out more about this. And where is Deepak? Do we have access to him? Have you called Rohan Naik? Does he know about this? Find out more.' Rohan was the security in-charge for GB2 and had extremely strong relationships with the police and the law enforcers.

Mansi didn't know which question to answer, for there were too many of them. 'I have told Rohan. He is trying to find out. I am only surprised why no one from his family told us about it. Why didn't his wife call us yesterday? Very surprising.'

'You ask Rohan to call me...NOW!' he said, before hanging up even as he read the last line of the article. '...The role of GB2 in the entire episode is yet to be seen'. What the hell! How could they even insinuate that someone at GB2 or GB2 itself was involved in supporting the naxal movement!

And then he looked at the bottom. The name struck him. He picked up his phone and dialled Mansi.

'Hello Mansi.'

'I am just calling Rohan. Give me two minutes.'

'No, not that. Wanted to check on something else.'

'Yes, Ronald.'

'Do you know Karan Panjabi? I recollect Sherlyn mentioning this name to me a few times.'

'Yes. He used to work with us.'

'Is this the same Karan Panjabi who has co-written this *Times of India* story?'

'Oh! I didn't see that. I know he had joined Citibank when he quit. I don't recollect anyone mentioning that he has quit Citibank to join the media.'

'Why did I think that you would not have discovered this?' Ronald was sarcastic. 'Can you please check on that?' The stress on 'please' was not missed. He was frustrated with Mansi and her team.

'I will check on both these things, Ronald.'

'Great, thanks. Please get someone to start working on a briefing note and a press release. I am sure the press is going to be after our blood the moment we get into office. We should have a denial ready and cleared by legal and compliance teams by then.'

'Sure, we are already working on this. Me and my team are in office.'

'One more thing. Has any other newspaper carried this article?'

'No, Ronald. This is a kind of scoop for TOI. An insider at CBI has leaked this story to *The Times of India*. Since they were the only ones to have this story, they carried it as a scoop and have made this a front page news item.'

As he kept the phone down, Ronald knew that this was going to be the biggest challenge he had dealt with in his life. Almost immediately he went for his shower. It was going to be a long day in office. It was better to get in quickly. Rohan called. Hurriedly, he took a briefing and hung up, promising to call soon.

After a quick shower and a hurried cup of coffee, he left for office. Enroute he connected with Rohan again.

'Any update, Rohan?'

'Not yet, Ronald. We tried calling Deepak's residence. No one is picking up the phone. We have sent someone to his house to find out more.'

'Just be careful, Rohan. No one should even remotely link us to this case. We cannot be seen to be taking Deepak's side in this issue. We are just trying to find out the details so that we protect our interests.' Ronald was clear on how to defend GB2.

'Yes, Ronald. I will take care of this. I will be in office in fifteen minutes and will brief you in detail when you come.'

'Ok. Be careful.' Ronald disconnected the call.

The fifteen minute drive from home to the MG road office of the bank was very stressful for Ronald. He was driving the car himself. His driver normally came by 7.30 a.m. That day he had left for work a good hour-and-a-half before that. The roads were empty. Marine Drive was dotted with a number of morning walkers, each trying to outdo the other. 'Mumbai has taken to fitness like never before', he thought as he focussed on the road and drove past the Churchgate station on his way to office.

In *The Times of India* office, not too far away, the scenes were different. It was a big story that they had broken that day. Such a big story, and being the only newspaper to carry it, made it even more special. Anindya Mukherjee or Andy as he was called by everyone in the industry, the chief editor, was in his room, looking extremely gleeful. With him were the two men who powered the article – Bhaskar Ghosh and Karan Panjabi. The former was an old TOI hand while the latter had joined them only a week back. In fact, he was hired from Citibank to be the banking editor of their TV channel – ET Now. As a part of the regular induction into the group, he was on attachment with Anindya for a week. When this story broke out, Anindya requested him to assist Bhaskar, who was an expert on Naxal affairs but according to his own confessions, had little or no knowledge of banking.

'Folks!' screamed Andy in joy. 'We have cracked it. This is a fabulous story. No one else has a clue. We are the only ones to have brought this out. Great work, boys.' He turned towards Karan and continued, 'And Karan, Bhaskar has seen many such successes in his career as a journalist. You are lucky to have got this exposure in your first assignment. And you have demonstrated that you have it in you to succeed. Well done, Karan. You have a long way to go.'

'Thanks, Andy. I will always give it my best,' Karan tried to be humble.

'I am sure. Anyway, well done, folks. I know you haven't slept the whole night in anticipation of this story. You guys deserve a well-earned break. Go home and get some rest,' Andy suggested.

'Thanks, Andy,' both of them said in unison and turned to exit the room. As they were nearing the door, Andy stopped them.

'Listen, folks, journalism is not about breaking a story before the others. It is about capitalising on the same and ensuring that everyone remembers that we were the ones to tell them about something which no one else did. We have made a good beginning. We must not let go of this opportunity. When you get back in the afternoon, I need to know from the two of you a plan on how we are going to build on this lead and how will we follow it up.'

'Yes, Andy,' said Bhaskar. And Karan just nodded and came out of Andy's large but cluttered cabin.

'Karan,' Bhaskar called out when he saw him heading towards the main exit to the building.

Yes, Bhaskar?'

'Where are you going?'

'Home...will sleep for a while and then come back by twelve.'

'Haha...you must be kidding, my friend.'

'Arre...why? Even Andy asked us to go home, take some rest and come back with a plan.'

'Karan, Andy wanted the plan by early afternoon. Remember he leaves at one and comes back by 6 p.m. If we have to give it to him by 1 p.m., we have to work it out now, before we head out. Or we will never be able to meet his deadline,' Bhaskar wisely suggested.

'Gawwwddd!' Karan moaned before he turned back and walked towards Bhaskar. 'Come let's go,' and they headed to the conference room. Karan let out a big yawn as they entered the large conference room.

By the time they came out in the next one-hour, they had a rock solid plan. When they presented it to Andy, he was thrilled. 'This will surely interest the readers. Who wants to read about the tragic stories of the Naxals? The glamour of the foreign banks will keep all of them enthused. And when that glamour gets juxtaposed with the thrill of the Naxal revelation, it will be fabulous. Let's put this in action,' Andy said excitedly He again looked at Karan and smiled, 'Karan, this is really good. It puts lot of onus on you as it lays emphasis on foreign banking in India. If you are able to deliver on this, you will become a star.' He walked up to Karan and hugged him. 'One last word of caution. While we will give the public what they want, we will not report anything which we believe we cannot corroborate, or which is unconfirmed. If it is a hypothesis, we will state it so. If it is a pragmatic hunch, we will make a judicious choice, but we will not indulge in character assassination.'

'Yes, Andy. Don't worry on that count,' Karan assured him.

'I am saying this because I know that Deepak and you did not get along. It is said that you even quit your job because of him. I do not want that bias to reflect in your reporting. This may be your opportunity to get back at him but I do not want this to be used as one.'

Karan was shocked. How did Andy know about all this? Every word of his was true. When he was writing out the report last night, biases had crept in because of his hatred for Deepak. But Andy, knowing about the background was surprising. 'Sure, Andy,' was all he could say as he turned to leave the room.

Back at GB2, by the time Ronald reached office, Ramneek Chahal, Manish Bhalla, Rohan Naik and Mansi were already there. They huddled in his room and shut the door. Sherlyn had come in, too. Ronald had called her as an after-thought just in case calls came in from the regional offices in Singapore.

'Let's begin the debriefing. Rohan, tell me all that you know.'

For ten minutes Rohan briefed the team on everything that had happened. The media had reported only about Deepak's arrest for being a Naxal sympathiser. It did not talk about the details. About the killed Naxalite in RaniBodli, about the credit card in the name of Francis, about the possible and proven linkages between Deepak and Francis. The nitty-gritty were missing. The CBI had not provided the details and hence the paper had not carried the same.

Rohan had found out all this information from his contacts and passed them on to the entire team. They were all equally shocked. Deepak had the reputation of being a politically savvy worker, but he was definitely not the one to be associated with those battling the government, with those employing unconstitutional means to achieve their goals. However, it seemed that their perceptions were incorrect and Deepak was all that they thought he wasn't.

'Ok, has anyone been to his house yet? While we cannot be seen to be linked to this issue, we need to make sure that the family is comfortable. We can't let the family of an employee suffer till the time that he is proven guilty. Even if he has been taken into custody on account of a non-work related issue.' Ronald tried to demonstrate his human side. Everyone realised that this was just a lip service to make sure that no one faulted him.

'Yes, Ronald. Someone from my team visited his apartment in Chembur this morning. We were not allowed to go in. It's a sanitised area. There is a large posse of police personnel posted outside his house. A number of TV outdoor vans were also parked there. After his arrest, it looks like his family has gone into hiding. There is no one at home. Unless the CBI has taken them into custody for their own safety,' Rohan said.

'Or maybe for interrogation,' added Mansi.

'Possibly,' echoed Ronald. 'And Mansi, will you use your contacts at least now and see what the media is planning. I want to know what they propose to do. We need to protect our brand. We need to safeguard our interest. Deepak may be involved but we cannot allow ourselves to be dragged into this issue. And that reminds me, where is the briefing note that I wanted to send to Singapore?'

'That will be with you in five minutes. Rajesh Krishnamoorthy is working on it,' Mansi answered.

'Ok, make sure it is comprehensive and covers all the information that we have.'

'Sure, Ronald.'

'Thanks. We will all assemble here again in the next sixty minutes. And Mansi, can you please ask Joel to come in, too? I want HR to be completely in the loop.'

As all of them were walking out, Ronald called out to them.

'Folks...Do you think Deepak is guilty?'

'I don't know,' said Rohan. 'But the way it has unfolded it looks like he is definitely involved. Guilty or not, I can't say.' He refrained from being judgemental.

Ronald just nodded his head as the others walked out of the room.

The day was too hectic for Ronald. Rushing from one meeting to the other, from one conference call to the other, he did not know when the day ended. The press had come calling more than once and each time they were sent back with a press release. Mansi and her team had drafted a crisp press note which just said that the matter was subjudice and hence the bank would not comment on it. The release also went on to say that they were working with the regulatory authorities to get to the bottom of this and would share the details with the press as appropriate.

Savitha was continuously trying to reach Deepak on Sunday but his mobile was switched off. She spent the entire night wondering what had gone wrong. Nervously, on Monday morning, she packed her daughter off to school and got into her car. She drove all the way from Bandra to Chembur, to Deepak's house, only to see it surrounded by hordes of people, almost all of them from the media.

She quietly made a hasty retreat and returned home. She did not know what to do. It was best to wait and watch.

The whole of Monday, Deepak spent at the CBI office at an undisclosed location in Mumbai. He was interrogated repeatedly on his relationship with the referee. How did he get to know him? Where did he meet him? What all did they discuss? The CBI had a number of questions to ask him. Deepak had answers to many of them. When Deepak did not know the answer, he was tortured mentally. The CBI had already pronounced him 'guilty' and was trying to get the most out of him. It was a harrowing experience.

By evening on Monday, Deepak had become the most well-known GB2 banker in the country. Almost everyone who watched TV knew his name. All the channels carried this story as the lead. A foreign banker involved with the Naxalites and being a Naxal sympathiser made for very interesting viewing.

By evening CBI came out with a press release in support of the story. They fed the media with the necessary fodder. The fact that Deepak was a supporter of the Naxal movement and had a role to play in the massacre of innocent policemen in RaniBodli was put out to the press at large. The story of Francis and the Omega watch was given out to the media.

As Ronald had expected, there was pandemonium at GB2 headquarters. Everybody from the regional office to the global headquarters in New York were keen to know what the story was and what steps were being taken to reduce the negative impact that this story could potentially have on the brand. To make matters worse, Christmas holidays were about to begin and almost all the seniors were expected to be on leave for over three weeks. Everyone wanted to make sure that they had covered up their bases and gathered as much data as was required to keep their seniors happy. No one really came forward to help Ronald solve the problem – they just wanted to know what he was doing to fix it.

The whole thing was becoming too frustrating for Ronald. But as the CEO of the bank in India, there was no running away from it. By afternoon, the RBI had inquired about what was going on. Mansi, along with Saurabh, made a quick trip to the RBI and reassured them that GB2 management was on top of things and there was nothing to be concerned about. It was a mere issue of non-compliance by one of their staff members. It was not a systemic issue but more a matter of personal integrity and that the judiciary was dealing with it. RBI bought their explanation.

That evening, Mansi called Bhisham. 'Bhisham, that Francis fella...'

'Yes, what chaos he is creating for us? But Mansi, do you think Deepak could really be involved?'

'These days it's difficult to tell, Bhisham. Anyway, leave that. The police will figure that out. Bhisham, I called because Ronald wants to know if the card of Francis is a delinquent card. The data that came to us in the morning suggests that it is not. However, I wanted to check with you.'

'I expected this question. I have seen the statements. No suspicion. He is a very good customer. High spender on the card. Pays every month and is what we call a transactor – a customer who spends on the card and pays the entire amount almost instantaneously...does not revolve on his card, in other words he does not carry forward the outstanding by paying a minimum amount due.'

'Oh, in short, a very good customer. That's good. I will inform Ronald.' Mansi did not understand a word of what Bhisham had said. All that she could make out was that Francis's card was not a delinquent card.

'Thanks, Mansi. Call me in case you need any help. Do you want a note for Ronald on the performance of Francis's card?'

'Of course, it will help. Why don't you send it to Ronald?' and then she paused. 'Wait. Send it to me first. I am putting together something for Ronald on this. I will give it to him along with the other papers.'

She then called up Ronald almost instantaneously to inform him that Francis was a non-delinquent, high spender but a transactor. A good customer who banks would die to keep on their rolls!

'Something seems fishy here. If he is such a good customer, it is difficult to digest that he would be involved in such activities. Can you re-check?' Ronald seemed suspicious. Mansi just muttered something into the phone and hung up, leaving Ronald wondering if everything was as clear as it looked.

'Sherlyn,' he called out. 'Can you please call Rohan Naik and also get the fraud head, Inder on line? It's urgent!I need them on a conference call.'

Sherlyn called back almost immediately. 'Ronald, both Rohan and Inder are on line-2.'

'Thanks Sherlyn.' Ronald walked to his desk to pick up line-2.

'Good evening, folks,' he said. Both Inder and Rohan chorused, 'Evening Boss.'

'Any progress on the investigation?'

'Inder, you want to take the lead?' Rohan clearly had not done his homework. Probably the criticality hadn't sunk in yet.

'Sure, Rohan.' Inder began his download. 'Ronald, we checked this gentleman's card performance. Absolutely clear performance. We have retrieved the application form, photograph and his KYC. They all seem to be in order. We have not been able to match his picture with that of the killed Naxalite because we don't have the picture of the Naxalite.

Once we have that and also the forensic report of the passport copy, we will be able to confirm if the passport was genuine.'

'By the way, we have requested the CBI for a photograph of the killed Naxalite. They have said that they will provide it soon. They have their own protocol to follow,' Rohan added.

'Ok, great. As far as the card is concerned, the spending is reasonably high. Around 35–40,000 per month. The customer spends on his card and almost instantaneously pays up. He seems very conscious that he does not have to pay any penal charges or interest. Very good customer.'

'Have you sent someone to the customer's house?'

'Not yet, Ronald. We will do it soon. Since the CBI is investigating this case, we did not want to be seen to be interfering with the probe and that's why we have been going slow on external investigation. We have rather been focusing on the details that we have on hand.'

'Thanks. Keep it low key and let me know the moment you find something fishy. Irrespective of what time of the day or night it is.'

'Sure, Ronald,' Inder replied.

Ronald was not happy. He felt that he was dealing with a bunch of incompetent people. A feeling shared by almost everyone who comes into foreign banks in India from overseas!

Back at the TOI office, Karan was at his desk trying to finish his article which was scheduled to appear in the paper on Tuesday. This was as per the plan given by Karan and Bhaskar to Andy. He was almost through his first draft when the ring of the phone at his desk disturbed him. 'What the fuck!' he exclaimed as he stretched out his right hand to pick up the phone. He was desperately trying to focus as he had to finish the article and send it out.

'Good evening, Karan here.' He didn't sound as if he was too keen on entertaining the caller.

'Hi Karan, how are you?'

'Who is this?'

'It's me, you idiot! How can you forget me?' The caller seemed slightly annoyed.

'What?' There was silence for a few seconds.

'Karan, you still there?'

'Oh God! It's you. What a surprise! And why are you calling me on my land line?'

'I did not want to take a chance and call you on your mobile. You reported the story first. What if they are tracking your mobile? That's why I called on the board line. In fact I came back home to call you because I was worried that they might be tracking calls in and out of GB2.'

It will, however, take some guts to tap phone lines in and out of *The Times of India*.

'You sound as if you are about to reveal something gory and sinister?'

'Maybe.'

'What?' Karan couldn't believe. 'Tell me it is not about Francis or whoever the fella is?' he continued after a few seconds.

'Not on the phone, Karan. See me at the Café Coffee Day outlet in Kalaghoda in twenty minutes.'

'Wait! Wait! Wait! I am just finishing my story. This has to go to press in the next one hour. Let me finish and then come.'

'Karan, this can be the story of your life. You decide what you want. I can either meet you in the next twenty minutes or else I will see you the week after next. I am flying off to the USA tonight for a two-week holiday. You decide.'

'But I have just completed the first draft of my piece, silly. Give me at least ten more minutes,' Karan persisted.

'Ok, thirty minutes, at Café Coffee Day. I will wait for ten minutes. If you don't come, I will go home and see you in two weeks' time.'

'This better be good, buddy.' The phone was disconnected by the time Karan spoke the final sentence. He looked at his watch. It was 7.45 p.m. He was already late for the next day's cover story. He quickly looked at the article. It was a seven on ten. He could do a better job if he had the time. But the guy on the phone had him hooked. Maybe there was something *sinister*.

He emailed the half-baked story to Bhaskar and requested him to take a look at it before sending it to Andy. All the first page stories were personally read and passed by Andy. This was to make sure that there was no reputational impact to the newspaper. Andy read Karan's article and cleared it in one go. Karan is a genius, he thought and began reading other stories.

Karan in the meantime rushed to the Café Coffee Day outlet at Kalaghoda. It was a good ten minutes from where the *Times of India* office was. He stopped a cab outside his office and hopped into it. The driver started haggling. Cabs in Mumbai never came easy for short distances.

By the time the cab pulled outside Café Coffee Day, it was 8.20 p.m. He was five minutes late. Thankfully he had been given a grace of ten minutes, and he was well within the grace period. Hurriedly he hopped off the cab, gave him a fifty-rupee note and rushed into the café. He didn't even wait to take the change back from the cab driver.

CCD at that time was almost empty. Kalaghoda and its surroundings were predominantly office locales which would be extremely crowded during the day. However by the evening, these lanes and bylanes would look deserted. Everyone would have left for home, and 8.20 was hardly a time for coffee.

There were about five people in the CCD outlet at that time – all in different corners of the café. He looked around, as if hunting for his prey. And there he was. In the farthest corner where it was reasonably darker. Brooding over his cup of coffee was this guy whom he had seen a couple of years ago.

'Hey, how are you, buddy? What a surprise?' The last he had seen of Amit was when he was in the mortgages role in western India. Amit was the credit head for mortgages at that time. He was Deepak Sarup's guy.

The guy gave Karan a very nervous smile. It looked as if he was extremely scared.

'Hi, Karan,' he responded.

'Hey, what's up? Is everything ok? You don't look good,' Karan asked him.

'I am fine, Karan. Except that I have been wondering for the past twenty-four hours, if I should do what my conscience tells me, or what my organisation demands of me as an employee.' Karan responded to his statement with a confused look.

'You know, Karan, two years back when Deepak was auditing you in mortgages, I played a role in fixing the audit. On Deepak's insistence I fudged some data on valuations and legal opinions and that was held against you. No one knows about it except Deepak and me. You weren't even given an opportunity to defend yourself. The dice was so heavily loaded against you that you didn't have a choice but to look for greener pastures outside GB2.'

'I am aware of all this. At that time I did not have the backing to fight the battle with Deepak and the credit folks. But why are you bringing this up now? I am done with all that...long ago. Don't tell me you called me all the way to apologise!!' Karan tried to lighten the atmosphere.

'No, Karan. What's happened has happened. It cannot be changed. I called you now to give you something which may be of interest to you. People at GB2 have given these papers a cursory glance only and hence they have not been able to get to the bottom of this. I know if you see this, you will be able to crack it in no time. Nobody has seriously looked at the data in the office.' He then opened his bag and pulled out a brown envelope and handed it over to Karan. 'This might be of use.'

Karan accepted the envelope which seemed to contain about fifteen to twenty sheets of papers. 'What's this?' he asked Amit.

'I can't say anything more, Karan. You just take a look. Call me on my wife's cell if you need to reach me. Do not call on my mobile or my land line,' Amit suggested.

'Sure, buddy. Noted. Thanks for your help.' Karan then signalled to the service boy to come and take their order. Before he could come in, Amit got up, 'I need to go, Karan. If anyone sees me with you, I will be in trouble.' He stood up and shook hands with Karan. 'See you, my friend.'

Karan pointed to the visiting card lying on the table and said, 'I didn't know you moved to compliance and regulatory reporting. When did this happen?'

For the first time that night Amit smiled. 'I moved to a new role almost immediately after you left. I couldn't bear the thought of being in that team especially after I fudged data and you left the bank, frustrated and dejected. When this job came up, I applied and got through. I have been here for some time now. We are now required to keep a copy of all the data sent to regulatory authorities, that's how this came to me. And, when some junior guy in operations sent this data to CBI without even looking at it, I knew this could mean trouble. On reading this story in the newspapers this morning, I knew this would blow up. And, when I saw your name at the bottom of the story, I felt I could help you. Karan, I could get sacked for this.'

'Thanks, buddy. Let me see this and come back to you.'

'Take care, Karan,' he said and left quickly.

Karan couldn't wait till he got back to office to open the packet. He tore it open hastily. Inside there were a few photocopies. There was a letter from CBI addressed to the CEO of GB2, a response form the bank to CBI along with a number of documents that they had asked for. In the file Karan found some photocopies.

- Application form
- KYC – Passport copy which was used as the residence proof and identity proof
- Photograph of the customer
- Photocopies of twelve months' credit card statements

And a few other documents. All of them related to the credit card of Francis D'Silva.

He sat there, staring at those documents. Something was not right. He kept looking at them again and again. He turned them over, changed the sequence, scanned them top to bottom, but couldn't figure out what was wrong. Four cups of Macchiato went down his throat. He was trying very hard to concentrate. The papers that had just been given to him were telling a story. But what was it?

He went through it sheet by sheet. The application form could hardly be called an application form. It was not completely filled up. A number of fields were blank. Usually such half-filled application forms would have been declined. There was a lot of overwriting on the form; the permanent address was missing and even details of loans and cards from other financial institutions were missing. The residence address given in the application form seemed to be incomplete. How such an application could get approved remained a mystery for Karan.

Next came the KYC document. In the case of Francis, his passport was submitted as proof of identity and residence.

He looked at Francis D'Silva's passport. It seemed original. The font on the passport was normal. The perforations on the passport looked genuine. But as he kept staring at it he was getting an uncomfortable feeling about its genuineness.

It needed just one moment of brilliance for everything to come flashing in front of him. But that moment was eluding him so far. He thought it futile to look through the balance documents repeatedly. He asked for the cheque, paid it, generously tipped the waiter and left.

Back in office, he called Bhaskar and sought a meeting. Bhaskar was an expert on Naxalism with hardly any experience in banking. So from a banking coverage perspective, Bhaskar was of little value. However, the plan that they had presented to Andy on how they were going to leverage on this story had a large banking angle to it.

Bhaskar was in Karan's cabin in the next ten minutes.

'Thanks, Bhaskar.'

'Yes, my friend, why did you call me here?'

'How was the CBI press conference?'

'It was routine. They just gave out a release…not much information. They did say Deepak is not cooperating and has been mostly silent. They said that they are trying to extract information from him, but it will take some time.'

'Hmm…what about the computer they seized from his residence?' Karan asked.

'Most of the files are password-protected. Forensic experts are working with computer experts to break the code and open up the machine for inspection. That will throw up more light on the activities of the team.'

'Ok...anything on his family?'

'Oh yes, how did I forget that? They said that after Deepak's arrest they fear a security threat to the family and so they have shifted his family to a safe location and are giving them security cover till the investigation is over. They also clarified that the family is currently not being treated as a suspect. They even said the preliminary investigations indicate that Deepak was operating alone and did not have any accomplices.'

'Bhaskar, we already know most of what they have told us. Their inferences are largely based on what the bank gave them.' He handed over the entire packet to Bhaskar which was lying with him till now. The latter looked through the entire set and frowned. He did not understand a word of what was written in them.

'Can you explain these statements to me? I can't understand anything.' He handed them back to Karan. They were not the usual statements sent to the customer but screen prints taken off the banks core banking system. Karan himself had taken some time to understand them, as screen dumps contained codes and internal references to the bank's internal accounts, and was not particularly in a user-friendly format like a normal credit card statement.

'Why are these like this, and not like a normal card statement?'

'Probably, because statements pertaining to periods beyond a year are normally archived. When CBI queried on Francis's account, some smart guy in the operations team would have found a quick fix. Instead of ordering the statements from the old documents

etrieval unit, which would have taken three days and multitudes
of follow-ups, he would have decided to take a screen dump and
end it to the CBI.'

'Hmm...,' Bhaskar shook his head. It was too difficult for him
o comprehend.

'Ok,' Karan began. 'Let's look at the card transactions for the
month of July 2008.'

Date	Location	Merchant	Debit (₹)	Credit (₹)	Balance Outstanding Cr : Credit Dr : Debit
Transactions for July					
5 July	Kolkata	Ghosh General Merchants	42,800		42,800 Dr
8 July	Hyderabad	Cash Deposit		43,000	200 Cr
12 July	Raipur	Fanaa Kirana Stores	47,624		47,424
13 July	Cochin	Cash Deposit		48,000	576 Cr
27 July	**Monthly statement for July generated – Outstanding Amount**				576 Cr
Transactions for August					
18 Aug.	Raipur	H N Supermarket	48,000		47,424 Dr
21 Aug.	Kolkata	Cash Deposit		48,000	576 Cr

21 Aug.	Jamshedpur	Gems Rice Merchant and Wholesalers	45,600		45,024 Dr
26 Aug.	Bhuvaneshwar	Cash Deposit		46,000	976 Cr
27 Aug.	**Monthly statement for August generated – Outstanding Amount**				976 Cr

*Credit card statements are far more complex than what has been depicte
here. It has been simplified for easy understanding

'On 5 July, he had bought stuff from Ghosh General Merchant
for ₹42,800. On the eighth, he paid ₹43,000 into the account i
cash. Again on 12 July, he bought some groceries. In fact, I suspec
groceries because the shop has a name which sounds like a grocer
store. He bought goods worth ₹47,624.On 15 July, he paid ₹48,00
into the account. His card statement gets generated on 27 of ever
month. So when the July statement was generated, he had a credi
balance of ₹576 in his account.'

'Interesting,' said Bhaskar.

'What's interesting about it, Bhaskar?'

'Why would he buy groceries for such a large value twice
month? No household needs this kind of supply.' Karan was surprise
by this piece of information.

'Hmm...interesting question. Maybe he was buying supplies t
feed his entire band of villagers and tribals.'

'Possible!' Bhaskar paused for a few seconds and then suddenl
asked, 'What is his credit limit?'

'Three lakh.'

'Then why is he paying ₹43,000 and ₹48,000 twice in a month? Both these transactions are well within his credit limit. Even if he had paid ₹100,000 at the end of the month, after the statement is generated, he would not be charged any interest?'

'Yes, Bhaskar. All credit cards give you the facility to spend upto your credit limit. If you are within your credit limit and pay the entire outstanding before the due date, no interest is charged. And you normally get three weeks from the time the statement is generated, to make the payment. Assuming that Francis had not paid up but incurred both the expenses in the month, his payment due would have been ₹91,000 and he would have had to pay the amount within three weeks of his statement generation date. And had he paid the entire amount, he would not have had to pay any interest for sure.'

Karan was a little surprised by Bhaskar's simple question and asked him, 'But tell me, Bhaskar, which credit card do you use?'

'I don't use any card, Karan. I don't understand these calculations, so I always use cash. And worse, these days income tax authorities are closely tracking the spending on cards. I don't want to unnecessarily come under their scanner.'

Which world are you living in, Bhaskar? The tax authorities normally raise their antenna only if you spend more than two lakh per annum on your card account, or if you pay over ₹50,000 in cash whenever you make a payment into your card account. Otherwise the tax authorities don't even look at it.' Karan smiled in disbelief.

'Maybe...I belong to the old school of thought.'

'Hahaw...,'laughed Karan.

'Ok, coming back to Francis. His behaviour is very unlike the Naxalites. Naxals are always short of cash. They keep looking for sympathisers for funding, and options to raise capital. They indulge in looting, extortion, etc., to raise money to buy arms and to feed the poor. They even commit murders when their ends are not met. It is suspected that the Naxal movement is funded by a section of the cash-rich mining industry. A significant number of mines in Central India are located in the Naxal strongholds. I know for sure that a number of mine owners pay protection money to these Naxals. Sometimes it is in cash, sometimes in kind. That said, the Naxals are always looking for money. I cannot think of a stage in the evolution of the Naxalite movement when they have had ample cash and resources,' Bhaskar said.

'Ok, how is it relevant?'

'Karan, you idiot, tell me, will someone short on cash ever pay the full amount before time, especially when the amount involved is well within your credit limit. If Francis was hard pressed for cash, he wouldn't pay ₹48,000 and 43,000 into the card account well before the due date.'

'I see your point,' Karan's eyes lit up.

'Can you see if he has done this in other months, or if July was an aberration?'

Karan looked through the entire statement for the year. Every transaction made was succeeded by a corresponding payment well before the due date. There was not a single statement in the last one year when he had to pay anything at the statement date. Moreover, every month there were two or at best three large value transactions. He turned towards Bhaskar.

'Bhaskar, every single spend is succeeded by a payment within the next four days. Not a single instance of a delay beyond four days. Throughout the year there have been eight transactions. Apart from the one in July, all others are small in value.'

'Hmm...not the mark of a man who needs money to run his Naxal movement! Clearly he is not paying the money himself,' Bhaskar said.

'Then what could it be?'

'I don't know. You are supposed to be the banking expert.' Bhaskar winked at him. 'Anyway, I am leaving for the day. Will talk to you tomorrow.'

'Goodnight, Bhaskar.'

Suddenly Bhaskar stopped and looked back at Karan as if he had forgotten to mention something. 'Friend, Andy liked your piece for tomorrow. I have written another update on the basis of the CBI press release. We are carrying your article and mine on the front page, with a small tagline which says – You read it first on *The Times of India*. You have arrived, my friend. Well done!'

'Thanks, Bhaskar. I look forward to your guidance.'

'Ok, thanks. By the way if I take a credit card, which one do you recommend?' Bhaskar asked.

'GB2 has a good proposition. You must look at it.'

'Ok...and you said I won't be caught if I spend less than two lakh per annum, or if I pay less than ₹50,000 in cash whenever I make a payment. At least I won't have to quote my PAN number anywhere, for any transaction. Right?'

'Yes, Bhaskar.'

'Ok, thanks. Take care. Goodnight.'

And Bhaskar left for the day leaving Karan holding all his papers, wondering what to do with them. The discussion with Bhaskar rang in his mind. He thought through it again and again. There was some meaning in what Bhaskar had said. Karan was sure that he knew a lot more than what he projected. It was very unlikely that he did not know about credit cards, leave alone the basics that Karan mentioned to him.

Two things kept harassing him during the entire discussion with Bhaskar and even after that. The first one was on Francis paying the spent amount almost as soon as the expense was incurred on the card, especially in view of the fact that the Naxals were always short on cash. And secondly, why were all transactions in the 38-45 K range? There was something in Bhaskar's smile, which told him that he knew it all. What was it? The sparkle in Bhaskar's eyes, as Karan was explaining the transactions in the card statement to him, was not normal.

What could it be? He was so close to nailing it, yet so far from it. Why was that moment of brilliance eluding him?

His concentration was shattered by the beep on his mobile. Someone had sent him a message. He glanced at his phone kept on the table next to him. The screen of his iPhone displayed 'text message – Bhaskar'. Next to it were two buttons. One displayed 'close' and the other displayed 'view'. He touched the 'view' button. Bhaskar's message opened on his screen.

Still thinking? If you really want to be an investigative journalist, you need to think fast. If you can't get to the bottom of this by tomorrow, let me know. I will tell you where you went wrong. Cheers, goodnight.

What the hell was this? He was right. Bhaskar knew what the issue was. That guy was too smart. Here Karan was struggling to decipher the head or tail of these documents and Bhaskar had within minutes figured out what the problem was. He was slightly embarrassed that Bhaskar had upstaged him in solving the mystery of the transactions. But he was now more determined to succeed. He had to get to the bottom – he was not going home till he cracked the puzzle.

After another twenty minutes with those papers, Karan gave up. He tried calling Bhaskar but he didn't pick up his phone. Giving himself one last chance, Karan went to the coffee machine. He picked up a cup of coffee and headed back to his desk. His body wanted him to give up but his pride didn't let him.

He picked up the transaction list again. He looked at the spent amount again and then at the payments made. There was a 100 per cent correlation. Why would that be? Why would anyone spend on a card and make a payment within the next three days? If he had cash to pay, then why even incur the expense on the card? He might as well have paid in cash and bought the goods. Merchants normally give discounts on cash purchase over and above what they offer when someone buys things on a card.

One transaction in particular perplexed him. On 18 August, there was a purchase transaction in Raipur for ₹48,000. The payment corresponding to this purchase was made on 21 August. And there was another purchase made in Jamshedpur for ₹45,600 on 21 August. What was surprising was that, as per the transaction list, the cash payment into the account was made in the Kolkata branch. The money had been deposited in Kolkata whereas the customer was in Raipur and Jamshedpur on those two days. 'Wait! Something is not right here,' he said to himself and looked back at the transactions.

Was Francis in Raipur? Or was he in Kolkata? Was he in Jamshedpur? There was something fishy there. Was this the moment of brilliance that was eluding him? The customer was based in Mumbai. Francis's office and residence according to the application form were in Mumbai. There were transactions in Raipur and Jamshedpur and payments made in Kolkata. Didn't seem normal!

He then went and looked back at all his transactions in the past six months. Particularly the payments into the card account. And there it was! Staring at him right in the face. He had found the problem. He knew what had happened. The documents were so clear. He had cracked it. It could not have been anything else. When he would come out with these findings in the papers, he would be the king.

He called Bhaskar. When Bhaskar didn't pick up the call, he decided to send him a SMS.

'Bhaskar, I think I have cracked the problem. I will talk to you tomorrow morning. I am amazed at how you could figure this out before me. Hats off to you! I am proud to be working with you. Thanks. Goodnight.'

Within the next 15 seconds he received a message on his phone which just said,*' ☺, we will talk tomorrow. Well done. Goodnight.'*

As Karan shut down his desktop and picked up his jacket from the chair to leave, he took one last look at the credit card transactions of Francis. Staring at it the last time, he tried to just make sure that he was not missing out something. He had looked at that paper so many times that day that he could now rattle off all the numbers in the sheet without even looking at it. He put it down and walked out of the room. He reached the lift lobby, still lost in thought about Francis and his exploits. He pressed the button to call the lift. It was in the second basement and he was on the sixth floor. The lift took some time in coming up. His mind space was completely overwhelmed by the transactions.

Was there was more to it than what he and Bhaskar had figured out? And then it hit him hard. He started sweating. The wall next to the lift supported him when he felt dizzy and almost fell down. Thankfully there was a bottle of water in the lift lobby with a dispenser. He grabbed a glass of water and gulped it down.

'Oh my God!' he said to himself. 'This is not what we thought it to be. It could be worse.' He started to get scared. It could be big enough to knock him and Bhaskar out. He had to get help. He urgently dialled Bhaskar. He wasn't picking up. Karan composed himself and walked into the lift, which the liftman had held for him. At that hour, it was unlikely that anybody else would want the lift.

Karan got into his car and drove out of the Times building and drove towards the suburbs. As his car sped on the JJ Flyover, he decided to take the next course of action only after consulting Bhaskar and Andy. It was too big for him to take a call on his own.

Tuesday, 15 December 2009

GB2 Offices, Mumbai

Ronald McCain was a harassed man. If it was only *The Times of India* on Monday, the newspapers on Tuesday were splashed with stories about Deepak and GB2. Stories about how the banks had relaxed their stringent hiring criteria and about how easy it was for anti-social elements to get into banks dominated the media space. *Times* carried an article about the CBI findings and the information shared in the CBI press conference. Alongside that article on the front page, was an article. 'The Deepak Sarup that I know'. It was an article by Karan Panjabi.

The article focused on human fallibility. It spoke about Deepak's aggressiveness and his uncontrolled desire to win and how the same could have led him astray. It spoke about how he enjoyed organisational support in almost everything he did. In the end the article left the readers with a question, and an interesting one at that. Was Deepak Sarup a Naxal sympathiser before he joined the bank, or did the Naxals find him an easy target given his attitude, ambition and organisational credibility, and brain-washed him into subscribing to their ideology? 'As of now the law enforcers are working on the former hypothesis, but it might be worth exploring the latter, too,' Karan had written.

'Sherlyn,' screamed Ronald McCain from his office. He never believed in using the intercom. When she heard him scream, Sherlyn came running in. 'Ask Rohan, Inder, Saurabh, Bhisham and the entire investigating team to see me right now. If they are not in the office, get them on a call'. Ronald had just got off a video conference with the Group Public Affairs in New York and they wanted to be sure that GB2 was on the right side and there was no wrongdoing or laxity on its part. They had to be updated in the next thirty minutes as the Group CEO in New York was about to address a press conference.

All of them assembled in his room within the next five minutes. At Bhisham's behest, Savitha joined in through video conference from her office in Malad. As Bhisham was not confident to handle Ronald all by himself, he requested Savitha to join in. She was the lone person on a VC while all the others were in Ronald's cabin.

'So what have we got here?' Ronald was not in a good mood when he kicked off the meeting. No one spoke. Everyone kept looking at each other, waiting for the other person to start. No one wanted to say anything stupid and be drawn into this debate. When no one spoke, Savitha started. She was in a peculiar situation. Everyone was staring into the video screen in order to avoid Ronald McCain's stare and thus she felt that everyone was looking at her and expected her to speak. However, she was ready with her story.

'Ronald, we have reviewed all the documents pertaining to the credit card of Francis D'Silva and have noticed some anomalies. Firstly, the passport copy given to us was fake. Our forensic team had visited the residence address given in the application form and on the passport and found that even though such an address existed, the Francis D'Silva who lived there passed away three years ago. And the photo on the passport copy is not his. The copy of the fraudulent passport has been made so brilliantly that it passed the fraud check that we do during the course of our approval process. While the card seems to have been acquired on a fake passport, all the other documents are fine as they have been certified by the corporate where Francis worked. The fraud seems to have escaped early detection since the performance on his card was impeccable. Not a single delayed or missed payment in the last twelve months and every time the customer has paid up 100 per cent of his outstanding. This makes us believe that there was no intention on the customer's side to defraud the bank. Possibly the sales guys, in their zeal to get the customer a card, helped him with a fake passport,' Savitha said. It was very normal in any bank for the credit teams to pass on the blame to the sales guys in case of a mess up. Savitha was doing nothing different.

'Are you saying, Savitha, that there is no way that we could have detected this fraud? I am sure there would have been warning signs. Our mails or credit card statements sent to this address would have returned. Wouldn't that have been a trigger?' Ronald asked impatiently.

'Yes, Ronald. That would surely have been a trigger. In this case, however, the card got delivered to the customer's office and all his statements are mailed to an email address. As a part of our green initiatives we are getting most of the new customers sign up for email statements.'

'Hmm...how are the other cards from the corporate performing?'

'We checked that as well, Ronald. In fact we track the performance on these cards every month. At the time of approving the deal we had mandated a monthly tracking of the portfolio and had even set up benchmarks. As per that approval condition, the performance of cards from this corporate is tracked and reported every month. I am happy to state that all the cards are performing brilliantly. In fact they are performing in line with the best portfolios. It's a high spend and low default group of customers for us. Ideal, Ronald. Its an ideal portfolio. One thing important to be mentioned here is that the corporate has shut down. They have gone out of business in India and have exited the country. We sent someone to the corporate to check on this yesterday. This is the feedback we have received. Unfortunately we do not have any corporate bank relationship with Symbiotic Technologies, else we would have known earlier.'

'Then why don't we withdraw the damn cards from all their employees? How many of them are there who still have our credit cards?' Ronald was getting worried.

'Ronald, it's about 900 of them. I do not think we can withdraw the cards facility because of two reasons. Firstly, there is no performance deterioration. They are performing well. And secondly, the cards were issued as personal cards and not as the corporate ones. As long as the customers keep paying us back, we will be drawn into trouble if we withdraw the credit card facility to them, especially now that this issue has come in public domain, withdrawing the cards immediately may not be looked at kindly.'

'Hmm...ok. Let's deal with Francis first. We will then figure a way of dealing with the others,' Ronald said.

A knock on the door disturbed them. She had been trying to reach him on the intercom, but he was so engrossed in the call that he didn't notice.

'Yes, Sherlyn?'

'I have a call on hold for you. Line 2.'

'Who is it?' Ronald didn't want to break the discussion with Savitha and the rest.

'Karan Panjabi from *The Times of India*.'

'Please put him on to Mansi. She is handling the press.'

'He says it is urgent. He needs to speak with you.'

'Tell that fucker that I will talk to any one but him. At least for the five years that he worked in this organisation, he should have had the courtesy of calling us before putting that damn story out on Monday morning. I have no intention of talking to him. Tell him that. He can do what he wants to do.' Ronald was indignant.

'Yes, boss.' Sherlyn went out of the room.

'Karan, I am sorry. Boss doesn't want to speak with you. He is still upset with your Monday article,' Sherlyn informed him.

'That was my job, Sherlyn. You know that. Why can't you explain this to him? Tell him that I want to tell him something which might be of interest to him.'

'I tried, Karan.'

'Please try one more time. Go and tell him that he will regret it if he doesn't speak with me,' Karan persisted.

'Shut up, Karan. You want me to threaten my boss?'

'No, sweetie. I am not asking you to do that. But please...it is very important that I speak with him.'

'Can you wait for thirty minutes? Let him finish what he is doing and I will speak to him after that. He will be alone and also would have cooled down. .

'You said that he will be alone after this call. He has no other meetings lined up.'

'Not as of now...definitely not till twelve. The next meeting after this is a call with Singapore at noon.'

'If I get there now, will you get me an audience with him?' Karan asked.

'I will try.'

'Thanks. I am coming there.'

In the next twenty minutes a puffing and panting Karan had reached the fifth floor office of GB2. Sherlyn gave him a warm hug as she took him into a conference room on the side. Karan was still a popular guy at GB2. When he was working for the bank, he was a soft-spoken guy who would never rub anyone the wrong way, until provoked to the extreme.

'What is all this crap, Karan?' she asked him.

'There's more to what meets the eye, Sherlyn. That's why I want to meet him. Did you tell him that I would be here?

'No, I did not because had I told him, he would have refused to see you. At least now, I can tell him that you are here and ask him for an audience. Now you wait here. I will be back in a jiffy.' Sherlyn left for her boss' room.

Within three minutes she was back. 'He says he doesn't want to see you. The organisation is very fussy about what word gets out and he doesn't want to quote anything to you beyond the brief that is to be put in the press note this evening.'

'What nonsense! Tell him that if he doesn't see me, he will be up shit creek. People are taking him for a ride and he doesn't realise that. Tell him that I am here because I still have my loyalties towards this organisation. I quit this place not because I wanted to, but because I was frustrated with the politics here. The same politics will take this bank down. It is in his own benefit that he listens to me. There is a racket out here, which he needs to control and fix.'

'Thank you, Mr Panjabi.' The thundering voice made them turn around. It was Ronald. 'I appreciate your concern. However, I would like to place on record that we have a competent team investigating this issue and would not like to engage with the press in an informal manner. Let it not be lost that you covered a very important piece without informing us. What makes you believe that we will have the same trust in you?'

'Ronald,' began Karan, 'I can only tell you what I have learnt. It will help you. We will in no manner alter our coverage or investigation to suit you. If you are interested in listening to me to protect your bank, you allow me to speak. Otherwise, I am wasting my time.'

'Thanks for coming here personally.' Ronald turned his back towards them, and held the conference room door open. Sherlyn was standing there, looking at the two of them, wondering whether to stay or leave.

Ronald showed no interest in what Karan was saying. Probably, the fact that Karan was an ex-employee added to his frustration. Ronald stood there stoically as Karan picked up his laptop and looked towards Ronald once again. It almost seemed like one last appeal.

'You are committing a big mistake, Ronald. Your own people will mislead you to protect their skin. I know I am not experienced or capable enough to preach to you, sir, but this is larger than it looks. You might need an external party to set it right for you. That might not be us, the press, but you definitely need some help here. If you change your mind, please do call me. Sherlyn has my number.' Saying so, Karan stormed out of the room.

'Bullshit!' barked Ronald, as he saw the back of Karan disappearing into the lift. 'I am glad he doesn't work for us anymore.'

'Ronald, he was one of the better ones we had. One thing he had in abundance was integrity. He was not a manipulative or political guy, and that worked against him. He was honest, Ronald. If there was any guy I would put my money on in these times, it would be him. But you are the boss.' Sherlyn left Ronald in the conference room and walked towards her desk. Her emotional plea, too, fell on deaf ears.

Back at work, Karan returned to polishing his report. He had a strong hunch – a very strong one. But it was not proven. He was feeling for his erstwhile employers and that's why he had spoken to Andy and Bhaskar. Only after getting them on the same page as he was had he tried to speak with Ronald. His conscience was now clear. He had made an attempt to forewarn GB2 but Ronald was not willing to hear.

A knock on his cabin door woke him up from his thoughts. It was Andy.

'How sure are you, Karan, about what you are saying? About your hypothesis?' Andy asked.

'Andy, it can't be anything else.'

'Do we have evidence? We cannot go to town on this story without any evidence. It's something which has far-reaching implications. Apart from you, it has the potential to tear me to pieces, if we get this wrong,' Andy warned him.

'I am aware of that, Andy, and I have thought this through. I have considered all the possibilities and I am reasonably confident.'

'He is right, Andy. There can be no second possibility in this. If you disassociate yourself from GB2 and look at it dispassionately, you will realise what the real problem has been.' Bhaskar joined them.

'Why isn't GB2 realising it then? They, too, have smart people' was Andy's reply

'Maybe they, too, have found this out Andy, but they are not telling anyone. Ronald was extremely defensive today...just not willing to open up,' Karan explained.

'Or they still have some people on the inside, who work with Deepak and cover their tracks pretty well,' added Bhaskar.

'Hmm...but this time that's not going to be easy,' Karan added.

Andy was not convinced. 'Look folks, if you guys want me to give you a front page positioning, which this story will get given its explosive nature, I want you guys to get me some evidence. Even if it is not documentary, get me any verbal, circumstantial evidence...or something which convinces me that what you are saying is 100 per cent correct. In this case even a 99.9 per cent won't do. I acknowledge that this is a possibility, a very very strong one at that, but it's too big a chance to take without any evidence.'

'I understand, Andy. We will get you the data by the evening,' Karan promised.

'That sounds more reasonable.' Andy left them.

Bhaskar turned to Karan. 'How will we get evidence? This is more a gut feeling than a possibility. While we presented an extremely confident picture to Andy, we are ourselves not 100 per cent sure about this.'

'Wrong, Bhaskar...I am 200 per cent sure. You are not. But do not worry. By the time we go to press, I will have enough to convince both you and Andy. I know how this place operates.'

After Bhaskar left, Karan got to work. He picked up his phone and dialled a few numbers. He had to work his way through. The first few calls yielded no result. He didn't give up. He had to make sure that he had enough evidence by the end of the day to convince Andy to carry his piece in the paper the next morning. He tried to call Amit, the guy who had given him the documents in the first place.

'Karan, am not too sure if I can help you right now. I told you, buddy. I am in the US now on a two-week holiday. I can try to help you once I am back. I am not even carrying my laptop or my remote access keys. Sorry mate, I can't help you out this time,' Amit said.

Karan had reached a dead end. How was he to get the information required to substantiate his story? He had no clue. His mind was like a completely blank screen. He couldn't even speak to anyone about how to get this data. People were just too scared to talk to him. Probably everyone in the cards team in GB2 had been told to stay away from him. There were only a couple of hours more for Andy to close the cover page for next day's edition. Andy would be on his head soon. He needed to think out of the box. If the 'Francisgate' didn't go up on the first page of *The Times of India*, Andy had to find an alternate story.

Just to divert his mind, so that he could start afresh, he picked up his iPhone 3GS and logged onto Facebook. He would do that very often of late. Whenever work got a bit boring for him, or monotonous, he would just access Facebook for five minutes or so; surf around to see what his friends were doing around the world, post a few messages, refresh his mind and get back to work. Earlier he had an iPhone 2G, but ever since he upgraded to a 3GS, internet access had become a lot faster. Accessing Facebook on a 3GS was not as frustrating as it was on a 2G.

'Totally mind-numbed and blank,' he wrote and pressed the 'share' button to update his status.

He went to the washroom to freshen up, washed his face, rearranged his clothes and walked back to his cabin, stopping on the way to pick up a cup of coffee. Back at his desk, he logged into his PC, his mind still distracted and slightly distraught at not being able to find a solution to his problem. He needed some basic evidence on his hypothesis before he could get Andy to agree.

He clicked on MS Outlook to open his mailbox. He was expecting a revert mail from Bhaskar on the wording of his article.

'42 unread messages' claimed a pop-up when he opened the mail box. 'Oh shit!' he exclaimed. He had been into his new job for only a few days and he was beginning to get stressed. 'Who said banking is stressful and media isn't?' he thought. He scanned through the 42 unread mails in his inbox and moaned. Too many mails to read but none of substance! He minimised the window and blankly stared at the screen of his iPhone, lying next to his laptop, wondering what to do next. Suddenly it struck him. Something was wrong! Did he see it right? Or was he hallucinating?

He quickly sat up straight, glanced back from the iPhone to the laptop and pressed the icon for opening MS Outlook, and it popped up in front of him. He hurriedly scrolled down and there it was. A completely unexpected message. Something which beat even his wildest imagination. He had forgotten her, knocked her out of his life. They were best of friends for three years, and were in a serious relationship in the last of those three years. But that had all been forgotten. In the last twelve months they had not even been in touch. This was the first message from her in a long long long time.

The MS Outlook index page showed an unread message from Facebook. The subject line gave everything away. It said – 'Kavya Pereira sent you a message on Facebook.'

A message from Kavya was always special. More so, if it came after one long year. He clicked and opened it. 'What happened, baby? Is everything ok? Just saw your Facebook status.'

They had parted ways amicably, and even though they had not kept in touch, they had always tracked each other through common friends. They hadn't even removed each other from the friends list on Facebook.

She had seen his status update and had got worried and pinged him. Karan had programmed his Facebook profile in such a way that in case someone sent him a message, an alert would pop up straight in his office email inbox, too.

As he stared at the message, he wondered how this could have happened. Was this some kind of divine intervention? He loved her a lot when they were together. It was a silly misunderstanding that had driven them apart. He was over with that.

But strangely, it was not her getting in touch with him and reestablishing contact which he thought was 'divine'. Her message was a god-sent opportunity. Why didn't he think of her earlier? Could she be the answer that he had been searching for such a long time?

He immediately took out his mobile and dialled her number. A popular Black-Eyed Peas song played on her cell. *I gotta feeling that tonight's going to be a good night.* He knew that she liked that song. Even the song told him that it was going to be a good night. Maybe she was indeed the answer.

There was no response from the other side. 'Please pick up,' he pleaded. 'I need you now, more than ever,' he said as he disconnected the line and dialled again. His heart sank as he felt his last hope slipping away from him. He sank into his chair, wondering what he would do now. The morning's discussion with Ronald had pissed him off and this article was his way of getting back at Ronald, albeit in a very mild manner.

He was busy cursing Kavya for not picking up the phone when a strange noise filled the room. It was the noise of a phone ringing – a strange ring tone. He looked around. There was no phone in the room except his.

And then he suddenly remembered. 'Oh shit! It's my phone,' he said to himself and pulled it out from his pocket. It was Kavya. He hadn't changed the ring tone that he had set on his phone to identify Kavya's call. So much time had passed since he had last spoken to her! No wonder he had even forgotten the ring tone he had specially set for her. Hurriedly, he picked up the phone.

'Hi, babes.'

'Hi, Karan.' Her sweet voice reverberated on the phone.

'How are you doing, Kavya?'

'I am good. You tell me what happened? For the first time I found your Facebook status very cryptic and negative. Something had to be dramatically wrong. I got worried.'

'You still love me?' Karan took a chance.

'Shut up, Karan! Not all over again...we will leave this topic for some other day. Tell me what happened?'

'Are you still in office?'

'Yes...was packing up to leave when I saw your call.'

'So when did you move out of your phone banking role?' Karan asked.

'Over a year now, Karan. Why?'

'You had access to the core banking system then.'

'Yes....'

'Core banking as in banking accounts, loans and cards,' Karan reiterated.

'Yes, Karan. But why are you asking?'

The core banking system was the system GB2 used for maintaining customer accounts and records. Kavya was a supervisor in phone banking and was called upon to answer customer queries regarding all products. Hence she was given a system access to customer accounts relating to all the banking products. A year back, Kavya left the phone banking team in retail bank and moved to the commercial banking business. It was a move upwards with a significant increase in money and position. Her role was still the same, though she was now accountable for customers in the small and medium enterprise (SME) and mid-market space. Hence her system access had not been modified.

'Do you have access to the cards system even now?'

'Well, I haven't checked it in a while, if you want I can check once and get back to you.'

'Can you check now, I will hold.' Karan was being very mean. He was speaking to her after a year, and he had already moved onto what he wanted from her. Thankfully, Kavya didn't seem to mind.

'Karan, what is the issue?' she asked. 'What is the hurry?'

'There is a problem. I had come to meet Ronald about it today.' Karan narrated the entire episode to her.

'Ok, I have understood. I had heard about Deepak's arrest. Poor guy! But if he is involved, it suits him fine.' She, too, hated Deepak. All the games that Deepak was playing with Karan were on when she was dating him. That impacted her, too. 'So what do you want me to do?'

'Kavya, I want some help, and the only person who can help me is you.'

'Tell me...I will help you only if you promise me that if I lose my job you will give me a monthly salary till you are alive,' she said laughingly.

'Haha...of course, why not? I am sure you know that I am willing to keep giving you my salary till the day I am alive, even if you don't help me,' Karan, too, laughed, making a clumsy effort at flirting.

'Look, the Francis D'Silva I told you about worked for a company called Symbiotic Technologies. I have observed a strange pattern of spending and payments in his card. I want you to check and tell me if a similar pattern is seen in other cards in Symbiotic.'

'And how do you think I can do that?' she asked, a bit surprised.

'You need to run a query and find out the number of cards in which the office address is mentioned as "Symbiotic Technologies",' Karan guided her.

'Ok then.'

'Do this quickly please, I will hold,' Karan requested her.

'No, I will call you back the moment it is done.'

Within five minutes Kavya called back. 'Karan, I am through. There are 968 cards with Symbiotic Technologies as their office address.'

'Do you see any delinquent card? How are the cards performing?'

'Let me see...,' Kavya quickly went through the report to see if there was any card which had defaulted on payments.

'No, Karan, not even a single card is delinquent. Each of the 968 cards is active. It's a great portfolio.'

'Hold your horses, Kavya. This is not normal. In any portfolio there would be a few cards which slip payments once in a while. Symbiotic credit cards are very clean. There is not a single delinquent card. And normally when things are way far from normal, there has to be something more to it. It raises eyebrows.'

'Hmm...Karan, you are right. Now what?'

'Kavya, I want you to pick out ten of these cards and check their transactions. Tell me if you notice any trends...specifically the one I told you.'

Kavya took some time in going through ten randomly selected accounts. She kept mumbling something on the phone all through. Karan didn't respond. This went on for over fifteen minutes, after which she came back on the phone.

'Karan, this is rubbish.'

'Why, what happened?' he asked.

'Everything that you were implying is correct. The problem is a lot bigger than what everyone thinks it is.'

'You mean to say that my inference can be correct?' Karan asked her, positive she would say yes.

'You are bang on, Karan! It cannot be anything but what you are saying. Wait...let me check ten more accounts.' Kavya hurriedly checked ten more random accounts from the lot of 968 Symbiotic Technologies employees.

'It's the same story, Karan. Just the same! You must tell Ronald about this.'

'I tried, babes. I did tell you that I came to GB2 this morning to tell him about it. He refused to entertain me.' Karan felt angry with Ronald yet again.

'That's really bad, Karan.'

'Hmm...but who will tell him? I had all the intent to help him. He didn't listen. Sherlyn told him, too. I guess this is the problem with these goras. They think we Indians are a bunch of incompetent idiots,' he grumbled.

'Haha...you are telling me, Karan? I still work for a gora bank.'

Karan was happy that she laughed candidly. It meant she was still comfortable in his company. He, too, had realised that going away from her was a mistake. Maybe this was an opportunity to set things right.

'Kavya...?' he asked with the coyness of a newly-wed.

'Yes, Karan.'

'What are you doing this Friday?'

'Nothing...why?'

'It's been ages since we went out for a drink. Let's catch up on the lost time. If you need to get home fast, let's meet early. What do you say?'

'Friiiiiiddddaaaayyyyyyyyyy...we will see how it goes.' Kavya started thinking.

'Please don't say no...pleasssseeeee!' Karan fervently requested.

'Haha...ok, we can meet on Friday.'

'Thanks, babes. Will catch you soon,' a thrilled Karan literally kissed the phone as he kept it down. He still loved Kavya and pined for her. He always cared for her. That day he got to know that she, too, cared for him. He went back to Facebook and checked his account. Hers was the only message based on his Facebook status update.

Once the phone was back on the cradle, life swung back to the present. Andy, Bhaskar and the *convincing* remained on his mind. But now Karan had a better story to tell. He rushed to Andy's room, almost knocking a few people on the way. He was already ten minutes over the scheduled deadline. Andy was in his room, finalising the pagination of the front page. With him were a couple of others who had come to him for his sign-offs for the stories to be carried the next day.

'Andy, I need five minutes. I have juice for you,' Karan said hurriedly.

Andy nodded and the rest of the people left the room. Bhaskar joined them in a few seconds. The five minutes that Karan had asked for extended to a good forty-five minutes. Andy was shocked. Bhaskar was not. After all, hadn't Bhaskar needled Karan about the real problem last night? At the end of the conversation, Andy picked up the intercom, dialed an extension and waited patiently for it to be picked up.

'Hello,'

'Hey, Sharma. Andy here. No change. We go with the old front page layout,' he gave staccato instructions.

'Yes, sir...just in time. We were about to go ahead with the changed format.'

'Thanks, old man.' He kept the phone down and looked at Karan and Bhaskar. 'Well done! We will rock tomorrow.' Then he looked at Karan and asked, 'Are you scared, son?' Karan was stumped for a minute, wondering if he should really have been in the first place.

Mumbai

'Global Bank of Greater Boston involved in massive money laundering scam. Over 100 crore of money routed to fund Naxalite operations'

This headline on the front page of the country's most widely circulated daily really woke everyone in GB2 to a threatening reality. Ronald was shocked out of his wits when he saw the morninger. It was the same guy – Karan Panjabi – at work. He was now ruing those five minutes the previous morning when he had been extremely rude to him. Maybe this was what Karan had wanted to tell him about. But Ronald didn't allow him to speak.

He read the entire article again.

A massive money laundering scam, with far reaching consequences, has been unearthed by our correspondent today. It is suspected that over 100 crore of funds have been diverted to the Naxalites through the account books of Greater Boston Global Bank. While it is early to say if there has been any connivance on the part of the bank officials, the recent arrest of Deepak Sarup, an alleged Naxal sympathiser, does raise questions on the sanctity of the seemingly untouchable foreign banks in India.

The modus operandi followed here is very simple. A Naxal sympathiser sets up a company that acts as a front. The company acquires credit cards for its employees through a hungry and ever-willing bank, Greater Boston Global Bank in this case. The bank, in its eagerness to issue cards and meet its monthly targets, compromises on processes and documentation requirements and ends up issuing credit cards to benami parties, who don't exist at all.

These cards then are used by Naxal operatives to transact and buy weapons and food and groceries to feed their large contingents and troops. The transactions are smartly monitored by a cell of militants, who then inform the sympathisers pan India. This network of sympathisers then pay into the respective credit card accounts at various locations in cash. This too raises eyebrows because not a single payment into the 968 card accounts is of value more than ₹50,000. It may be prudent to point out that fifty thousand is the threshold beyond which one is expected to quote a PAN number while making a cash deposit and these transactions tend to get monitored by the tax authorities. The Naxalites have smartly ensured that cash payments into these cards never crosses ₹50,000, effectively laundering over 100 crore without getting noticed. While this does away with the requirement of quoting a PAN number while making cash deposits, any surveillance by the income tax authorities, on account of the customer spending more than 2 lakh a year is suitably nullified by the fact that the customer is non-existent. Who will the IT notice get served on?

Take the case of Francis D'Silva, the Naxal commander who was killed during the massacre of 55 innocent SPOs in the Ghauli forests in Ranibodli. A credit card with a credit limit of three lakh was recovered from his body.

A critical examination of the conduct of the card account in the last twelve months reveals that he has spent an average of one lakh every month. Payments have been made on time, every single month, always in cash.

What also surprises here is that while the customer, i.e. Francis D'Silva, was supposed to be based in Mumbai, the transactions were in Kolkata, Raipur and Chhattisgarh and the payments into Francis's cards have been made in cash at the branches of GB2 in Hyderabad, Chennai, Mumbai and even in branches like Thiruvananthapuram and Cochin. For instance on twenty-first of August, Francis spent ₹45,600 at a grocery store in Jamshedpur, and the same day a ₹48,000 cash deposit was made into the card account in the Kolkata branch. Such instances can be justified as a one-off, but if all transactions in Francis's account follow a similar pattern it leads to questions on the modus operandi and even on sources of these funds.

If one individual namely Francis has followed such a modus operandi, it can be termed as someone defrauding the bank. However if in all the 968 credit cards issued to benami employees of Symbiotic Technologies, a bogus company, the same modus operandi is followed, it points to a large scale money laundering scam.

Unaccounted cash from Naxal sympathisers made its way every month through this operation to fund the Naxalite war against the nation. The average money routed through each of these 968 credit cards was one lakh a month that makes it close to ₹9.7 crore to fund Naxals through this scheme. In twelve months the money which has changed hands is in excess of a hundred crore.

The most shocking lapse seems to be clearly on the part of GB2. Reserve Bank of India has stipulated that banks collect certain mandatory Know Your Customer (KYC) documents from customers before they open any account. The originals of these documents are to be sighted by the bank employee before any account is opened. This process needs to be followed for issuance of credit cards, too. However in the case of Francis D'Silva, the credit card seems to have been issued by GB2 based on the KYC document (passport) provided by his company, without a bank official sighting the originals. No verification of the residence address was carried out.

Alongside this article is attached a copy of the forged passport of Francis D'Silva, which formed the basis of the card issuance. The photo on the passport is completely different from the photograph of the individual who was killed in Ranibodli. (Real photo released by CBI in inset.) It is suspected that the entire lot of 968 cards issued to Symbiotic Technologies followed this lax process.

It is now clear that the cards delivered to the HR executive at Symbiotic Technologies, a fraudulent company, never reached the employees. In fact it was never intended to. In fact there were no employees in Symbiotic – there were only co-conspirators.

These cards made their way to the Naxals of central and eastern India and became a mode of laundering black money from sympathisers to support the Naxal cause. Arms were bought, food and rations were procured using the card as a front and the same was funded subsequently by unidentified Naxal sympathisers in cash. A brilliant game by the Naxalites to beat the banking system in the country.

This raises the following key questions:

1. Why did GB2 not follow laid down procedure on KYC when they issued cards to employees of Symbiotic Technologies?
2. Why weren't such large-scale cash transactions into a particular set of customer's credit card accounts identified through internal control processes of GB2?
3. Was GB2 only a conduit for routing of these funds or were employees of GB2 or the organisation itself a willing partner in the entire scam, in return for financial gains?

Most of these questions remain unanswered. However we are confident that as days go by and more data becomes available, we will be able to get to the bottom of this scandal, which threatens to rock the foundation of the world's largest democracy.

CBI today released two pictures of the alleged Naxal killed in the Ranibodli massacre. The picture on the left is the actual picture of the Naxalite while the one on the right is the picture as it exists in the passport of Francis D'Silva (courtesy GB2). CBI has requested that anyone with any information on the Naxalite should immediately contact the Anti Naxal Cell of CBI at 123455678. You may also contact the offices of this newspaper at 2222222222.

This newspaper headline created a furore both within and outside the bank. Within the bank, the entire PR machinery went into a tizzy. The reputation of GB2 as a compliant bank and as a solid process-oriented bank was shred to bits by the front page of *The Times of India*.

Ronald was livid. He was furious at his team, particularly Saurabh, Bhisham and the fraud team led by Inder, for not informing him at the right time. He was shocked that what they could not figure out with their massive databank was easily identified by someone from outside who had limited access to their data. 'This is another failure of the India GB2 team,' he screamed. 'We have serious credibility issues in the region which have been aggravated by this report.'

He looked at Bhisham and said, 'I want the fucker who is responsible for this failure to be brought to task. Do you understand? I want heads to roll.' He then turned towards Inder. 'And, Inder, I want a complete report on Symbiotic from you. You have only twenty-four hours for it. Now come on, guys, time to get moving!' he shouted. Little did he know that Inder's report would say nothing different than what was already there in the papers!

Andy was extremely thrilled with the reaction to his morning story. He had gambled with the story. In fact his career was at stake. It could have backfired if it had turned out to be plain speculation. But it was Karan's conversation with Kavya which had convinced him about the veracity of the story. If even one of the credit cards that Kavya had checked had not followed the same transaction pattern, he would have withdrawn the story. With 20 random cards displaying the same transaction pattern, it was prudent for him to go ahead. In the worst case, he could have been pulled up for exaggerating the facts but no one could deny that there was definitely a huge problem which needed to be fixed.

In Karan, he saw a rising star; someone who had full faith in his convictions and had the potential to deliver the goods when it mattered the most. This story had even raised Andy's own stakes within the group.

That evening Karan, Bhaskar and Andy were at Indigo in Colaba where they celebrated the exposé over a drink. It was a nice resto-bar in the lane next to Café Leopold. Andy laid out the newspaper on the table in front of them.

'Guys, many, many years from now, when you will be old and taking care of your grandchildren, you will reminisce this day and the thought of what's happened today will give you extreme joy. It will be one of the most successful wins of your career. Mark my words! It can't get better than this. Foreign banks, government, Naxalites, money laundering and threats,' Andy spoke.

'Threats?' both Karan and Bhaskar called out in unison.

'Haha...yes. Thakurta came to meet me this afternoon. He doesn't want us to steal his thunder. Wanted us to go slow,' Andy told them.

'What did you say?' Karan asked him.

'It doesn't make sense to be belligerent, guys. I called up our management to see what support we have. Never enter into a battle without any cover. If you are destined to lose, don't ever try to battle. Wait for an opportunity where you are sure to win.' Andy said philosophically.

'That's all fine but what did you say?' Karan was getting impatient with the lecture.

'I told him to mind his own business. We will do our job the way our readers want.'

'He bought into it?' Karan asked.

'No, he didn't, but you can't fuck around with the media. Can you?' Andy smiled as he said this. And then he looked at the front page of *The Times of India*. He looked at the two pictures on the front page. One was of Francis D'Silva released by the CBI and the other of Francis D'Silvas as his passport copy picked out from the document given to GB2 while applying for a credit card. 'Whoever you are, Francis, you will be kept alive by the media for long.' And then he looked at the bar where a couple of cute-looking ladies were ordering their drink and waved out to the barman. Within minutes their drinks arrived and they celebrated their famous exposé.

Thursday, 17 December 2009

The Day of the Summons
Mumbai

RONALD had not expected a summons from the RBI so soon. The newspapers had speculated about this mess-up only a day back. And the governor of the RBI had already served him a notice. Everyone knew that RBI had taken a very categorical stand on KYC documents and account holder details, but he didn't expect them to give him a show cause notice, which seemed more like a threat. And the accusation levied on them – waging a war against the nation – was shocking. At the least he should have been given an opportunity to defend the bank before the harsh notice was issued. The problem with these notices was that they normally made it to the records. And long after the issues died down and problems fixed, they still remained on record and came back to haunt at the most inappropriate of times. Ronald was worried about this impact, too.

But there was no point worrying about it because it was a fait accompli. RBI had issued a warning letter and sought answers from GB2. He had to now figure out how to handle this issue.

Bhisham, Inder and their respective teams along with Mansi, Ramneek and a few others were waiting for Ronald as he came back from the RBI.

Thankfully the Francis issue was relegated to the third page on *The Times of India* that day. It was largely because of an unfortunate mishap. The speeding Sealdah-bound Uttar Banga express had rammed into the rear of a stationary Bhagalpur-Ranchi-Vananchal express, at Sainthia railway station in Birbhum in West Bengal early Wednesday morning. Over 65 people were killed in this accident. The railway minister had started making noises about the possible causes of the accident. Naxal activism was also being suspected as one of the possiblities. Even the dumbest of souls would know that this was because of a signalling error rather than the Naxals.

Ronald showed the letter from RBI to Saurabh. 'This is why I was summoned by the Governor,' he said looking at the others. 'So what does our investigation show?'

Bhalla walked in. He was a little late for the meeting and apologised.

'Bhalla, Anything new?' asked Ronald, turning his attention towards him.

'Ronald, without going into the details, everything that the newspaper says is true. Symbiotics is a fraud company. It does not exist any more. We have seen small companies like these being set up fraudulently in the past but have never seen such a large-scale organised fraud. We got misled by the presence of the organisation in the virtual world, sexy websites, visits by senior management and their façade of a threat of losing the deal to Citibank. In fact we have a relationship with a company called Symbiotic Systems in the UK. At that point in time, we were misled into believing that this company was a sister concern of the British company. Having said that, we have got all the approvals from our credit folks. Bhisham has approved it himself. In fact he put in some additional checks as well just to be sure.' He then looked at Bhisham and said, 'Bhisham, would you want to add something?'

Bhisham was cornered. He couldn't say anything but accept that they had approved this transaction. 'Yes but...,' he was about to say something when Bhalla cut him short.

'Ronald, in fact only after receiving the written approval from credit did we close the deal with Symbiotic. Even they took their time in considering the proposal and granting their stamp of approval.'

The blame game had begun and Bhalla had won round one. Now even if Bhisham spent hours talking to Ronald to convince him that he was being framed, Ronald wouldn't believe him. He was, in a matter of minutes, a condemned man.

Back in the offices of TOI, the mood was remarkably different than the boardroom of GB2. The TOI team was upbeat. They had clearly stolen the lead over most of the other newspapers. The public loved it. Who wouldn't? Who doesn't want to see the big and mighty take a tumble in the battle against the Naxals?

Karan had agreed with Andy that the article for Friday would be on the frauds in the mortgage business and how it was possible to launder money by taking loans from banks. It was fast becoming Karan's week at the newspaper. He had just got out of a meeting with Andy and was casually flirting with his secretary when the phone on her table rang. She picked up the phone.

'Yeah, he is here. Do you want to speak to him?' she asked the caller.

'You want me to tell him this...oh, ok...I will let him know. He will call you. Ok, take care,' and she put the phone down. Karan had no idea what the caller was saying.

'There is someone at the reception for you, love,' she told Karan.

'Who would it be? At this hour?' He looked at his watch. It was past six in the evening. He hadn't even completed the article he had to write.

'Dunno,' She shrugged her shoulders. 'Apparently, he wouldn't even tell the receptionist his name. He is insisting that he will only see you and no one else.'

'Ok. Can you please check with the reception if he could wait for 30 minutes? I will just complete and send the article for tomorrow's edition and then meet him.'

'I will, but maybe you would just want to see who it is. Maybe it is urgent,' she said

'Babes, nothing is more important than this money laundering Naxalite case. Nothing...,' He smiled at her. 'Will you please let the guys at the reception know that I will be down there in thirty minutes?'

'As you say.' She called the reception. 'Karan will be down in thirty minutes. He is in a meeting. Will you please ask the gentleman to wait?'

Karan rushed to his desk. He had to complete and send the article to the editing desk in the next thirty minutes. Even though he was already behind deadline, the newspaper was very tolerant towards him since he was leading the Naxal story. He opened the top drawer and pulled out his cellphone. He had left it there for charging. There were fourteen missed calls of which twelve were from the some unknown number. However, If someone had tried to call him twelve times in ten minutes, it had to be important. He dialed the number. It was picked up in the first ring.

'Mr Panjabi?' the receiver of the call asked Karan.

'Yes, who is this?'

'Hi, I am Jinesh Shah. I am waiting for you at your reception.'

'Oh, it's you. Sorry, I didn't recognise you. Have we met earlier?' Karan asked him.

'No, we haven't. I need to see you for five minutes.'

'Mr. Shah, thanks for coming all the way. But I am slightly busy. Can we meet tomorrow morning?' Though he had committed earlier that he would be down in thirty minutes, he was now trying to wriggle out of the meeting.

'Mr Panjabi, what I have might be of interest to you. I am not too confident of going to the CBI, so I came to you. I would rather have the press know before the CBI. I am safe that way.'

'What are you talking about?' Karan seemed interested now.

'You printed those two pictures in the newspaper this morning. I might be able to give you some insights into the guy.'

'What?'

'Yes, I have met this gentleman.'

'When? Where? Who is he? How do you know him?'

When Karan rattled off so many questions, Jinesh slightly clamped up. 'Look. I can't talk on the phone. I am at your reception and there are too many people around. Can we meet in person? I have left my coffee shop to my employees and come here to see you. I also need to head back.'

'I will be there in five minutes.' Karan slammed the phone down, logged into his PC and quickly skimmed through the article he had written. He didn't waste time in rereading the entire article. He pressed 'send' and off it went. And as promised, within 5 minutes he was at the reception.

He looked around. There were about nine people sitting at the reception. He couldn't make out who had come to see him. No one seemed like the guys who would he would normally interact with. Not that profile. From the corner of his eyes he looked at the receptionist. She tilted her head, moved her eyes to someone sitting right in front of him. Though Karan didn't read her signal well, he had narrowed down the search to three of the nine people. He looked at all of them and called out.

'Jinesh?' it was less of a call out and more of a question.

The most innocuous looking man stood up. 'Mr Panjabi...', he said.

'Yes, please call me Karan. Good to see you, Mr Shah.' He shook his hand. 'Let's go inside.' He guided him towards a conference room. Jinesh looked very shaken and worried. The creases on his forehead made him look at least a few years older than his age. He kept looking over his shoulder as if he was being followed. Something had shaken him up and it was showing on his face. It didn't take Karan much to figure this out and he was sensitive to Jinesh as he led him into the conference room at the far end of the corridor from the reception.

'Please come in', he said as he opened the door of the small room. 'Please be comfortable.' And he gave him a big smile that instantly put Jinesh at ease. 'It's safe in here.'

Karan sat away from the door and made Jinesh sit with his back facing the door. From that position Jinesh could not see the people walking through the corridor and that helped to add to his illusion of security.

'Mr Shah, please feel comfortable. No one can reach here without our permission. No one can even listen in to our conversation,' Karan tried to assure him

'Hmm...I hope you will not call the police.' Jinesh seemed apprehensive.

'Not right now, for sure, because I do not know anything.'

'Thanks for meeting me at such a short notice.'

'It's ok, Mr Shah. So what do you do these days? You said you run a restaurant. Right?'

'Not a restaurant, I run the franchise of Costa Coffee in Juhu.'

'The one near Amitabh's bungalow?' Karan asked.

'Yes, yes, that's the one.'

'Hmm...it's a new one. I have been there a couple of times.'

'Yes, that's the story which I wanted to tell you.'

'Yes, sir, I am waiting.'

'About two years back I used to run a completely different business. I ran an Internet café. It was a flourishing business. I had about 20 computers and almost the entire student community in and around Juhu came to me. Mine was a reasonably well-known Internet café but everything changed one day.'

Karan had seen that internet café earlier. It was actually a rundown, sleazy internet café, but just as is the case with children where everyone feels that their children are the best, even in business everyone feels that his shop is the best and Jinesh was no different.

'What had happened?' Karan wanted to know

'There was a man who came to me one day in March 2008. I had people around me and was slightly busy. He said he wanted to use my internet café. I was quite happy to let him in. Then he told me that he wanted to use it on a day when there would be no one in the café. I told him that there was not a moment during the day when all the terminals were free.'

'This was in March 2008?'

'Yes.'

'Do you mind if I take notes?' Karan asked.

'Not at all. But please don't record our conversation. It scares me,' Jinesh requested him

'Sure. Sure.... Go ahead.'

'When I told him that there wouldn't be a moment during the day when all the terminals will be free, he went away. Probably he went looking for other places. Before leaving he called someone to take directions to other Internet cafes in the area.'

'Hmm...'

'When he didn't find any such internet café which would be free all through the day, he came back to me.'

'When did he come back?'

'Within the next two or three days.'

'Why did he come back to you only?'

'Maybe he went to the others too. But I would like to believe that he came to me because mine was the only one which had a small private enclosure.'

'Ok.'

'This time he came with an offer.'

'An offer?' Karan raised his eyebrows.

'Yes. He asked me if I would shut down the internet café for a day. I was surprised and asked him why he would want me to shut down my café for a whole day. It would mean a loss of revenue for me.'

'Strange.'

'That's when he made a deal. He said he would pay me the double of the revenue lost during the day. Which meant that he would pay me double charges for the twenty internet terminals. It was an offer I could not resist. Suspecting that he would not pay later, I asked for advance which he agreed to.'

'How much was that? This would have meant over 10,000 rupees for the day, right?' Karan guessed.

'Hmm...more than that. And it was difficult for me to refuse. See, I make that amount over a week, sometimes even longer. My café used to normally run at 40 per cent occupancy and he was paying me double the charges for all terminals that day.'

'Understood.' 'He came back the next day. He brought his laptop and other equipment, which were small in size and fitted into a small bag. They looked like routers, scramblers and some hi-tech stuff. He said that he was working on a top-secret deal that couldn't be disclosed. He looked polished and smart. Spoke good English. So I was taken in and agreed to his condition of not recording his entry in my register. The rules required me to maintain a register marking everyone's entry and exit and also to take ID proof from clients who use the internet cafe.'

'Hmm...then?'

'He started his work at around 4 in the afternoon. He connected his own laptop. I think it was a brand new one. He kept working at it for a long time. I went in a couple of times, but every time he shooed me away. He didn't even eat or drink. He took his stuff inside with him and shut himself off from everyone.'

My deal with him was till 10 p.m. He expected his work to get over by then but unfortunately it didn't. The connection was far too slower than what he thought it would be.'

'Did you ask him to leave?' Karan was getting impatient. He wanted to know the core issue. He was wondering what was it that Jinesh was trying to tell him. But he didn't want to cut his flow. It's just that he wished he knew the end before he saw the complete movie.

'I went inside to tell him that the time is up and he needed to leave. He didn't seem to be interested in stopping what he was doing. A variety of cables and equipment were spread around him, all connected in some way or the other to the laptop. He couldn't have stopped. He knew that I was a businessman, always on the lookout for means to make money. It had worked once when he gave me double the tariff for using the café. This time he dangled five notes of ₹1,000 each in front of me. He said that he was very close to finishing his work and would need to be around for an hour more. This was around 10 p.m. I could make out he was downloading something. I glanced at the screen, it said 12 per cent downloaded. It was something to do with passports because the file name was "Passport Mumbai".'

'What? Passport Mumbai?' Karan was surprised.

'Yes.'

'Ok.' Though Karan was excited, he soon composed himself. It could have been anything.

'I stepped out and waited. I was getting worried because police patrols that area after 10.30 p.m. There are a number of dark alleys which are frequented by couples who come there, park their cars and do improper things. So patrolling is intense. I was worried that some police constable might see the lights on and come in for a check. And then I would be in trouble. If I had known that he would go on for so long, I would not have given him the internet café.'

'You gave it to him for the money. Didn't you? I think you would have given it even if he had told you he was going to work late. Don't complicate it by putting on a virtuous façade.' The moment Karan said that, he cursed himself. He was not there to win a debate with Jinesh.

Jinesh thought for a moment and then said, 'Maybe.' Thankfully he didn't take offence. He continued, 'As I had feared, within minutes a couple of beat constables came and started pushing me around. They wanted me to shut down the café. I pleaded with them and sent them on their way. I spoke to the person inside and I shared part of the booty with the cops. They gave me ten minutes and said that they would be back after that.'

'Did they come back?'

'Yes. They came back in fifteen minutes and this time, they started acting tough. They became abusive. I think they had gone to drink and came back after downing a few pegs. It was becoming difficult to control them. I went in and requested the guy again. He blankly refused and said that he had paid money so he expected me to manage everything. By the time I came back the policemen had hunted and found where the power box was. I tried arguing with them but they didn't listen. They pulled out the fuse for the building. The lights went off. The computers were all on UPS, his laptop was on battery back up. I did not have spare UPS points near the private cubicle so the guy had connected his equipment to the normal power. I guess everything got switched off. I ran down. I did not want him to trip over anything and hurt himself. By the time I reached there, he had gone. As I was entering the room, I heard a small blast. The table he was working on was burning and everything around it was clean. It was a localised blast which destroyed any trace of what he was working on. He had disappeared through the back door. By the time I came up, the police constables had also disappeared, happy that they had the last laugh.'

'Did you mention this to anyone?'

'No, I did not tell anyone. I was so scared that I would get implicated in something and I did not tell anyone about it. I closed the café for a few days. The bomb blast had scared me. A couple of days later a few people from Crime Branch came and interrogated me and asked me if I had noticed any suspicious activity around that area in the past few days. They were with me for a few hours, confiscated all my PCs and disappeared. That scared me even more. I decided to shut down the internet café permanently and do something else. Over the next six months, I bought the neighbouring property and opened up a Costa Coffee outlet.'

'So why are you telling me about this now? What made you come to me?' Karan asked

'Because of your article in today's papers.'

'What?'

'The guy who had rented the café from me was none other than the guy in the picture on your front page.'

'What are you saying?'

'Yes, Mr Panjabi, he was none other than the alleged Naxalite who was killed. He was up to something crooked. I don't know what it exactly was but I am now worried and so I want to cooperate and tell everything to the police and CBI. However if I tell them now, I am scared they will implicate me in something and put me behind the bars. I would rather tell you so that the media knows everything before the police.'

'How do we believe you, Mr Shah?' Karan voiced his skepticism.

'I have a picture to prove this. In fact the first time he came in, I had people around me. There were a couple of people from the webcam company who were giving me a demonstration of the video camera to be fixed to the computer screen.'

'Video camera? Why?'

'You see, many internet users would come to chat with their girl friends, family and other acquaintances, so we keep using it. I had a webcamera attached with five of the twenty workstations. The webcam company was selling me webcams for the remaining fifteen. It was purely a matter of chance that the video camera was on when this Naxalite had come to see me for the first time. It recorded his movements and also the conversations. When I did the deal with him later, I retrieved the file and saved it securely. I just wanted to play it safe.'

'Was he not aware that the computer was recording him?'

'No. After the blast and the fire, I kept the file in a secure place.' Jinesh pulled out a USB drive from his pocket and handed it over to Karan. 'If I go to a TV channel with this, they will pay me lakh for it. But in this case I do not want to make money. I just want to protect myself.'

'You are forgetting we too have a TV channel. Don't worry, we will get them to pay you whatever it is worth,' said Karan, reminding Jinesh that they were a full-fledged media house.

'Will you give me a minute, Mr Shah? Please don't move out of this room.' Karan ran out of the conference room to see the contents of the USB drive. On his way he called Andy and Bhaskar and requested them to come to his room immediately.

Andy and Bhaskar were with him in a jiffy. He plugged the USB drive into his computer and double-clicked on the MPEG file. The film started playing. All three of them were shocked. Jinesh was right! The entire discussion of the suspected Naxalite with Jinesh during his first visit to the cafe was captured on tape – Francis asking for the internet café to be vacant when he wanted to use it, Jinesh selling him the merits of his internet café. Almost everything was clearly visible on tape. It was surely the guy who was killed in the RaniBodli massacre. The Naxal commander, the referee.... It was him on the tape.

'Bring him to my cabin.' Andy, too, wanted to be a part of this conversation.

'No, Andy. He is comfortable with me. Let me handle this. If you want, I will dial you and keep my phone on during the entire conversation. You will be able to hear everything. Otherwise we may end up scaring him and he may not tell us anything,' Karan tried to dissuade him.

'Hmm...its ok. You talk to him and let us know what he says. Keeping the phone on might make it too obvious and put him off.'

And Karan went back to the room where Jinesh Shah was waiting for him. This time he went with his laptop. 'Yes, Mr Shah, you are right. This indeed is the same guy. But what was he trying to do?' Suddenly, Andy's secretary barged into the room. She had a cordless in hand. 'Andy wants to speak with you right now,' she told Karan.

Karan took the phone. 'Yes, Andy,' and he walked out of the conference room talking on the phone.

'Karan, I think we must get Thakurta into this. While we have had our share of glory in this case, this might just be getting out of hand. It may be bigger than what we can handle. What do you think?' Andy suggested.

'I would second that, Andy. You asked me yesterday if I was getting scared...I think now I am beginning to get scared.'

'Ok...let me try to call him. You keep Jinesh engaged while I try and reach out to Thakurta.'

'Sure.' Karan returned to the conference room where Jinesh was waiting for him.

'Sorry, Mr Shah, It was my boss on the line. Had to go,' Karan said.

'No problems.'

'Mr Shah, what you have given us today is extremely important. Would you mind if we use this clipping in our news channels (Times Now and ET Now) and cover this in the newspapers tomorrow? We will compensate you suitably for this. Andy, my boss, will close out the financials of the deal with you.'

'I see no problem in that. But do you think there will be a liability on me? I should not land up in trouble.'

'Unfortunately, Mr Shah, I don't think I am the right person to answer that. You will have to seek legal counsel. However, we will in, all our coverage, state that you had come forward on your own with this information. That will ensure that the law enforcers are liberal with you in case they interrogate you.'

'So, what do you suggest me to do?'

'What I can probably do, Mr Shah, is to talk to our legal advisor and get him to meet you. He can advise you on your way forward. But his advice to you will be entirely on a personal basis and the newspaper does not take any responsibility for that.'

'Sure, I understand that.'

'Would you like to wait here while I call him and see if he is free?' Karan asked.

'Ok, I will wait here,' Jinesh agreed.

'I will be back in a moment.'

Karan walked out of the room and asked the receptionist to connect him to the legal counsel of the newspaper. Karan spoke with him briefly and within five minutes Lalit Khaitan, the legal counsel of Times Group, was with Jinesh. Karan left for his own room. He had a bomb of a story now. Something that would blow the audience away! This story was fast becoming the newspaper's domain. They had the first-hand information on this story even before the CBI or the law enforcers got a wind of it.

In the meantime Andy reached out to Thakurta.

'Mr Thakurta, this is Anindya Mukherjee here?'

'Yes, Mr Mukherjee, how can a meager soul like me help you?' Thakurta still seemed peeved at the way his conversation had gone with Andy the previous day.

'Mr Thakurta, there is something which we have unearthed that might interest you. We could ideally have carried out the story tomorrow morning but that will hamper your chances of getting to the bottom of the issue. Will it be possible to for you to meet ne? We can take you through it and then take a call on the course of action.'

'Ok, when do you want to meet?' Thakurta was a little surprised that Andy was singing a reconciliatory tone, but he obliged.

'Now!' said Andy.

'What?!! Now?' He paused for a while. 'I have just reached home.'

'Sir, it is something which you will surely be interested in knowing before we publish it. I leave it to your wise judgement.' Andy was not going to beg and plead with Thakurta. He was doing him a favour by giving him the information. If he wanted it, he better come.

As expected, Thakurta arrived in thirty minutes. He too, was very concerned about this case as it signalled the resurgence of Naxalite sympathisers in urban India and that was a dangerous trend, which everyone in the government wanted to quell.

Karan, Bhaskar and Andy gave a quick rundown to Thakurta on what Jinesh had told them. Thakurta was listening intently to the entire episode. He had come alone. The moment they told him that Jinesh had seen the file with the name containing the word 'passport' being downloaded, Thakurta suddenly perked up.

'What? Passport?' he asked them.

'Yes, sir. The downloaded file had something to do with the Mumbai passport office,' Karan responded.

Thakurta pulled out his phone and called someone. None of the other three in the room knew who he was speaking to. Within 45 seconds he cut the call.

'When did you say this guy met Jinesh?' Thakurta asked.

'In mid-2008.'

'Hmm...Jinesh is telling you the truth guys,' Thakurta gave a wry smile to the three of them and shook his head. 'He is in fact telling you the truth.'

'Ok. So now you know something we don't,' Andy interjected when the silence continued for a while.

'Guys, what I am going to tell you will not make it to your newspapers till I give you explicit approvals. If it does, I know how to deal with it.' Thakurta warned Andy and Karan before his revelation.

'What is this about, Thakurta?' Andy asked.

'First tell me, is this acceptable or not?'

Everyone looked at Andy who just nodded.

'In the middle of 2008, there was an unsuccessful attempt at hacking into the passport office website and stealing the data pertaining to passport holders in the Mumbai passport office. It was around the same time this bloke is talking about. We couldn't identify the location from where the hack was tried because the guy used complex communication routers and left us with an intricate maze of web addresses to resolve, which we were never able to convincingly do. We confiscated computers, raided premises, which include your guy's café, but we were not able to convincingly arrive at a conclusion and hence never made this public. A number of people are under surveillance on this issue, and I am sure your guy would also be on that list. These could be surely related.'

'I have never heard about it.' Andy was surprised.

'That's because it's classified. Even in our database it shows as a *suspected* breach,' Thakurta replied.

'Oh! This gives the story a completely different twist. So our man here may actually be telling us the truth. The Naxalite did try to hack into the passport office website. Once he was unsuccessful, they found some other way to get the data and then used the same data on passports to apply to GB2 for credit cards under Symbiotic Technologies. The passport numbers and the passport holders' names on documents supplied with the credit card applications would have been genuine, but the photograph on the passport was forged. This would dramatically reduce the chances of the bank's fraud processes picking out the passport as a fraudulent one. What a game! A big game this is! But one thing I can't understand, Andy,' said Karan.

'And what is that?' Andy asked Karan.

'How did a large bank like GB2 with best global practices and stringent risk controls fall prey to this? Despite all the "love and affection" I have for Deepak I don't think he is a criminal. I do not think he would have been party to this at all. Somewhere deep down, my conscience says this. What beats me is that an organisation like GB2 can make such a large slip-up. Very, very strange.'

'We can never tell, Karan. Appearances are deceptive,' Thakurta argued.

'But this could also mean that while you have identified the lapse in the case of one Symbiotic Technologies, there may be many such cases and thousands of benami cards floating around across the banking system in the country,' Karan said, suddenly aware of how big this could be.

'Yes, you are right, Karan. Let's however first deal with Symbiotic and the related issues before we get to the other ones,' said Thakurta.

'Ok, let me now show you the video that Jinesh had recorded. First and exclusive visuals of Francis in flesh and blood!' Karan then swiped his hand on the track pad of his laptop to get his screen into action. The USB was in his hand. He plugged it in and waited for the clipping to come up on screen. It was a clipping of Francis walking into the shop. Thakurta looked at it intently. His eyes went wide in surprise even as his face became red with anger. He went through the clipping carefully – kept forwarding and rewinding the frames to make sure that he had not missed anything.

The story was clear: Francis came into the internet café and spoke to Jinesh.

'Bump up the audio. I can't hear him clearly' instructed Thakurta.

'Here...use this', said Karan, handing him an earphone. The laptop was not connected to any audio system and hence he could not have amplified the sound beyond his laptop's maximum.

From the conversation, it was clear that initially Jinesh had refused to give him the internet café when he wanted it all by himself for a day. There was no debate. His request was outrightly refused by Jinesh Shah. Then the person took out his phone and pulled out a piece of paper from his shirt pocket. The paper had someone's number. With the paper in his right hand and the phone in his left, he dialled a number and waited for the call to be picked up.

'Hello.'

...

'This guy here refuses to let out the café for a full day.'

...

'Ok. Where else can I go?'

...

'Next to Alfa store in Vile Parle? How do I get there? Is it too far from here?'

...

'Hmm...there are three of them? ...ok, ok...I will go there. If I am not able to get it there then we will see what to do.'

The video captured what he spoke but what the person on the other side spoke remained a mystery. It was a short conversation where the person asked for some directions to another internet café in the neighbourhood. After a chat for a couple of minutes, he disconnected his phone and walked away.

'Who was the person that Francis spoke to? That person could be the vital link in this case,' Thakurta looked at the three of them and said. He decided to see the clipping again. This time he put the video on pause when he reached the part where Francis was speaking on the phone. He rewound the clip repeatedly and viewed the frames where Francis took out the phone and dialed a number, desperately trying to see if the dialed number was visible from any angle. It was not. Even when he magnified the screen freeze, he was not able to readout the complete number. All he could make out was that the first four digits of the number that Francis called were 9820.

'Half of the Mumbai city has 9820 as the first four digits of their phone number,' Andy said, looking at Karan who just smiled wryly in return.

Disappointed that he was not able to get the telephone number, Thakurta lost interest in the clipping. He was about to stop the clip as it played for the twenty-second time on Karan's laptop, when he froze. The clipping ended just as Francis finished his call and disconnected the line. The moment Francis finished the call, he moved the mobile phone away from his ears, brought it in line with his eyes, and pressed the red button to disconnect. It was a new phone, and he was slightly ill at ease using it. His fingers hadn't gotten used to the phone and he had to visually see the placement of the button every time he used it.

Thakurta played the end of the clipping yet again and stopped the clipping at the instant when he moved the phone away from his ears and brought it in line with his eyes. He froze the frame and zoomed into the area over Francis' right shoulder. The computer took some time in pixilating the area. An hour glass image appeared in place of the cursory arrow which marks the cursor. But that disappeared within 3 seconds. And when it did, the phone was visible very clearly.

Even though the screen was partly hidden by Francis' right cheek, a large portion of the screen was visible – bang in front of him. His expressions were a mix of shock and joy. On the screen, clearly visible, were the last six digits of the number Francis had called. He was ecstatic. He now had all the ten digits of the mobile number of the person Francis had spoken to.

'Gotcha! This will be very useful for our investigation,' Thakurta said to himself as he tore a piece of paper from the notebook lying on the table to write it down. 'Let me quickly give it to the investigating team to figure out whose number this is.'

Karan, took out his iPhone. He, too, wanted to note it down. 'It will be useful,' he said to himself, even as he started keying in the number into his iPhone. The hand holding the phone was shaking with excitement. He had never done anything like this in his life.

He entered the number and was about to save it in his contacts when he noticed that he had pressed one digit incorrectly. Wiping the number off his screen, he tried to save it again. He keyed in all the digits carefully, one by one. The moment he reached the last digit and entered it, a new text appeared on his screen. The text showed that the number already existed in Karan's mobile phone contact list. His face went pale. Below the number appeared the name of the person whose mobile number Francis had dialed.

The name of the contact really threw Karan off-balance. He couldn't believe it. For a moment he thought that he had keyed in the wrong number. He looked at the number again. It was the same. Then how could this happen? It was almost impossible. The name of the contact had to be incorrect. Something was dramatically wrong.

He looked at the screen once again, simultaneously glancing at the number written on a piece of paper by Thakurta's side. It matched. The entire clipping was played again. He stopped at the point where the first four digits were visible. They were the same as he had taken them down in his notebook. By the time he looked up Andy and Thakurta were mid-way to the conference room where Jinesh was patiently interacting with the lawyer.

'Andy, Andy...this is crazy,' he screamed when he saw that Andy was getting into an elevator. Andy stopped abruptly.

'We have a problem here, Andy. You, too, need to see this Mr Thakurta,' Karan said hurriedly.

'What happened, Karan?' both Thakurta and Andy exclaimed, almost in unison.

When Karan told them what he had just seen, both of them were flabbergasted. Was he serious? Could this be true? This had much larger implications.

'This is outrageous. Nothing but a systematic rape of our systems. We do not know how many such individuals exist all across. We could be up against a system full of fraudsters. I told you. Deepak is not the kind of guy who would indulge in these things. His integrity was never a suspect. Yes, he was strong-headed but not someone who would take the entire system for a ride. It looks like he has been used as a pawn,' Karan said.

'Maybe, Karan. But he may still be involved. What this shows us is that there are others involved, too, but it doesn't absolve Deepak of all the wrongs. What you just saw proves beyond doubt that there are others, too!' Thakurta now had a worried look on his face.

'What are we going to do now, Mr Thakurta?'

'What we have seen just now is reason enough for us to treat this individual as a suspect and take into custody,' said Thakurta, referring to the person whose name was blaring from Karan's phone. 'We should initiate a search of the suspect's office and residence to see if we recover something. The Public Security Act gives us the right to detain a person indefinitely if we think the person is a threat to public security,' Thakurta told them.

'Human right activists call it a draconian law,' Andy added Karan had no clue about it.

'Look, Andy. Whose side are you on? Make up your mind. You called me here to tell me to take action on this new information of yours. And now you are also handing out a threat. What is it that you want to do?' Thakurta was clearly irritated.

'I was just making you aware, Mr Thakurta.'

'Ok, here is a deal,' Thakurta said. 'I am going to take a team to the suspect's residence. I am within my right to conduct a search of the residence, provided the suspect is present during the search If the suspect is at home right now, I will be able to do something Do you guys know where the person lives?'

'What if the suspect is not at home?' Karan asked.

'We will have to wait till tomorrow. We can then pick the person up from office and head straight to the residence and conduct a detailed search. Maybe we will find something.'

'Can we keep a watch on the house tonight? I will surely be able to get the address for you. If we notice something suspicious or if an escape is attempted, we can anyway take the suspect into preventive custody. Else we can pick up the suspect for questioning tomorrow. Let's keep the bank in the loop. I will talk to Ronald again,' Karan suggested.

Thakurta thought for a moment and nodded. 'Only because of you and the wonderful work that you have done, Karan.'

That night Karan called Sherlyn on her mobile. 'Sherlyn, I need Ronald's residence number...need to speak to him urgently. He needs to know something which is going to happen tomorrow morning

Please!! Do not ask me for the details now. Will you give it to me?' Karan pleaded. Sherlyn obliged him but caveated it saying, 'Please do not tell him that I gave his number to you.'

'Thanks, Sherlyn.'

The next call that Karan made was to Ronald. Ronald was quite receptive this time. He had paid the price for not listening to him earlier. When Karan narrated the entire story to him he was stunned. It took some time for the reality to sink in. He now knew why, despite all the controls, it never worked. How Symbiotics took the entire bank for a ride despite their world class processes! He had one request in the end. 'Karan, can you please speak to Thakurta and make sure that no one creates a scene in office.'

'Ronald, are you ok if I get Thakurta on the line as well? You can then directly tell him how you would prefer it done.' Ronald agreed.

Karan then got Thakurta on the line and the modus operandi was agreed upon. The CBI was indulging Karan and Andy because they were the guys behind the entire investigation. They had the choice of going public without passing on the information to Thakurta. But they didn't go down that path, and for once Thakurta was indebted to them.

GB2, Ronald McCain's Office
Mumbai

Ronald McCain was a nervous man as he entered his office that Friday dressed in smart casuals, the colours of which oozed an energy which belied the inherent stress in his mind. He had never done this before.

His last few days had begun with discussions on the Symbiotic case and ended with the same. On Friday, too, like every other day he called Mansi, Bhisham, Saurabh, Ramneek, Rohan and Inder for a discussion on the Symbiotic issue. He had called them early on Friday morning and asked them to come prepared with their respective team members involved in the investigations. Updates to Global HQ went twice a day, given the sensitivity of the case. A complete debriefing was necessary before formulating a response. 'And don't forget, this is an in-person briefing,' he told everyone. No one was prepared for this. This sent everyone scurrying to their respective team members asking them to travel to Ronald's office for a briefing at 9.00 a.m.

At 9.20 a.m, everyone was in his office. Armed with their updates, they had come with their respective teams. Ramneek Chahal had come with Bhalla, Bhisham had come with Savitha, Mansi had come with Rajesh Krishnamoorthy and so on.

The discussion started but Ronald was too distracted. The only thing running on his mind was the discussion with Thakurta and Karan the previous night. How was he going to explain this to the Global Head Quarters? They would not take kindly to this. He kept looking at his watch.

At 9.45 a.m., the door opened and Karan, Andy, Thakurta and a few officers from CBI walked into Ronald's room. Two of them stood blocking the door to make sure that no one exited the room without their permission.

'Hey Karan,' Ramneek began but when he didn't get the same response from him, he backed off.

Rohan Naik was the guy who figured out that something was not going according to the plan. 'What's going on, guys? How did you get in?' He asked them and when Thakurta didn't even look at him, he desperately started screaming for Sherlyn. 'Sherlyn...Sherlyn, can you please call the security.'

Sherlyn peeped into the room but Ronald waved her away, 'It's all right, Rohan. They are here with my permission. Not that they need it.'

Rohan didn't understand. He just looked at Ronald, wondering what was going on. Bhisham instinctively came closer to Savitha. The protective male instinct took over.

Ronald then looked at Thakurta and nodded. 'Please go ahead.' Thakurta didn't really need to have waited for this signal from Ronald. He turned to the officer to his right and nodded. A nod that symbolically urged the operation to begin. The officer was joined by a team of two and all of them moved towards Bhisham. A few steps, and they were right in front of him. Everyone was wondering what was going on. Two firm hands gripped Bhisham.

'What's going on?' He screamed. But it was more out of panic than anger that he screamed. He had a scared look on his face, but only till the hands that gripped him, shoved him to a side only to release him. The lady officer took a step forward and held Savitha, who was too shocked to respond.

'Savitha,' it was Thakurta who spoke sternly. 'We are taking you into custody under the Public Security Act. You are suspected of furthering the cause of Naxalites and, in the process, waging a war against the nation and also working with anti-social elements to overthrow the legally elected government of the state. You will have to come with us. We do not want to use any force, so please do not make us change our minds.'

Everybody in the room was beyond shock. Savitha – a Naxal sympathiser. It was unimaginable. Some in the room knew that she was seeing Deepak but never expected her to be involved in the case. She was so far looked upon as a simple girl who fell in love with the wrong man. She was the victim. Deepak could have been lured into this line by Savitha and Francis.

Thakurta looked at Ronald and said, 'Mr McCain, thank you for your support. We will be proceeding against her in the cases of money laundering and fraud against the bank, too. I would leave it to you to figure out how you would like to manage this internally.'

Savitha didn't offer any resistance. She quietly stood where she was, held firmly by the CBI officers. Thakurta looked at the lady officer and nodded. 'I will see you back at the headquarters,' he said. As if robotically programmed, the lady led Savitha out of the office, into a waiting lift, and then straight into a car parked outside the MG road office of GB2.

Karan then looked at Ronald and said, 'Sir, we would like to speak with you in private if it's ok with you.' Ronald looked at the others, who quietly walked out of the room.

'Mr McCain,' began Thakurta, 'The moment Savitha left her house this morning, we entered her house and conducted a search. Under the law I can be in the dock for doing this. But I took a chance based on this gentleman's hunch.' He pointed to Karan. 'His hunch seemed to be correct.'

'I didn't understand, Mr Thakurta,' said Ronald.

'During the search we found interesting facts about Savitha. She has a history. She is a part of a very carefully planned racket where she had been planted into your organisation with a long-term strategy. A marriage photograph, which we found hanging in her bedroom, shows that Savitha is none other than the wife of Ganjali, the Naxal leader who was the first Naxal to engage in a jihadi-style suicide bombing in Malkangiri in Orissa way back in 2004. I have been handling the Naxal wing of CBI for over a decade now and that's how I remember Ganjali's photograph very clearly. I am surprised how your hiring checks didn't figure that out. What concerned me even more was that your organisation hired her after Ganjali's death.'

'We also recovered a number of documents from her home which had the names and addresses of people who we were already trailing because we suspected them to be Naxal sympathisers. Incriminating literature which was distributed to like-minded people to turn them into sympathisers for their cause was found in abundance. You would be surprised to know that we even recovered three revolvers from her residence, which is good enough to keep her in custody as we go about gathering more evidence against her.'

'Sir, I suspect that there could be multiple Symbiotic Technologies in your bank and hence it might be worthwhile to check all accounts where cash is being paid in. Transactions which these Naxals conducted on their card accounts were of a specific nature. Hence it will be easy to identify.'

'Can you please check that and let us know if there are more of such accounts so that we can take action? You might want to block all these cards immediately.' It was Thakurta.

'Sir,' added Karan, 'when she was in mortgages, the loans sourced by her and her team showed a significantly higher delinquency than the others. We initially thought it was due to credit-related and underwriting issues. However, now it seems prudent to revisit all the loans that she had sourced. Those were large ticket loans and you might have a significant amount at risk if they were obtained by fraudulent means. Investigating those may give Mr Thakurta some vital clues in the battle against the Naxals. It might give some insight into where the money is being routed to.'

'I am sorry we may be sounding like telling you how to run the bank but that's not our intent. We are just cautioning you against all that has happened,' said Thakurta as he thanked Ronald and made his way out of the building. Karan and Andy also moved out.

Ronald was left in the room wondering how he was going to handle one more blow up and how was he going to pacify the RBI. While this saga seemed to have ended, it was just the beginning of yet another uphill climb for him.

The Journey Ends

SAVITHA, after being taken into custody from McCain's office, was headed straight to CBI office where she was charged under the draconian PSA act. Her fate was sealed the moment her name was displayed on Karan's phone when he had keyed in the number from Jinesh Shah's video clipping. Both she and her husband were ardent Naxal sympathisers who had come to Mumbai from Malkangiri. Ganjali, with whom she was married off by the village elders, had given up his life for the Naxal cause, and that was when Savitha had vowed to keep the flag flying high. She took on the cause of providing infrastructural support for the Naxal cause by infiltrating a bank and helping the Naxals raise and transfer money from their supporters to the Naxals' fund. Symbiotic Technologies was a brilliant plan hatched by Anakadundhubi and Savitha. Deepak was unwittingly sucked into the plan.

She faced the prospect of being in jail long enough to forget what a career at GB2 would feel like. Even if, at some stage, the antiquated law of the country let her free, she was unlikely to ever find a job in another bank. She was not in love with Deepak and what happened to him obviously didn't matter to her. Her daughter was condemned to lead a life in an orphanage in Panvel, on the outskirts of Mumbai.

Deepak Sarup, after spending three months in jail, was released on bail as the CBI didn't have enough evidence to name him in their chargesheet. Savitha's arrest took the attention off Deepak Sarup, which made life easier for him. After Savitha was taken into custody, Karan's newspaper ran a series of articles on how Savitha could have beaten the system and how she set up Deepak by pushing him into a friendship with the referee. Karan's crusade to prove Deepak's innocence paid off. Even though the court cases were still on, Deepak was a free and relieved man now.

However, he was facing challenges of a different kind. Going back to GB2, an organisation where he was accused of frauds, was always going to be awkward. Taking moral responsibility for the large-scale frauds which happened in his regime, he quit GB2. However, he was struggling to find another job. The financial services was a small sector in India and almost everyone knew about Deepak's reputation. Stories of the politics he indulged in with Karan, including the infamous SMS episode, had become folklore in the industry. Fearing that he would vitiate the atmosphere, no one really wanted to hire him. Karan helped him out by giving him some odd jobs at the TV channel but that was proving to be difficult and unsustainable. Last heard, he had joined a small-time credit bureau as its project manager. A big comedown from where he was in GB2! But isn't life a big leveller?

Karan came out the strongest from the entire episode. His stock rose to dizzying heights within the Times group. He was the banking editor for their TV channel ET Now. He was also offered a plum position in the editorial board of *The Times of India*. The pain of leaving GB2 and even Citibank was soon forgotten and he was heralded as the upcoming star of the media industry. Kavya's re-entry into his life was permanent. The two of them met that Friday, the day Savitha was arrested. What (re)started with Kavya saying 'we will see na' ended with them seeing each other permanently. They eventually got married and settled down in their own apartment in Pali Hill in Bandra.

Francis, the referee, or was he Anakadundhubi or Kishore? No one knew. His real name, his real identity, was something which remained a mystery till the very end. All that was known about him was that he was a commander in the Maoist camp. A typical example of a village boy picked up at a tender age, brainwashed and called upon to serve the cause of the Maoist rebels. Joining hands with Savitha, he had brilliantly manipulated Deepak into unknowingly working for their cause. Though the fraud was detected and the manipulations curtailed in GB2, how many such Anakadundubhis were lurking around in the country was anybody's guess!

Ronald McCain wrote back to the RBI after the dust settled on this issue. The RBI took a very strong view of the issues that GB2 had had in the past and took the extreme step of writing to the bank's board in UK, cautioning them against any recurrence of such issues. It said that it was treating the money-laundering episode as a failure on the part of the bank to control, detect and report illegal transactions and was not treating it as a war against the nation as its initial letter might have suggested. But it also said that any repeat of such laxity would call for suspension of banking license in the country.

Ronald, after spending two challenging years at the helm in GB2, when last heard, was counting the days for his exit from India and to bring to an end this infamous saga that happened once upon a time in the Greater Boston Global Bank.

RUPa 8|12|15